SWEET TEA FOR TWO

Center Point
Large Print

**This Large Print Book carries the
Seal of Approval of N.A.V.H.**

SWEET TEA FOR TWO

Genell Dellin

CENTER POINT LARGE PRINT
THORNDIKE, MAINE

14 MAY 14
Center Point
33.95 (20.37

This Center Point Large Print edition
is published in the year 2013 by arrangement with
The Berkley Publishing Group,
a member of Penguin Group (USA) Inc.

This is a work of fiction. Names, characters, places, and
incidents either are the product of the author's imagination
or are used fictitiously, and any resemblance to actual
persons, living or dead, business establishments, events, or
locales is entirely coincidental. The publisher does not have
any control over and does not assume any responsibility for
author or third-party websites or their content.

The text of this Large Print edition is unabridged.
In other aspects, this book may vary
from the original edition.
Printed in the United States of America
on permanent paper.
Set in 16-point Times New Roman type.

ISBN: 978-1-61173-737-0

Library of Congress Cataloging-in-Publication Data

Dellin, Genell.
 Sweet tea for two : [A Honey Grove Romance] / Genell Dellin. — Center
Point Large Print edition.
 pages cm
 ISBN 978-1-61173-737-0 (Library binding : alk. paper)
 1. Homecoming—Texas—Fiction.
  2. Farm foreclosures—Texas—Fiction. 3. Life change events—Fiction.
  4. Coffee shops—Fiction. 5. Man-woman relationships—Fiction.
  6. Texas—Fiction. 7. Large type books. I. Title.
PS3604.E4447S94 2013
813'.6—dc23
                                                      2013001221

For Nancy Yost

SWEET TEA FOR TWO

One

Sometimes it's all right to leap before you look.

Lilah Briscoe was sending mental messages to her beautiful, black-haired granddaughter, Meri, instead of doing what she was supposed to be doing, which was organizing the League of Women Voters' ice cream booth on the Rock County Courthouse lawn. Meri Briscoe and the handsome young rancher Caleb Burkett were in love.

Lilah knew that before they did. She also knew that it was the deep, rare kind that lasted a lifetime, no matter what happened in the relationship.

Now she was worried about what might happen if Meri couldn't relax and trust it. Lilah was afraid these two weren't going about it the right way, and she knew if they lost each other, they'd both be devastated.

Caleb didn't need this message. It was his nature to leap first and look later.

Really, Lilah knew him better than she knew Meri. She'd helped his mother raise him and he'd spent lots of time at Lilah's Honey Grove Farm.

Ironically, Meri, Lilah's own blood kin, hadn't been at Honey Grove since she was six years old. And her mother, Lilah's only child, Edie Jo, hadn't raised the little girl at all. She had also kept her away from Lilah and told her that Lilah didn't want to see her, which was a lie.

Caleb had fallen for Meri the minute he met her. He was crazy about her.

And Meri about him.

They were right for each other, Lilah had known that since the moment she introduced them, but now she wasn't sure they were going about it in the right way.

She couldn't stop watching them. They were over there, closer to the middle lawn of the grand old courthouse, laughing and joking around while Caleb's twin, Gideon, tried to help them set up the booth for Honey Grove Kitchens, the business Caleb and Meri were partners in with Lilah. Meri was hunting for the perfect tree to shade their table and Caleb and Gid had to keep moving it for her. The table would be the perfect way to advertise Honey Grove Kitchens, particularly the little café they'd recently opened as part of the larger business. Situated in the front corner of the old building they'd renovated on the Square, it was the perfect place for folks to stop and enjoy a bite to eat. It would help to make Honey Grove Kitchens—or HGK as everyone had taken to calling it—a success.

Lilah shook her head. More concerned about Meri and Caleb than the business at the moment. Since Meri'd been dragged all over the country until she was abandoned by her no-good mother,

her lifelong dream—all through high school and college and law school—had been to have a man who loved her and a family of her own.

Oh, Lord, help her know it's Caleb. Help her trust him.

Lilah watched them and put her whole heart into wishing the best for them.

Lord, help Caleb know she loves him. Help him know he can settle down.

One or both of them might come to her for confidences still yet.

Lilah knew better than anybody else in the world, including them, that neither one had the sense God gave a wooden goose about how to make decisions in their personal lives. Everybody needs somebody to go through life with, and they'd both had a hard time so far. Finding home would be such a blessed relief for them both.

Plus, Lilah had to admit she had a selfish bone. She wanted her granddaughter, who had inherited Lilah's violet eyes and strong energy, to be married and happy and settled here in Texas so she'd never live far away from Honey Grove again.

"What're you doing, Lilah? Planning the wedding in your head? That's not yours to do, you know. It's Meri's."

Lilah gave a little start. She'd been so far gone she'd nearly forgotten Doreen was here. But here she was, that was for sure, and using her snippiest voice, too, the one that always grated on Lilah's last nerve. The two of them were what the girls nowadays call frenemies, and had been since kindergarten.

She turned and saw that Doreen, too, was homed in on Meri and Caleb. Of course. Since they were one of her favorite subjects for gossip. And that tacky remark had been a trick to try to worm it out of Lilah if they were making any plans or not.

"Well, if you've heard there's gonna be a wedding, you're way ahead of me."

"I worry about our Meri," Doreen said. "That Caleb's the handsomest devil in Texas, I'll give you that, but a leopard can't change his spots and—"

"Any man can settle down when he finds the right woman."

Lilah glared at her. "And be honest. What you're worried about is selling a wedding dress and some bridesmaids' dresses and one to me and no telling how many guests. Face the facts, Doreen. Those two are the kind to elope, I'm thinking."

Doreen cackled. "Oh! So you *do* know something you're not telling."

"No, I do not."

But the image of Meri and Caleb standing at the altar brought, somewhere, way back at the farthest edge, the tiniest something to niggle at Lilah's mind. She couldn't name it. Just *something*.

To push it away, she said, "And you know full

well that I'll not sit here and hear one bad word against Caleb."

She tried to keep back the next words that leapt to her tongue, but they jumped off it anyway.

"*And* you know full well that you have no right to say 'our' Meri. Meri is in no part yours. Just because you stole my own daughter from me doesn't mean you can do the same with my granddaughter."

Doreen just had to have a little trouble brewing all the time or she wasn't happy.

Now, she just shook her head like Lilah was the most unreasonable thing she'd ever seen.

But one thing about Lilah, she wasn't one to look to the past. Once Doreen had made apologies for being such a troublemaker in Lilah's life, Lilah had forgiven her completely and put the past where it belonged.

But the big *but* was, every time they were together Doreen made it plain as day she hadn't.

"Face it," she said, "here lately, we've spent way too much time together."

Lilah was the one Doreen had asked for when she and Lawrence had that big car wreck. Somebody pulling a six-horse trailer had sideswiped them up by Plano and put Doreen in a wheelchair and then on crutches.

And Lilah had gone to her immediately. She would always help others out of her sense of Christian duty. That was the unbreakable code of this country and Lilah had made it her life's work to honor that code through and through.

Doreen depended on her. Yet she was jealous of her, too.

Especially of the fact that Lilah had become partners with Meri and Caleb and was supervising the bakery and kitchen at the new business, Honey Grove Kitchens. The whole thing had been Meri's idea, starting with her noticing that so much storm-damaged produce was going to waste every year. They had begun by using it in casseroles that they then froze and sold, and in baked goods that called for fruits or vegetables, like Lilah's famous zucchini chocolate cake. Now they'd branched out into selling baked goods and they'd be serving breakfast and lunch in their new café. Doreen had always loved being the only businesswoman in their class from school. Lilah had told her for years that Honey Grove Farm was a business, too, but Doreen had turned a deaf ear to that.

And, probably, if she'd thought about it, she resented that the farmers loved HGK for doing them a good turn, buying damaged foods they would otherwise have to plow under as a total loss.

Doreen seemed to forget that the farm had been a business all these years and Lilah had been running it for the last twenty of them.

Yes, she and Doreen had forgiven past sins

against each other, true, and in public, too, right there at the First Baptist Church the day Raul's Restaurant burned to the ground, but that didn't mean they were suddenly best friends. How could they be? There was way too much water already gone under the bridge for the two of them.

Yet they would always help each other. The code was doubly strong for people you've known all your life.

Lilah stepped away from the wooden table with the League of Women Voters' sign on it that they'd set in front of their lawn chairs and went to the card table behind Doreen which was set over the ice cream freezers to be another barrier between them and the sun. She would just keep her mouth shut for a while and stop worrying about Meri and Caleb. She would unwrap the paper bowls and napkins to be ready when people started wanting ice cream.

Doreen made a move like she was going to help. Lilah hoped she wouldn't. It'd take her ten minutes to wrangle her crutches and get up out of that lawn chair and then she wouldn't be able to do anything with her hands because she had to hold on to her crutches.

Lilah needn't have worried. The helpful gesture was a fake. The sloping green lawn that surrounded the Rock County Courthouse was already swarming with people coming and going and spreading out picnic blankets and carrying in coolers and setting up their own chairs to listen to the candidates' speeches. The whole Square was buzzing with the excitement of the traditional election campaign kickoff, so Doreen did not intend to take a chance on missing a single detail. Her head was whipping from side to side, she was trying so hard to watch it all.

"Don't get up," Lilah said. "Doreen, you're not well enough yet to help serve ice cream. You should've stayed home like I told you."

Doreen didn't even hear that. She was looking back down the low hill to the Square itself where there was a sudden commotion.

A bunch of people parted for a small, open Jeep to drive through—right across the sidewalk!

Lilah stared, the paper bowls forgotten in her hands. Flying the Texas flag on one side and the Stars and Stripes on the other, the Jeep came bouncing up the gradual slope of the courthouse lawn at a good little clip.

Too fast for the terrain and the number of people scattered around.

There was a man driving and a woman standing up, waving. They had loud music playing "The Eyes of Texas."

What in this *world?*

"Who *is* that?" Lilah said, rushing over to Doreen's chair to get a better view as the Jeep swerved around Kelly Collier, who was carrying a box of his brochures. Kelly was one of four candidates running for sheriff.

"What are they thinking?" Doreen said. "Driving on the grass like that?"

She stiffened. "Why, my *goodness!* It looks like *Lawrence's* Jeep . . ."

Sure enough, on the side of it, there was the magnetic sign, SEMPLES REALTY. Lilah recognized it as the vehicle Lawrence used to show his customers hunting campsites and fishing camps and such.

"It is!" Lilah said, and she wasn't proud of it—not at all—but this tickled her something fierce. Here was Doreen, who'd made a career out of poking her nose into everybody else's business and she didn't even know what her own husband was up to.

"Doreen, who is that woman he's with? Is that some celebrity? Look! It must be. She's got a little dog clutched up there at her bosoms."

Her very *considerable* bosoms, as shown by the low cut of her red dress. She was waving to everyone with her other hand like she was a Hollywood star and smiling to beat the band.

"She looks familiar, sort of," Doreen said. "Who *is* that?"

"Oh! Oh!" She clapped both hands to her face. "It's Missy Lambert! She filed to run against the Judge. You know! She retired from her newscasting job to do it."

Then Doreen lost the power of speech (which, to Lilah's knowledge, had never happened before) and gaped at the spectacle openmouthed.

The Jeep rolled past their League of Women Voters' booth with Lawrence holding on to the wheel with one hand and Missy's leg with the other, trying to help her keep her balance and not fall out of the vehicle. The woman was so desperate for attention—probably she was addicted to it from so many years of being the grand marshal of parades in every little town for miles around—that she was actually *standing up* in the passenger seat!

Lawrence didn't have a hand left over to wave at his wife. In fact, he gave no sign he even saw Doreen as he rolled past with a huge smile on his face.

Neither Doreen nor Lilah could take their eyes off the Jeep, so they both saw it when, the next minute, the little dog squirted out of Missy's clutches. The dog saw its chance when she twisted to the left to wave at some demented fan (some man, of course, who was hollering her name).

Instantly, Missy forgot about him and started screaming like a peacock, reaching in vain for the little Yorkie, but the dog shot past Lawrence and over the top of his door to hit the ground running.

"Stop! Stop!" Missy hollered.

Lawrence stomped on the brake. Missy lurched

toward him and he caught her but she reared back the other way and scrambled out her side of the vehicle screeching, "Simone, come back. Here, Simone! Oh, somebody please catch her . . ."

"Oh, yeah, there he goes," Doreen muttered.

Sure enough, Lawrence cut the motor and piled out on his side. He ran ahead of Missy, who was hampered in the chase, partly by being on the other side of the Jeep to start and even more by her stiletto heels.

They were that nude color that was so stylish right now. Which surprised Lilah, since her dress wasn't, not so much.

The dog was headed straight for Caleb and Meri, who were finally in the process of actually setting up the table to advertise Honey Grove Kitchens.

Lilah smiled as she looked at Meri. That girl was determined to do this right and make sure everybody that showed up today knew about the HGK café. She'd brought no telling how many samples of baked goods to hand out. Thank the Lord, both Caleb and Gideon appeared to still be speaking to her. Maybe she'd settle in, once the table was up, and enjoy the day.

Simone was making a beeline for them as if she knew the boxes stacked on the ground there held cookies and muffins. Maybe she could smell them.

Lawrence was fairly fast, for a man his age, and

Missy Lambert was no slowpoke, even in heels, and lots of other people were trying to help, but none of them had a chance of catching the dog. That little thing was a wonder. As she ran, her short legs were just a blur.

"I never saw a dog that fast," Lilah said.

Doreen didn't answer, of course. She was up on her crutches now, moving around so as to keep an eye on Lawrence, such a look on her face it'd stop him in his tracks if he could see it.

Simone must not have scented the cookies, after all, because she veered off toward two horses with teenaged boys slumped in the saddles cooling off in the shade. Taking a break on their way through town to the fairgrounds and the youth rodeo, no doubt.

The tiny dog charged them, barking with a vengeance, aiming for the horses' heels like she thought she was a Border collie.

Lawrence, Missy and assorted adults and children who'd joined in the chase sped up, but they didn't have a chance. One of the horses stood still long enough to throw a halfhearted kick at her, but then the other one spooked, so he did, too. They bolted across the lawn, both riders hanging in there, but barely. They had no control.

Merciful heavens! They could wreck the entire ice cream social in a heartbeat.

Sure enough, the chaos that followed was amazing. People scattered, tables fell, political bunting and brochures whipped up into the wind and flew in all directions, while the noise of so many people laughing and yelling and hollering advice to the young cowboys only scared the horses more. They thundered right on downhill toward the street.

That little Simone was a stayer, now. She tried to keep up with her prey but her legs were getting tired and by the time the horses reached the street, they'd left her in the dust. When she gave it up, she turned to look for Missy, who, by now, was stopped and bent over (hanging out of her dress, of course) to try and get her breath. The minute Simone spotted her, she gave out some weak yips and headed for her waiting arms.

Lawrence was standing over Missy and he beamed at the reunion, putting his arm around Missy's shoulders in congratulations.

Doreen forgot all about the League of Women Voters and ice cream and started hobbling off to get her hands on him. Poor guy. He was in for a world of hurt.

Lilah looked at him, shaking her head in sympathy.

"So," a deep voice said in her ear, "how'd ya like them apples for a campaign kickoff that'll be talked about for years to come?"

She turned to find Elbert Carlson, known all over the county as the Judge, standing at her shoulder.

"Well, you sound like you're trying to take the credit for all the fun," Lilah said. "You oughtta be worried instead. Haven't you noticed it's your opponent that furnished the entertainment today?"

He just smiled. Elbert always did have a sense of entitlement but nobody was quite sure where he got it from.

"And she presented a very nonjudicial image as she did so," he said. "Right? I've been the Judge for a long time. So I'm thinking she won't be hard to beat."

Lilah shook her head. "You may be wrong about that, Judge. Folks nowadays like their politicians to be entertaining."

He chuckled. "Yeah, but they know me. They know I'll take care of them."

Lilah smiled. "Too old-fashioned," she said. "You need to try to be a little more 'with-it,' Elbert."

He patted her shoulder. "Well, then, maybe you could help me with that. You *are* planning to support me in this campaign, aren't you, Lilah? Us older-but-almost-with-it folks have to stick together, you know."

She raised her eyebrows and gave him her straightest look. "That depends entirely on how you'll vote on the re-zoning of Jones Orchards."

He widened his eyes under his shaggy brows. Too shaggy. That came from not having a wife to keep him well groomed. Honestly, what was Hank the barber thinking, letting one of his clients walk around looking so unkempt?

But then, Elbert's hair hadn't been cut lately, either, so maybe she shouldn't blame Hank.

"You've had enough time to think about it," she said, pressing him to make it clear she was serious about this. "Where do you stand on the re-zoning, Judge?"

He shook his head. "You know I can't make a decision on that before I study both sides of the question."

"I can see how you don't want to lose the votes of either side," she said, "but you don't have to pussyfoot around with me. I won't tell a soul but I'll work my heart out for you if you give me your word you'll be against it."

"What if I honestly don't know?"

Oh, Lord! His tone just gave her the willies.

"Look, Elbert, I've already heard that the reason Missy entered the race is to help get that zoning changed. And you know as well as I do that's the truth. Her people are all builders up there in the north end of the county, and just think of the business they'd get if Rock County starts getting covered up with new houses."

So. If the Judge decided to be a yes vote, too, all the folks wanting to keep Rock County centered in agriculture would not have a real choice for county judge. Honey Grove Farm would be sunk. With Jones Orchards just across the road from it, the entire neighborhood would go residential before a person could say Jack Robinson.

"Well, if that's the way you feel, I honestly don't know who I'm supporting for judge."

"Aw, come on, Lilah. You're the queen of the county and you know it. People listen to you."

"And what I'm going to be telling them is we need to keep our farmland for farms if we're going to feed the world . . . and if we're going to keep our tax revenue up when the big-city folks come out to enjoy a day trip to our quaint town, as they like to call it, and hang out at the farmers markets buying their organic, natural, local food."

"I just don't know yet. I haven't had a chance to really look into it."

He gave her his most charming earnest look. "You know me, Lilah. We've known each other all our lives. You can't *not* campaign for me. You always do."

"I will if you'll give me your word."

"I can't do that now."

She smiled. "Sorry, Elbert."

He looked into her eyes for a long minute.

"I'm not giving up," he said. "Let me take you to dinner Friday night and we'll talk through all the pros and cons."

She gave him a narrow look. "That's a little bit elaborate, isn't it? We see each other around the Square . . ."

"No," he said. "Let's sit down and really discuss

this. I'll convince you to tell everybody in Rock County I'm the only man for the job. Besides, I'd love to go out with you."

"It wouldn't be 'going out.' It'd be a political discussion."

"Whatever terminology you like is fine with me," he said. "Political discussion it is. Now, what do you say?"

"I have a business and a farm to run. I never know what I'll be into by Friday night."

"I'll call you late on Thursday, see if we need to reschedule."

She shrugged. "We'll see how the week goes."

He truly was the candidate with the best chance to win. He was the incumbent and he was well liked and respected. So he *had* to come around to her point of view because her whole life was at stake.

Once those ugly, farmland-gobbling housing developments got started, they grew faster than mesquite brush could take a pasture.

"I'll be back by for some ice cream after I make my speech," he said, smiling sweetly. "I don't suppose you brought any peach pie to go with it, did you?"

Give him a challenge and maybe he'd rise to it.

"Even if I did, you wouldn't get a piece. Not until you promise to vote my way."

"I haven't said I won't, remember."

She nodded, smiling back at him. She'd bring

him around to her way of thinking if it harelipped the governor.

But he was an impatient sort, sometimes. Maybe she'd better go ahead and make sure of the chance to work on him in private, over a dinner that he wouldn't want to hurry through.

Which would be guaranteed if she were cooking it herself. Most men were fools for her chicken-fried steak with pepper gravy and mashed potatoes.

Alongside her buttermilk yeast rolls. And home-grown tomatoes.

But she mustn't suggest that. With the Judge making noises about "going out" with her, it'd be better not to ask him to her house. He might take it as encouragement along those lines.

And, after all, as her good friend Barbara Jane, usually called B.J., was always telling her, and Meri, too, she had to learn to be a taker as well as a giver and be gracious about it.

So she said, "On second thought, Elbert, let's go ahead and plan on Friday night. If something comes up, I'll let you know."

He twinkled. "Great," he said, patting her shoulder as he started off toward the speaker's podium. "It's a date."

A *date?* Lilah just shook her head as she watched him go.

Two

Meri stepped back, tilted her head and studied the angle of the table sitting in the shade of the tall live-oak tree. It *was* the best place—it'd be shaded all morning and nobody on the way to or from the courthouse steps where the speakers would stand could miss it.

"There's a pine and two post oaks behind the courthouse," Caleb drawled.

"No need for sarcasm," she said, flashing him a glance that turned into the usual long look because she couldn't stop herself.

The contrast of his sky-blue eyes with his deeply tanned skin and the sand-and-sun shade of his hair falling over the white strip of his farmer's tan always made her look twice. What woman wouldn't?

"This is perfect," she said.

"Thanks, honey," Caleb said. "All the girls tell me that."

Gideon said, "So I'm perfect, too, since we're twins, right?"

He snapped open another lawn chair with one hand and set it in the conversational circle he and Caleb were creating for their customers who dropped by for a bakery sample and wanted to stay for a little visit.

Meri shook her head at their silliness, but she

was smiling, too. They were charming, no denying it, even when they acted like two little kids. "Oh, yeah," she teased. "Here we go with the Burkett egos again. Y'all know I didn't say either one of you was perfect, but I must admit y'all have behaved perfectly today. Thanks for moving the table so many times for me."

Really. Nobody she'd worked with in the past would've done that so cheerfully.

"Yeah," Caleb said, "and now we've decided. Which is why we're setting these chairs out now. No more movin'."

She couldn't resist. She looked at the table again, tilted her head and stared at it thoughtfully.

"Meri. Did you hear me?"

"We-e-ell, on second thought . . ." she drawled, ". . . if there's a pine on the back lawn . . ."

Gideon and Caleb protested. "No! No more! . . ."

"You can't go back on your word. You said it was perfect."

They converged on her from opposite directions, using their smiles to charm her. Caleb's was impish and lively, Gid's quieter, thoughtful, almost sad, maybe. Fitting for their personalities.

"We do not need to move this cotton-pickin' table one more time. This right here is just fine," Caleb said.

But then, Gideon couldn't resist stirring things up a little more.

"Well, I dunno, Cale," he said. "Maybe we should. Meri, there aren't any huge, fierce dogs trying to gobble up your baked goods on the back lawn."

She felt her smile take over her face. This must be what it was like to have a brother.

Careful, Mer. You're not in their family yet. If you'll ever be.

"Will you *stop* it? The hospitality of our HGK brand would be ruined if we didn't have any samples to hand out."

"But you were so funny, scrambling like crazy to get the boxes out of the way of a dog the size of my hand," Caleb said. "I wish you could've seen yourself."

"You two didn't look too dignified, either, squatting there ready to catch her and be Missy's hero. Honestly, boys, I think she's a bit out of your age range."

They all laughed, and Meri felt the warmth of camaraderie grow inside her. It was satisfying to be the instigator of silliness for once. It was a new role for her but she was taking it on more and more as she relaxed into living in Texas.

In the whole community, really, she sometimes had this sense that she was part of a family, one bigger than her and Lilah.

She caught a fast breath.

Too soon to think like that. Take it slow. Be careful.

"Okay," she said briskly, "time to bring the rest of the stuff from the truck so we can get set up. Have y'all noticed that this crowd's growing by the minute? Here are hundreds of customers and we want to get every one of them to come through the door of our new café."

Caleb grinned at Gid. "You hear that y'all? My girl's talkin' like a Texan now."

My girl.

Caleb took her by the arm. "Let's go." He started them jogging downhill toward the Square.

"Hey wait," Gideon yelled. "I can't hang out here and watch a woman offload a truck. I'll go."

"Can't leave Meri here," Caleb yelled back over his shoulder. "She might decide she doesn't like the table in this spot after all."

"Oh, I see how it is," Gid yelled. "You lovebirds don't forget to come back, now. I've got more work to do today than just handing out cookies."

Caleb lifted his free hand to show he'd heard and they broke into a run.

Toward the bottom of the slope, Caleb let go of her arm and took her hand in his big callused one as they headed for the truck. Lately, he did that habitually when they walked together and it melted her every time.

Just before they reached the sidewalk that ran along the Square in front of his pickup, the smooth leather soles of Meri's new flip-flops slipped on the damp grass and she almost fell. Caleb caught her, turned her in his arms and hugged her right there, in public, on the Square in Rock Springs, Texas.

And she hugged him right back.

"Thanks for being so patient with me today, Caleb," she said. "Nobody else in my whole life has ever been so kind about my pickiness. I just wanted to find the perfect shade."

He chuckled, looking down at her with light in his eyes as he took a deep breath and then folded her more tightly into his arms. He rested his chin on the top of her head and rocked her gently. She breathed in the scent of him until it made her dizzy.

Finally, she pulled back and looked up into his beyond handsome face with its deep tan.

"Don't give me that look," he said. "It will get you nowhere."

But his eyes contradicted his words. The love—*was* it love?—that deepened his blue-eyed gaze weakened her knees. Literally.

She'd always thought that kind of talk was so silly. So far from reality.

She'd been so naïve for a woman her age. She hadn't even known this kind of feeling could exist.

"Right back at'cha," she murmured, using the phrase he'd started as a habit between them.

He grinned at her, shaking his head.

"Ah, my picky Meri. I hate to break it to you,

31

but your perfect shade's gonna move, honey. You do know you can't control the sun, don't you?"

She nodded solemnly.

He smiled and pulled her close again. His breath, warm against her ear, stirred her hair as he whispered, "But I *will* rope the moon for you if you want me to."

The words pierced her through.

The sound they made sent sweetness into her very blood. It tightened her arms around him. No one, *ever*, had said such a thing to her.

She hadn't even known it was possible that anyone ever could feel that way about her.

Meri tried to find enough breath to be able to think but her brain was mush and all her body wanted was to stay still in this moment in the sun, while vehicles and people swirled in the space outside their circle and could never get in.

"Hey, Caleb!" a man's voice yelled. "Looks like you're doin' all right!"

Meri startled and pulled back in time to see J.B., the builder, waving from his passing truck. He had a broad grin on his face.

Oh! Now the whole town would hear about this. Everyone would be talking about them and saying they were in love.

She didn't have time right now to be *in love*. She had a business to run.

On the other hand, with Caleb's arms around her, she didn't care.

She risked one direct glance up at him. A quick one. If she let it linger, she couldn't say what she might do. Her whole body was longing for the taste of his mouth.

The glint in his eyes made her smile but she turned and led the way on out to his truck, which was double-parked behind two others.

"You're gonna get a ticket," she said. "Haven't I told you not to do this?"

"Hub saw me do it," he said. "Besides, anybody wants out, they know it's mine, so all they have to do is give a holler."

The elderly Hub Morrison was a hanger-on at the sheriff's office who fancied himself a lawman and took it upon himself to direct traffic when needed. He lived to make sure that transgressors were punished whenever possible.

"Hub must like you," Meri said as she looked for the box with the tablecloth to go in their first load. "He never fails to hassle everybody else, especially Lilah and me. She's still mad at him for holding her and Dulcie up that day of the fire."

"Aw, most people just don't know how to treat him. Y'all ever bring him a chaw? A fresh twist of Redman goes a long way with ol' Hub."

"Hmm," she said as she stacked boxes of sample muffins and cookies on top of the tablecloth box, "bribing a volunteer enforcer of the law. I'll have to check the code for that. You might get yourself arrested and sent to Huntsville."

Caleb picked up a stack of plastic chairs from the bed of the truck. "Would you be my defense attorney? Would you come visit me? Maybe bring me a cake with a file baked in?"

She rolled her eyes at him.

"Hey, no kidding. Maybe we should start a line of those for the bakery. We could set up a mobile unit to deliver the cakes around to the various prisons after you get orders from girlfriends and wives."

"You're assuming they'd want the bad guys back."

He rolled his eyes. "You shock me, Mer. You'd want *me* back, wouldn't you?"

"*You* shock *me*," she said as they started back up the sloping lawn with their supplies. "I can't believe you're suggesting HGK take a position on the wrong side of the law."

He grinned. "My outlaw reputation's been suffering lately. I hate to let it die."

Meri laughed. But she made herself take note. Stories of Caleb's outlaw reputation included adventures with lots of different women, many of whom were still in Rock Springs and were still his friends, including the notorious, prominent and beautiful rancher Ronnie Rae Hardesty. She was the one who'd shot him in the leg years ago and caused the limp he lived with.

Gideon ran to meet them, took Meri's load from her and carried it to the table. Caleb set up the new chairs in another grouping near the trunk of the tree.

Swiftly, they spread the cloth on the table—pale blue gingham check like Lilah's favorite one at home, but embroidered at the corners with the HGK logo of bluebonnets and honeybees. They admired it, then unpacked the samples of baked goods onto the table. Meri stepped back and took a look.

"I'll go get the fresh flowers for the center," she said. "Then we'll take some pictures we can use for advertising . . ."

Gideon whipped out his cell phone. "First, let me get some of the two of you," he said. "Just to see how the light falls. Stand there, right behind the table."

So Caleb came to stand beside her. He put his strong arm around her and pulled her a little closer and she filled her lungs with the scent of his light sweat and his skin.

The ropes of his muscles across her back gave her a thrilling sensation to lean into and the sun melded them together in another private bubble of time. The breeze picked up, just at the instant Gideon started snapping. It stirred her hair. She glanced up at Caleb. His, too. She loved the way he looked with his hair messed up.

She couldn't stop looking at him. Just the sight of him made her draw a long, ragged breath. Twice in one day.

Two moments she'd never forget, no matter what happened in the future.

"Oh, look," Doreen trilled, "Gideon's taking pictures. I have to admit Meri and Caleb do look like they belong together."

Doreen's voice was one that really carried, and it penetrated Lilah's ears even while she was dipping strawberry ice cream into a bowl for Verna Carl as fast as she could. She glanced up.

"Well, I guess so," she said, using her best tart tone. "Nobody can deny they're both beautiful young people. Inside and out."

Doreen snorted, no doubt disputing whether that last thought applied to Caleb, too.

Lilah let it go so as not to get the old "Caleb Burkett's born to be a heartbreaker and a rambling man" chatter started up all over town again.

But Verna Carl didn't let any of that distract her from the reason she'd stopped by their booth, Lilah realized. She'd been looking at Doreen and now she gave her what could only be called a catty smile.

"Well, Doreen, it surely didn't take you very long to get to Lawrence after the excitement died down. I hope you let him know how tacky it looked for him to be holding on to Missy's leg like that right out in public."

Surprise jerked Doreen straight up in her chair and her face turned every color of the rainbow.

Lilah grinned to herself. Doreen was used to being the one dishing out the barbs instead of being on the receiving end.

"And just exactly what do you mean by that?"

Verna Carl threw up her hands and looked horrified. Sort of.

"Oh, now don't misunderstand me. I'm not hinting at anything. I haven't heard a word about them, but such behavior causes talk in this town. You know that."

Lilah was so interested, she topped the bowl with one more dip and it was one too many, then she had to grab another bowl right quick and save it from toppling off and being wasted. She handed Verna Carl her bowl and started saving the other dip herself without even knowing what she was eating.

The trouble between these two hadn't flared up for a long time. It started at the big Fourth of July celebration on the lake that year Mose Landry was in charge of the fireworks and accidentally caught his own fancy bass boat on fire.

Lilah's group were all teenagers then. Verna Carl and her sister were up on a flatbed stage, playing guitar and fiddle for Doreen, the teen-aged Miss Rock Springs, who was singing her heart out on "San Antonio Rose" (entertaining the home folks, yes, but also practicing for the talent portion of the Miss Texas contest, which she did *not* win) when, without so much as a "by your leave," Doreen stopped singing right in the middle of "Enchantment strange as the blue up above" and accused the two sisters of trying to drown out her voice with their "raucous" playing. Well. Her fiddling was Verna Carl's great pride and she never got over that insult. She and Lilah had always maintained the truth was Doreen forgot the words because she'd been thinking about how pretty she looked in all that makeup.

"He was trying to keep her from falling out of the Jeep," Doreen snapped. "He couldn't very well jerk her down to sit in the seat, now could he? She's a customer of his. She's looking into buying Tessie Harmon's house."

"Oh, my goodness!" Lilah said, through a mouthful of ice cream. She swallowed fast and almost got that ache down her throat from too much cold but that didn't stop her scare. "Missy must be pretty sure she's going to beat the Judge if she's already moving to Rock Springs."

Lord, but did Lilah have some work to do! She had to get the Judge firmly on her side and then campaign her heart out all over this county.

Verna Carl wouldn't let go. "So why was he driving her up across the grass in their own little parade? Lots of folks think that looked a little funny, too."

Doreen shrugged, trying to look like she wasn't bothered a bit.

"Lawrence said she needed a way to get all her

brochures up here to the crowd, so, of course, he offered the Jeep. We're a full-service realty company, you know."

"Right," Verna Carl said. "I just hope it doesn't cause bad blood between him and the Judge. I see he's even helping her hand them out."

"Times are hard," Doreen said. "What with the housing slowdown and all. People just aren't buying much because they can't get the mortgages. Lawrence has to do whatever he has to do. The Judge will understand, I'm sure."

That remains to be seen.

Lilah finished the ice cream and threw the dish away. *Yes. It would. This could be a very interesting election by the time it was over and all the votes counted.*

She took a minute to look around. Most of the overturned tables had been set to rights and the papers picked up already. That was good, because people needed to get their minds on politics as well as fun and excitement.

Doreen changed the subject and went to quizzing Verna Carl about her sister Margie's divorce after thirty-five years of apparently happy marriage, which, right now, was the talk of the town.

In Lilah's opinion, the shocking thing about it was that Margie waited thirty-five years to do it. That Buster Chapman was tighter than the skin on a tomato. He'd charge his own mother a dollar for a drink of water. It'd do him good to have to give Margie half of everything that he'd nickeled and dimed out of life so far.

But instead of putting in her two cents' worth, Lilah pretended to be cleaning things up and went back to her plotting while she had no customers. Yes. She'd stir up enough talk to reach the Judge's ears and make him think the majority of voters agreed with her.

Verna Carl finally went on her way and most people settled into their chairs to listen to the speeches. There'd be a lot of them, and not too interesting, since it was all the county offices up for grabs and most of the candidates weren't very good speakers. Not to mention that the incumbents had been saying the same thing for years in every talk they gave.

Lilah got two plastic glasses and scooped them full of ice, since ladies don't drink from a can in public, then she found two Cokes in the tub of ice and soda pop. She took one to Doreen and sat down in the chair beside her.

They had a moment of blissful silence while they poured their drinks, then Doreen said, "You know, Lilah, I'm worried about you. Are you sick or something?"

Well! That just floored Lilah. She stared at her.

"Why in this world would you say that, Doreen Semples? I turn out enough work for two women every day of my life."

"But you're not running Honey Grove Kitchens! The whole town marvels about it. *You,* of all people! You always boss everything, coming and going, but you're not in charge of your very own business!"

"Oh, my stars! I do *not* boss everything. I just usually know the best way to do things."

Doreen obviously didn't agree that Lilah usually knew best. She just took another drink, shaking her head in wonder. Really, she overdid the acting.

"Well, if it's any of *your* business," Lilah snapped, "I trust my granddaughter to run our business. And she's got a fine partner in Caleb."

"No. I don't understand it. At all. Meri's a lawyer, not a businesswoman."

Lilah got up and moved her chair deeper into what little shade they had left. The sun was getting serious now.

"I direct the kitchen," she said. "Recipes, preparations, processes, personnel. I make all those decisions."

Doreen wrinkled her perky little nose. Too perky now, with all those years around it on her face. "And that's it? It's just not like you, Lilah. You sure you're not sick?"

"No. I am not."

She gave Doreen her long, straight, killer look.

"Here's what you can tell your little bunch of hangers-on when they're sitting around your dress shop drinking coffee and talking about me: I decided to trust my granddaughter that night she did such a bang-up job of setting things to rights at the pie contest."

Raising her eyebrow for emphasis, she held the look while she poured some more Coke in her glass. Doreen could just put *that* in her pipe and smoke it.

It might be hitting below the belt to remind Doreen of that wonderful evening when Meri had verbally bested her so soundly in front of the whole town, but people who ask nosy questions need to be ready to get more information than they bargain for.

Doreen's face tightened. But not even the bad memory of a good trouncing could deter her from mining deeper into Lilah's personal life while she had the chance. And, of course, she didn't want to let talk veer back toward Lawrence and Missy.

"The decision you mentioned . . . you mean the decision not to boss her anymore?"

"I never really *bossed* her—"

Doreen snorted a little laugh. "Lilah, you—"

"Meri's too independent to take much bossing. And I had to teach her about farming and preserving food," Lilah said, gathering her dignity about her.

"Of course."

"No, what I decided that night was that Meri has great instincts and good judgment. She has a right to step out and use those qualities. A right to find out what she can accomplish in this world."

Doreen shook her head. "Hard to believe," she said. "I've known you all our lives and—"

"Believe it or don't," Lilah snapped. "You asked."

"Oh, now, don't go get all huffy. Do you think she's doing a good job? I guess so, or you'd take the reins away from her."

She shot Lilah her sly glance. "If Caleb would let you."

"Give it up, Doreen. I'm not going to gossip about the business."

Doreen hushed. She knew Lilah meant it.

She got up to move her chair out of the sun and Lilah helped her. While she was up, leaning on her crutches, Doreen looked for Meri and Caleb again.

"Maybe I should go over there and—"

"Stay right where you are. I haven't waited on you hand and foot ever since that wreck so you could go over there and quiz those young people within an inch of their lives."

Doreen sniffed and looked hurt. "Well, I appreciate all you've done for me, Lilah, but I have to say, for the sake of the record, that 'hand and foot' is a bit of an exaggeration."

Lilah grunted. "I get double credit for every hour because you're such a pill to deal with."

"That's no way to talk to a sick person. I'm not well yet."

"You nearly are. You'd better be thankful your leg was just broken in three places instead of smashed to pieces like we first heard it was."

"I am."

"Well, then, sit down and let's finish our Cokes in peace."

They did that and then Doreen went to the Church of God ladies' booth to visit with them and Lilah rejoiced in having a minute to herself. She leaned her head back and closed her eyes to enjoy the breeze and the shade while she had it.

But her mind was whirling like a windmill in a high wind.

The fate of Jones Orchards was the fate of Honey Grove was the fate of Rock County and Rock Springs. It wasn't just the farms and ranches that needed to be preserved. Rock Springs needed to stay just as it was. Small town life was a precious thing and it was dying out in too many places in this country.

If she should be fortunate enough to have great-grandchildren, she wanted them to experience Rock County just the way it was now.

She lifted her head and her eyes went straight to Caleb and Meri, over there handing out muffins and cookies and building up the reputation of Honey Grove Kitchens. They were gambling their youth and money on making Honey Grove Farm and Honey Grove Kitchens succeed. Neither one of them would've ever done that if they hadn't been trying to save the farm for Lilah.

Therefore, she *had* to stop that zoning change. That hussy Missy in her tight red dress had been all over the place since her grand parade entrance, handing out brochures with one hand and carrying that little dog in the other. All the men were goggle-eyed.

Could the birdbrain even set that little Simone down to wield the gavel if she should win the office? She had a law degree, yes, but she hadn't practiced the profession for years. There had to be an ulterior motive for her to get into the running right now, and Lilah *knew* in her heart of hearts that it was to push that zoning change through.

Well, she and her builder brothers could just think again. As long as there was breath in Lilah's body, she wouldn't give up. She'd make Elbert see reason or make the world look level.

Which sounded like yet another huge project on top of the dozen or so she already had under way. Right this minute, she'd rather think about something happy—young love, for example. She looked for Meri and Caleb.

Once she started gazing at those two beloved young people, smiling and laughing, she couldn't stop. They were so happy.

They really *did* look like they were perfect for each other.

And yet . . . there was that weird little feeling picking at her again. It tugged at her innards.

Oh, Lord. She hoped whatever it was, it didn't mean a thing.

Three

Meri ran slowly along Caleb's Indian River Ranch Road, the one covered with white gravel that led from the highway to the house. She needed to get the kinks out of her legs and her rhythm going before she increased the speed. It was hard to believe that lately she'd missed a few runs. Normally, she ran every day without fail.

Work (and worry) just consumed her sometimes. She had to remember that she always would feel better if she got in her daily run. Right now, a hundred yards from Caleb's house, she already felt a lift in her spirits.

She pushed aside her to-do list for the evening and concentrated on the rolling pastures dotted with trees and the endless sky overhead.

The considerable Texas wind was at her back, bringing the aromas of juniper trees and grass. She relaxed completely and picked up speed.

Until her cell phone rang. She dug it out of her pocket while she kept moving, swiped it and held it to her ear.

Caleb's voice said, "Hey, Mer. How about you turn around and come back this way?"

Disappointment stabbed her. "But Cale! I haven't had a chance to run for three days and . . ."

She bit her lip. *Quit whining, Meri.*

He had helped her with the supply orders and that was not on his list of responsibilities for HGK.

"Listen, babe . . ." he said. The warm honey of his voice slowed her blood. And her steps.

"The cattle I leased from Ronnie Buck for Gid and me to practice cutting with are climbing in and out of the pen. Next thing we know, one of 'em will cut a leg or go fall in the river and I can't afford any more veterinary bills. It seems stupid to pay for Doc's services when I could be taking care of my own animals, but I'm already working from can't see to can't see. That vet degree of mine will just have to keep on going to waste." He grinned. "Only thing good about that is it chaps ol' Jake's hide, for sure. Anyway, we'll just put 'em in the round pen for tonight and I'll have the boys fix the fence first thing in the morning."

"I'll be there in a minute."

"Meet me at the barn."

When she arrived, he had two horses in the cross ties and he was saddling one. Over his shoulder, he said, "Gimme a minute and I'll carry your saddle."

She started for the tack room.

"No way," she said. "I'd get a reputation as a sissy and never be able to live it down."

He'd known that she'd say that but his manners were habitual. It made her smile. Gallant. He was a gallant man and she loved that about him.

Among other things. Her smile widened.

Lilah had taught her well, though, and she didn't need any help. She'd been around horses enough by now that she could rely on her own knowledge as long as the demands on her were simple. She carried her saddle to the mount she often used at his place, a roan mare named Rosie.

"This is my first invitation to work cattle," she said. "Thanks."

He grinned at the teasing. "You're welcome. With that kind of attitude, you can learn new skills that might come in handy if that bakery thing doesn't work out for you."

"Not *even* a possibility," she said, smiling.

He laughed that deep laugh she loved. "Says the woman who worries and frets like a champion," he said.

"Not this evening. Now I'm a cowgirl just riding the range with her cowboy."

They mounted up, Meri stepping into the stirrup before he could come to give her a leg up.

He nodded, flashing that bright blue look at her. A caressing look.

"There you go," he said, chuckling. "I'm thinkin' this evening just took a turn for the better, cows or no cows."

She still couldn't believe how Caleb could

undo her. Her legs weakened in the stirrups. Some-how, without realizing it, she'd let her famous emotional control fade. And he had taken it.

If this was lasting love that she was feeling for him, then God help her if he didn't return it. But she didn't want to think about that possibility now.

They rode down one of the alleyways that ran between pens and pastures on the ranch near the barn. The fences that lined the alleys were almost as decrepit as the house had been before Caleb started working on it.

"I can't wait to really get these fences in shape," Caleb said. "They look so ratty. But you talk about expense . . . wow." He shook his head. "I can't get into that right now. Gotta get the house done first."

"You will. Just take it easy."

"Well. That's usually my line to you," he said. "What's happening here? We trading places?"

They looked at each other.

She fluttered her eyelashes at him in exaggeration. "Don't get used to it, cowboy. It's a temporary thing, no doubt."

"No doubt."

Laughing, they rode closer to the pen that held the cutting cattle. Meri stared at the cows in disbelief. Three of them were at the fence and as she watched, one stuck a leg between two lines of cable fencing strung between the pipe posts, then stepped through the space so fast it make Meri blink.

"Cale! Did you see that?"

Another one followed, trotting over to join the five or six head that were already in that pen. The third ran up and down the fence, apparently working up its nerve to try the same escape.

"Yep," Caleb said. "Whether I want to do it now or not, I've gotta replace that cable. It's so old and stretched it might as well not be there."

"I can't believe they can do that!" Meri said.

As she spoke, one of the two escapees ran to the fence and climbed back into the pen it had just left.

"Next thing you know, they'll be heading for the river," Caleb said. "That pen they're getting into has a hole. See it, there on the back? Soon as they find that, they'll be out on the range to play. That happens, we'll have to waste hours huntin' them down."

"Well, then," Meri said playfully, "let's round 'em up!"

They rode into the pen with the hole in the fence and Caleb sent Meri to block it with her horse. He herded the cows that were in there and pushed them out into the alleyway, except for one spotted one that ran to the cross fence and climbed back in with the original herd.

Watching that cow fade fast into the bunch of twenty or so that were milling around, as if she were hiding from Meri and Caleb, made them laugh.

"Okay, come on," he said, once he had urged his little bunch along the alley far enough to leave some room at the gate. "Watch these ones here and keep them from turning back. I'll get the rest of 'em."

Meri rode out into the alleyway and followed Cale's directions, sitting on her horse and watching her charges intently, moving only once to stop a black cow that turned around and started toward her. Ragged grass grew along the edges of the hard dirt pathway and that kept them busy. They all loved to munch on it.

Caleb pushed the larger bunch out into the alleyway behind Meri and she pulled her horse to the side so all the cattle could meld into one herd.

Then she and Cale drove them down the path toward the barn, swerving to take them up the small rise to the round pen that overlooked the old building.

"We'll leave 'em here tonight," he said. "Tomorrow I'll have the hired hands work on that fence. If we get the hole plugged, we don't care if they climb in and out all day long."

The two of them watched the cows begin to settle and then rode out. Caleb closed the gate of the tall round pen, which was made of boards set close together to prevent distractions. Cale had said it was where they started young horses.

He leaned from the saddle to drop the latch.

"So is that all we need to do?" Meri asked.

"Except for feeding the horses, cats and dogs, cooking supper, remodeling the kitchen and painting the fence and barn," he said, smiling at her.

"That is way more than I wanted to know."

"Me, too. Let's ride down by the river and watch the sunset."

Her lips parted to say there was no time for that, but she closed them again.

"Perfect," she said, and meant it.

As they rode along side by side, their bodies moving in the same rhythm as those of the horses, the whole earth seemed to gather around them as a green-and-brown cocoon of contentment. And all of it beneath an enormous sky streaked with reds and golds growing brighter with every breath Meri took, bright enough to light up the world with glory.

Safety. Meri felt safe and secure and satisfied. A rare moment for her, and she was grateful for it.

"You did a great job, Mer," Caleb said.

"Thanks, Cale. I never knew the work of a cowgirl could be so satisfying."

His answer was a murmured, "Whoa."

Both horses stopped. Close, very close together.

Cale leaned from the saddle to take her hand, pulled her toward him and kissed her.

Her whole body reacted with pleasure.

Then the moment was complete.

Four

Lilah gave the big sheet of piecrust dough one last hard swipe with the rolling pin, grabbed the cookie cutter and started cutting out tiny tart shells. Jewel, her kitchen manager, brought the pot of peach filling from the stove.

"You've got to quit this extra work," she said. "Whatever happened to 'when it's gone, it's gone'? Don't you know what that means? We put that note on the menus, remember?"

Coming from Jewel, who didn't talk much, this was a long speech.

And she wasn't done. "Just as I can't make enough cinnamon rolls for the whole town every day, we can't be expected to always have tarts on hand. So. They ate up all the tarts. We don't have to make more right now. Limited supply will make them even more popular."

She set the pot down with a thump and started fitting the dough into the tart pans.

"Just this one time," Lilah said, cutting more circles. "I want the Judge to have some and he's not here yet." She chuckled. "I'm trying to make him owe me."

Jewel snorted. "Impossible."

Lilah glanced into the café again, then through the window into the hall. Doreen was coming, heading straight for the kitchen.

53

"Jewel, there's such a crowd out there, I can't spot Meri. I need to tell her to keep track of which cookies are disappearing faster, the cowboy ones or the chocolate chip pecan."

Another snort. "That girl's already got a count in her head, you mark my words. She don't need you to give her orders."

Thank goodness Doreen sailed in through the door right then, so Lilah didn't start a fuss with Jewel. Who else in town but Jewel would be competent to manage the kitchen at HGK?

"Y'all got a good crowd for the HGK café grand opening party," Doreen trilled, "but then, what else is there to do in Rock Springs on a Saturday night?"

"Well, you could stay home and read your Sunday school lesson," Lilah drawled. "Look for a Bible verse about encouraging other people."

"That's exactly what I'm here for," Doreen said, "to give you encouragement and advice to build goodwill for your new business. Everybody's asking for you out in the café, so let Jewel do her job and you go mingle, okay? I'll do this cooking that you should've done before the doors opened."

And then Doreen, whose pushiness knew no bounds, actually picked up a spoon and started helping to fill the tart crusts.

Lilah surprised herself. Instead of snatching the spoon away, she let her be. The ones Doreen filled might be a little sloppy, but truth was, Lilah needed all the help she could get.

I've got more goodwill in Rock County than you can ever hope for, Doreen.

But Lilah didn't say the words. This was too happy a night. Doreen meant well—mostly. It was just her ingrained habit of telling other people what to do that made them hate her some-times.

And Doreen had a gossiping habit, too, so Lilah wanted to put out a positive message.

"I'm taking this big turnout as a sign that we can get some regulars in here for breakfast," she said. "I'm full of faith that we're going to sell desserts and breads like crazy, too. You know there's so many families where people are working two jobs and don't have time to bake."

For once in her life, Doreen was as sweet as the tarts.

"Yes, I do," she said solemnly, and she even raised her voice so Lilah could hear her over the music playing out in the café, "and Lilah, lots of them think your baking just can't be beat."

Lilah pulled back and stared at her in shock. "Well! Thank you so much, Doreen. I never thought I would hear you say that."

She grinned to herself, though. Doreen hadn't said that she herself agreed with that. She would never say that. Not as long as she had her right mind.

• • •

There really wasn't room in the café for dancing but when Meri put a Bob Wills CD on the player—she'd set one up permanently on a battered old secretary desk in the back corner of the room—teenager Dallas Fremont grabbed her boyfriend and pulled him out into what little space there was. Dallas and her brother, Denton, were two of Meri's and Caleb's favorite people.

Meri turned and opened her mouth to say the café was too small for dancing, but a group of the young people were already moving tables around and then Caleb came up behind her and took her in his arms. For a second, they just stood there spooned together, his warmth flowing all the way through her and his lips in her hair.

The old Meri would never have melted into an unexpected embrace on instinct, without a thought. Caleb. It was because the arms were Caleb's. Oh, yes, she did love him. If she dared.

And the song was "Faded Love." The old Meri would never have listened to such a romantic melody, either.

She turned in his arms and the old tune so filled with longing and love carried them out of the corner and through the little café into the hallway. They danced all the way down it, past the wall of kitchen windows and back again, holding each other closer all the time. He smelled so wonderfully citrusy and clean, he felt so strong and warm, he moved so sweetly to the lilting rhythm that she never wanted this dance to end.

But when the song was done, Caleb stopped. Meri looked up at him and he kissed her so thoroughly that all she wanted was more. And more. She stood on tiptoe and wound her arms around his neck and kissed him back until she was senseless.

Out of breath, they finally stopped and she buried her head in his chest. Tonight she wouldn't let herself think about what might happen next.

"Oh, there y'all are!" Doreen's voice trilled.

Meri and Caleb turned.

Doreen was coming out of the kitchen carrying a crystal platter holding a bowl of fresh tomato salsa surrounded by abundant layers of Lilah's handmade cheese crackers.

"You little lovebirds need to get to work," she said. "There's trays of pecan jumbles and lemon tea cakes that should be out in the café already."

Doreen leaned back against the doorjamb and looked at them sternly.

"I've been meaning to talk to y'all about being a couple in business," she said, "and I guess this is just as good a time as any. Your personal relationship can affect your business."

She raised her eyebrows at them as if they were naughty children. "Just like right now, for example. Also, the business can affect your romance or your marriage or whatever."

She paused so they could confess to marriage plans if they had them. That made her smile to herself, in spite of her rising irritation.

"I know because of working in the realty business with Lawrence from time to time. Y'all just have to be aware, always, that . . ."

Lilah, carrying a tray of brownie cupcakes and powdered-sugar covered snowballs, appeared beside Doreen.

"Oh, Doreen," she said sweetly, "would you please get that tray on out to the café and see if you can make things look good with the tables all moved around? I'll be there in just a second. Thank you sooo much."

Doreen left and Lilah said, "Y'all just try to have patience with her. She's had a big shock over Lawrence's scandalous behavior and all. I declare, she just cannot seem to resist telling other people what they ought to do. It makes me so mad, her trying to boss you two around."

Then she swept away toward the café.

Meri and Caleb looked at each other. With his irresistible twinkle, he muttered, "Reckon that could be a little bit of the pot and the kettle calling each other black?"

They burst out laughing and fell into each other's arms again.

Five

The feed store was busy this morning. So when Caleb backed his truck up to the dock and got out to go inside, he only waved at Denton Fremont and the other kids who worked there before and after school instead of helping them load his feed and joking around with them. They didn't have time for any of that today and neither did he.

Not enough hours in the day, what with Meri asking him to come help at the Kitchens with that order going to Dallas. He smiled. She was so excited about the new business and he loved watching her talk about it.

As soon as he'd finished helping her, he had to hit the road for the ranch and off-load the feed, put out the mineral blocks for the cattle and pick the most urgent of a hundred other jobs on the ranch that needed attention. Even though he really couldn't afford the expense, he was going to have to hire a couple of hands.

The place was too big for a man working alone, plus he wanted time to work on the house. That was what he was itching to do.

Most of the time. But sometimes he looked around and wondered what he, Caleb Burkett, was doing with a house in the first place.

He had so many responsibilities he hardly knew himself anymore. This unforgiving to-do list was only today's version. There'd be another one tomorrow.

He pounded up the steps that led into the store and pushed on the metal door, flashing back, for a split second, to when he was a kid and this was an old screen plus a weathered wood door that stood open all summer. A lot of little things had changed about Rock Springs and a whole lot of other ones had not. It really was amazing how much was still the same after all those years.

Del was there, at the counter just as he had been every time Caleb had ever come into the store. He had to go visit with him for a minute, of course, but he did manage to keep it on the weather and the ranch work and then get down to business before Del could start on one of his endless fish stories.

"Del, I'm thinkin' I need to add a couple more sacks of those high-protein pellets and a dozen mineral blocks to my order, okay? If you'll give the boys outside a heads-up about that, I'll pick up a coupla things inside here and then get outta your hair."

Del nodded and Caleb headed first for the cat food he'd promised to pick up for Henry, Honey Grove's loud, bossy cat.

He loved teasing Meri when she complained about Henry. She'd gotten really attached to him, but she hated to admit it. Caleb had always liked the cat that everybody else (except Lilah) loved to hate and now he had a real soft spot for him. Probably because Meri's hitting Henry with the car had led to one of their first meetings.

If she hadn't done that the day after her mother's funeral, and if Caleb hadn't been filling in for Doc Vincent at the veterinary clinic that week, they might never have made each other so mad that they'd had no choice but to see each other again. Close call. She'd been all set to go back to New York that afternoon.

Yet . . . he might've gone there to look her up. From the get-go, he'd been fascinated by her uncommonly beautiful, porcelain face surrounded by all of that black hair.

It was the air of reserve she kept herself wrapped in that got to him, though. The challenge of it. She carried herself like royalty to try to hide the pain in her eyes, but he'd seen it from the first.

Caleb jerked himself back to the business at hand, which was staring at the shelves of cat food in front of him. Which one had she told him was the only kind that picky ol' King Henry would eat? Science Diet Senior or was it Science Diet Hairball?

At his back, somebody growled, "What've you done? Gone to raisin' cats? Think you'll have better luck with them than cattle?"

Thank God he gave no sign of startlement but his stomach clutched like he was still a teenager.

He took his time turning around to meet his father's arrogant gaze.

"What's it to you?"

When the old anger flashed in Jasper's blue eyes, Caleb grinned. "Don't sweat it. Cats or cattle, either one, I won't be hitting you up for a loan."

His dad snorted. "At least you're smart enough to know *that'd* be a waste of breath. You're gonna need a big one since you're stupid enough to keep on trying to resurrect that old money pit of a house. Had any sense, you'd bulldoze it."

Somebody slowed down, passing by the end of the aisle. If Jasper didn't keep his voice down, the Scaly Alligators, Rock Springs' gossiping old men, would have something new to talk about.

But hey, who cared? Jake, as Jasper was known to most everybody in town, had provided untold hours of entertainment to the gossips in the past, and Caleb had done his own share of providing fodder for talk. He was long past caring what anybody said about him or the family, except for the fact that he knew their family's being the subject of gossip bothered his mother.

Plus, he should keep his cool anyway, no matter what. That always got to Jasper more than exchanging insults.

"Aw," Caleb said, "I kind of like the old house, now that I've got a new roof on it. When I get done, I'll call and you can come on out and take the tour."

Jasper snorted. "Hah. I won't live that long. You can't stick at anything long enough to finish it. You never have."

Ah, the old familiar words. Caleb had heard them from his father ever since he was old enough to remember but now, instead of stabbing him in the heart, they just thudded against the wall around it.

"I like ranching," he said.

"*You* can't ranch, you're not smart enough. Expenses'll eat your lunch. A couple of years—if you last that long—and you'll be filing for bankruptcy."

Caleb held his gaze. "You don't know me, Jake."

"But then, you *deserve* to lose the place after the sleazy way you got it."

Caleb managed to keep the expression on his face the same. "Like *you* never blindsided *me*."

"Not in public, I didn't."

Ah! That was the crux of it, right there. Jasper was one of the wealthiest men in Texas and believed he was all-powerful, and he wanted everybody else to believe that, too. Everybody had known he'd planned to buy Indian River at auction and develop it until Caleb bought it out from under him.

"You don't tell me *your* business," Caleb said. "Why should I tell you mine? You didn't even tell me you *wanted* Indian River—had to hear it from somebody else."

"Some old girlfriend busybody, no doubt. Who else'd go to the trouble to find you all the way out there in Wyoming? And *you* didn't want it, either, until you knew I was trying to buy it."

Caleb drawled, "You talkin' one of *my* old girlfriends?"

Jasper stared at him. His jaw twitched.

Caleb held the look for a significant moment before he turned back to the cat food problem. Jasper was livid. You could always tell when you'd hit a nerve with him because he got a white streak across his cheekbones.

Cale glimpsed Tol Weddle walking slowly down the other side of the rack of cat food. The champion tale-carrier of Rock County, ruler of the grapevine. Wouldn't you know it? No doubt Tol had been the person at the end of the aisle and he'd hung around to hear their whole conversation. It'd be all over town by ten o'clock this morning, exaggerated out of all recognition.

A new story about the Burketts would resurrect lots of old ones, including some about Caleb that might reach Meri's ears.

Oh, well. He'd warned her already.

So had a lot of other people, too, no doubt.

And if it wasn't this, it'd be something else that triggered the talk. People loved to watch the Burketts. Jasper had made a lot of enemies on his way to being top dog. He didn't care about that.

But he did care about having the last word.

"Stay out of my sight, Caleb, and don't speak if you see me. You're a disgrace to the Burkett name, you backstabbing little weasel. What you did to me on that Indian River deal is unforgivable."

Caleb felt that old clutch in his gut. Unforgivable. Now they were getting into familiar territory again.

Well, one thing was for damn sure: he'd prove Jasper wrong about him and the Indian River Ranch. Now he *had* to stick, no matter how restless he got. He had to make the ranch pay if it killed him. If he dropped in his tracks, working.

He grabbed the biggest bag of the hairball stuff and threw it on his shoulder before he turned around.

The store had fallen quiet except for the country music that was always playing—right now it was George Strait singing "King of the Mountain." Tol was still there. Jake was gone.

Six

Meri made change for Charlene Polston and her mother, Mrs. Dawes, who had come in for a treat on Charlene's day off at the Grab It 'n' Go. She apologized again and assured them that next time they came in, the HGK café would have plenty of cinnamon rolls.

"Don't you worry, we'll be back," Charlene

said. "We know y'all can't make everything every single day."

Her mother added, "And we just wish you all the very best on getting your first big out-of-town order out on time. My stars! That's a feather in Rock Springs' cap, sending muffins all the way to Dallas, now, isn't it?"

She gave Meri a congratulatory hug, even though this was the first time they'd met. Meri was becoming more accustomed to random hugs.

"And for a big natural-food outfit, too! You are making us so *proud!*"

"Well, they're not too big a distributor yet," Meri said. "They're a start-up like us, but they're looking at all of North Texas for their territory and natural foods are beginning to make inroads on everybody's consciousness, so this is a way for us to grow brand recognition, at least."

"It's a big deal," the woman assured her. "Even if you didn't grow up here, you were born here and I think you're going to be the one to put Rock Springs on the map!"

Meri forced a smile while she cringed inside. She had enough of her own and her partners' expectations on her shoulders without those of the whole town being heaped on top of them.

Why had she even told Charlene and her mom that there were no cinnamon rolls because all the employees were working on the special order?

And that that was also the reason she and Caleb were working in the café?

Because she was behaving like a native here. In Rock Springs, you might as well tell everything because no matter what the question, its citizens would ferret out the answer one way or another. Might as well just tell everything up front and save everybody time and trouble.

With a final pat for Meri, Mrs. Dawes and Charlene started for the door, stopping on the way, of course, to say something to Caleb. Meri smiled to herself. There wasn't a female in town, of any age, who could resist saying something to Caleb.

Meri looked through the window into the kitchen. Things seemed to be going as smoothly as they had since 4:00 A.M. on the muffins, both on the zucchini chocolate side of it and the blueberry peach side. Twelve dozen of each flavor to be mixed, baked, cooled, packed and shipped out to Dallas this afternoon.

Caleb was still pouring coffee for the customers at the six occupied tables even though he was in a fit to get back to the ranch. He wasn't showing it, though. He was playing the part of the perfect host, using his considerable charm, exactly as he should be doing. He was a sociable person and he was probably tired of working alone so much out at his ranch.

When Meri passed him on her way to clean off the empty table, he finished pouring with a flourish and turned to her. "Reminds me of our old concession-stand days."

She rolled her eyes at him. "Yeah. All one of them."

They both smiled at the memory. Uninvited, he had come right into the little concession stand and taken it over the first time Lilah had assigned Meri to sell Frito chili pies at a horse show. It turned out to be a good thing because Meri'd been so new to everything then that she'd never even heard of a Frito chili pie, much less how to make one. With Caleb's help, they'd made some good ones and brought in a lot of money for the Rock County 4-H Horse Club.

And that had been the day that led directly to this one. The seed of the Kitchens idea sprouted to life that evening amidst the smells of corn chips and chili as she and Caleb worried aloud about helping Lilah save Honey Grove Farm.

Now their salvage produce business was a reality. They had put every dollar Meri possessed on the line to start it, along with a lot of Caleb's money and Lilah's produce and labor and now they had a viable canning and freezing kitchen in operation, plus a bakery with a new café at the entrance.

Today's order from Dallas was an important step up the ladder to the level of success that would make all the risk worth it. Meri wanted everything about it to be perfect, so she'd splurged on some special packing cartons—gorgeous golden yellow ones with the HGK logo of bluebonnets, hives and buzzing honeybees. Those boxes should arrive any minute.

She looked at her phone. It was almost nine thirty. Jerry, the driver for Donovan's Delivery Service, had told her he'd probably be here around now. She'd already called him once, to check if he was running on schedule, but got no answer.

Thelma, the tiny, older woman who usually worked in the café, came back and took over the coffeepot from Caleb. "They're measuring to mix the last batch of each recipe," she said. "I'll take care of the café now if y'all wanna get out of here."

"All right!" Caleb said. "Thelma, you're an angel."

She chuckled, and raised her voice for the whole room to hear: "You two kids just remember—it took both of you to do my job and I'm twice y'all's ages."

Roy Streeter looked up from his second sticky bun and called, "You tell 'em, girl. Young'uns today don't know what hard work is."

Thelma nodded, which did not move one dyed-red hair on her head, and started toward him with the coffeepot. "That's exactly right, Roy. You still raisin' chickens?"

He held out his cup. "Yep," he said. "Too old to raise hell anymore."

That old saw got the usual laugh and the conversation in the room became general.

Caleb came to Meri. "I'd better get out to the ranch," he said softly. "Looks like everything's under control here."

Meri had hardly slept all night, worrying about what could go wrong on this watershed day at HGK, and now just the thought of his leaving made her feel exponentially more nervous.

That fact scared her. She didn't want to be so emotionally dependent, yet she couldn't restrain herself from protesting. "Oh, Caleb, please don't go yet. You have to look over the financials so we can talk about the estimated taxes, remember?"

He touched her hair and brushed his fingers along her neck. "I will, babe. Just not now. I gotta run."

Her temper flared, but she tried to hold it out of her voice. She'd already learned that Caleb didn't respond well to direct orders of any kind. "Are you sure it's not because you just don't want to? Lots of times, you just won't do what you don't want to do."

He shrugged, grinning. "You're not the first one to notice that about me."

"Well, then, maybe you should try to improve. That's childish," she said, holding back her disappointment to keep her tone mild. "Adults do what needs to be done and you have to do this sometime, so why not now? I want to get it in the mail. We can make a decision and you'll still be out of here in thirty minutes."

She looked him in the eye. "You said you would."

"*You* said I would. I don't have time right now."

"We have to get started paying the taxes or they'll be too much all at once."

"We will. But, look, babe, I've gotta unload that feed . . ."

Meri glanced through the window into the kitchen to see if things were still running smoothly then took a deep breath and fixed her most persuasive look on Caleb.

"Just hang in here for a few more minutes," she pleaded. "Please, Cale, help me out on this."

An irritated look crossed his face, but he wiped it off and tried to look charming instead. He didn't quite succeed.

"I told you, Mer. I trust you. Go on and write it up for however much you need. I'll sign it. But right now, I've got a fence to fix, besides all the feed stuff, and I just remembered I have a load of lumber coming for the house."

He leaned down and kissed her lightly on the mouth.

The tension knot in her stomach twisted itself tighter. She made herself concentrate on that instead of letting herself fall for the kiss.

Sweet-tasting as it was.

She pulled away. "You're a partner in this business. We need to make decisions *together* and—"

"Hey, Cale! You got a minute?"

They were standing in the café doorway to the hall that led to the renovated closet—now their office—in the old mercantile building HGK had bought on the corner of the Square. They turned to see J.B., the builder who'd done their renovations, coming in the front door of the café.

"I need to talk to him," Caleb said. "Excuse me, honey."

He was already turning away. She grabbed his arm.

"Oh! Now, listen, Caleb. Are you two talking about building the second kitchen? Already? Cale . . ."

He patted her shoulder. "Give me just a second, all right? I'll look at your papers in a minute," he said. "The ones spread out on the desk?"

"Right."

On the way down the hall to the kitchen door, she wondered exactly what her feelings for him were doing to her. She felt rattled and pulled in two directions and vulnerable for wishing he'd stay until they got the muffins all packed and off to Dallas. Really, they didn't need him.

But surely it wasn't the major reason she was insisting he look at the tax stuff now. Or was it?

72

She wouldn't think about it again. She and Lilah could pull this off, no sweat. Everything was done except the boxes.

Meri took her phone from her pocket and tried Jerry again as she walked into the kitchen. No answer.

Jewel screamed, "Oh, no! There went the last of the sour cream," and Meri whirled to see her standing frozen, staring at the floor as she reached out blindly to turn off the big mixer.

The carton had landed upside down. Of course.

From the other side of the kitchen, Lilah called, "Are you sure there's not another one?"

"Yes!"

"I'll run get some more," Meri said. She *needed* to run, she needed to get out and *do* something.

Lilah said, "Price Cutter doesn't carry the organic, remember? We may have to use regular—"

"No, we can't," Meri said. "All the ingredients have to be organic! It's on the labels and all the advertising, so that's nonnegotiable."

Lilah sighed. "Well, yes. Somebody might get sick from the additives in regular and it's too late to change the labels."

"I'll drive to Brenham," Meri said. "Y'all go ahead and bake all the zucchini chocolate ones—"

"No!" Lilah cried. "Wait! There's some at the house, Meri. I bought extra for that last trial run of the recipe. Go get it. It's in the very back on that top shelf of the fridge, if I remember right, and it hasn't been opened."

Meri rushed out and along the hall to the office for her bag.

Caleb was still talking to J.B. She interrupted for a second to tell him the news and ask him to keep trying to reach Jerry for her because service was spotty in several places along the road.

As she left the Square and turned out onto FM Road 2317, she tried Jerry again. No luck. This was beginning to cause the turmoil in the pit of her stomach to burn.

If they didn't have any boxes when the muffins were all done, what would they do? Lots of them were already cool enough to package. Jerry was supposed to pick up the filled boxes again in the late afternoon to take them to the San Antonio airport for a night flight to Dallas. They *had* to be on that plane.

Once Meri got to Honey Grove and found a cooler for the organic sour cream, she sat down for just a second to let Henry jump into her lap so she could scratch him under the chin while she tried Jerry again and thought about what to do if she couldn't reach him. There was something incredibly soothing about scratching a purring cat, although she still wasn't an animal person, not at all.

In spite of that, she and Henry were learning to understand each other. They'd been through a lot together.

He purred like crazy and, as usual, the sound did calm her a little. So did stroking his velvety fur.

No Jerry. With her free hand, she did an Internet search for Donovan's Delivery Service and called the main number. No answer there, either.

With a final pat and scratch, she put the cat down.

"Gotta go, Hen-Pen." Honestly, she was losing her mind, not to mention her dignity, but she had fallen into a habit of talking to the cat. Even using a nickname, yet! "You're in charge of Honey Grove. As if that's anything new."

She left, making sure Henry stayed inside. That was her unshakable habit to prevent another accident like on the day she'd run into him with her car. Which had scared her spitless. Caleb had been filling in for one of the vets on vacation, but he'd refused to keep the injured cat at the clinic. He'd expected her to change her travel plans and take care of Henry herself, which had made her so angry that her whole body had been shaking by the time she'd gotten back to Honey Grove.

She was angry at Caleb, now, too, but more disappointed and frustrated, she supposed. It always upset her if she couldn't mark off all the items on her to-do list every evening, plus she hated letting chores hang. The tax thing was almost done. Why not just finish it, for good? Be done with it? Fences and feed could wait for thirty minutes. Caleb would spend that long, at least, talking to J.B.

The least he could do was stay at the Kitchens until they knew for sure they'd have the boxes in time.

If not, what would she do?

She ran to her truck and headed for town again, constantly trying to reach Jerry.

No answer. He might've left his phone in the truck while he went up to someone's house, but this had been going on for far too long. It gave her a bad feeling that this was big trouble.

Her stomach clutched harder. It could be that they'd have to use whatever boxes they could find. Except for the fact there weren't enough in-house of any kind, plain or logo ones, for this order.

Surely Jerry would come through! Usually he ran ahead of schedule. Meri checked the time again. Jerry had said he'd have to pick up the packaged muffins by 6:00 P.M. at the very latest for them to make their flight.

She tried to call him again, got no answer and then, right there in front of Leroy's Beer, Bait and Ammo, she sent him a text even though she was driving.

Every nerve in her body tightened. She called Caleb. Maybe he'd talked to Jerry. No answer there, either. She texted him.

Then she realized she needed to calm herself. She didn't want to have a wreck. She managed to stay within the speed limit the rest of the way back to HGK.

Once there, she gave the sour cream to Jewel, and went straight to Lilah.

"I think I'll start calling bakeries in Brenham to see if they'll sell us some boxes," she said.

Her grandmother looked up from filling the last of the pans with zucchini chocolate batter. "Don't put the cart before the horse and spend a lot of money, now, Meri. Jerry's not that late, yet."

But all Meri could hear were the voices in her head.

This is all your fault. How could you be so incompetent?

You should've ordered them sooner.

You should've driven to Austin and picked them up at the supplier's yourself.

The whole town is excited about this. Think of the embarrassment if you can't fill this order.

"Here," Lilah said, both hands busy. "Get my phone out of my apron pocket and call LaDonna's Cut 'n' Curl. Then hold the phone to my ear."

Meri stared at her. *"What?"*

"Humor me."

Meri found the number, then did as she was told.

"LaDonna? It's Lilah. Look over there and see if Donovan's gone or just not picking up the phone?"

"He did? Okay, thanks. You having a pretty good day?"

Meri gritted her teeth while Lilah took time to listen to whatever LaDonna had to say. "Mm-hmm. That's good. Glad to hear it."

Finally, after almost a whole minute, Lilah said good-bye to LaDonna and to Meri, "Donovan put up his 'Gone Fishing' sign a couple of hours ago. He's gone for the day."

Meri wanted to scream. "I should've used UPS or FedEx. This is what I get for trying to give the business to a Rock Springs company. They go fishing."

"You did the right thing," Lilah said stoutly, but Meri could tell she wasn't into that whole-heartedly. "Don't worry now. It'll all work out."

Meri turned and started out of the room. "I'm going to see why Caleb didn't answer his phone . . ."

Lilah raised her eyebrows. "Cale? Is he here? I haven't seen him."

Meri ran straight to the office. Caleb wasn't there. Or in the café. The financial papers lay on the desk, untouched.

Her head started pounding. He hadn't done what

he said he'd do. He'd broken a promise. He'd deserted her.

That creepy old feeling reached for her with its cold fingers, whispering in her ear with its bad breath.

Abandoned again. What's wrong with you?

She grabbed the sides of the office doorway and fought back tears while she forced her mind to kick in and drown it out.

Get a grip. This is insane. Stop it. Just stop it!!!

She breathed deep for a little while, then forced her hands to unclench. She walked back to the kitchen, telling herself to shut her mind to everything else until this crisis was done.

Focus was one of her strengths. She could compartmentalize anything—she'd done it all her life, hadn't she? Compartmentalizing had kept her alive and made her successful.

And here was her Gran, looking at her with eyes just like Meri's except they were wise and kind. Looking at her as if she could read her mind.

"Listen, sugar," Lilah said, her tone so brisk it comforted Meri somehow. "If we have to buy more boxes, we will, but the other bakeries won't have the outside boxes for shipping. So why don't you check in the storeroom and see what all's there that we can use?"

Meri clapped her hands to her face. "We may have to make some. Oh, no. Won't *that* look pathetically small-town! I'll drive all night to take the muffins to Dallas in the flimsy bakery boxes before I'll do that."

"Go on," Lilah said, as she started filling a muffin pan, this time with blueberry peach batter. "Jerry'll get here, but it won't hurt to figure out what we'll need if he doesn't."

Meri started to go, then she lingered to watch Lilah finish with the last pan, scraping the bowl, adding a little bit of batter to the cups that were less full than the others. She didn't want to leave her and the bustling kitchen to go into the quiet storage room because she felt like a child again, one who didn't want to be alone.

She leaned against the worktable and tried to pull herself together. Caleb should be here to help her. Trusting a man to be your partner was a dangerous thing. She should've learned that with Tim.

She sent another text to Jerry.

Another to Caleb. Incipient tears stung her eyes.

She had to move and stop thinking. Maybe she could make shipping boxes. Even if she drove the muffins to Dallas, they'd have to be stacked with protection from damage.

Thirty minutes later, Meri had made two boxes that were acceptable and a list of exactly what they would need to make more. She fought to keep her mind on the details of the crisis and not on Caleb's putting his ranch ahead of HGK. This was business, this was her professional self-respect on the line, and she would step up, no matter what she was feeling.

"Gran," she said as she went out into the kitchen. "I'm heading to Brenham."

Lilah looked up from sliding the last batch of blueberry peach muffins into the oven.

"Listen to me, now. You be careful and keep your mind on your driving. No muffin order in the world is worth you having a wreck. Do you hear me?"

Meri promised, picked up her bag and opened the back door.

The steady rumbling of a big motor met her. It sounded like Caleb's truck.

She froze where she stood.

It *was* Caleb. He pulled up just past the door, turned off the engine and got out with his biggest smile on his face, his beautiful blue eyes sparkling.

"Caleb! Where have you been?"

Clearly, he was so pleased with himself and so glad to see her that it made her remorseful. Ashamed of herself for her lack of trust in him and the irritation against him she'd nurtured all afternoon.

Trust was just the hardest thing in the world for her.

"I've left you a dozen messages and texted you over and over! Where were you?"

The battered maroon van with DONOVAN'S DELIVERY SERVICE written on its side in gold scrolling letters drove up and, tires crunching on the gravel, stopped directly in front of her.

Caleb stepped back and made a sweeping gesture toward it.

"Bringin' in your boxes, darlin'."

Seven

Meri made the coffee, then leaned back against the counter to check her messages on her phone. Sometimes, but not always, she found a sweet "good morning" message from Caleb. Today it was all ads.

The old loneliness touched her but she pushed it away, looked at the ads for restaurant supplies she'd been getting lately and then she just stared into space waiting for the hot coffee and thinking about how scared she'd been yesterday when she couldn't get in touch with Caleb. She didn't like being so vulnerable. The walls she'd built around her heart over so many years were cracking apart. Loving someone made a person vulnerable beyond belief.

She fumbled in the cabinet for a mug, filled it and pushed the back door open, happy that Lilah wasn't up yet and she could have the porch swing all to herself. Her early mornings on the porch helped her pull her head together for the day.

Closing the door, she glanced at the swing, glimpsed somebody in it and startled. A little coffee spilled out but for once she ignored it.

Caleb's drawl came at the same moment. "Mornin', Meri."

He stopped the slowly moving swing and got up. "Looks like you need some help there."

Her heart was thudding from surprise. She didn't like surprises.

Yet she did like the personal "good morning" from him instead of a text. At least, she hoped it was "good morning" and not something serious.

"What are you doing here?"

They sat down side by side and sipped some coffee before he answered.

"Thinkin' about our first kiss."

"Really?" She smiled, the memory washing over her.

"Remember? We were standing right over there on the porch."

They both turned and looked as if they could see themselves.

"Yes," she said, her throat filling with emotion.

"We were soaking wet from the rain. I never had such a kiss in my life."

She nodded and managed to say, "Me neither."

He touched her hair, then moved a little away from her and leaned back into the corner of the swing. They looked at each other for a long while, washed in the early morning light.

The light breeze rustled the persimmon tree's leaves and moved the long, gauzy skirt Meri wore to be ready for the workday ahead. Birds were waking up and starting to chitter, from the barn one of the horses neighed.

"That kiss started something," Caleb said. "I think we need to talk about what."

A little frisson of fear ran through Meri. Yes, she was scared of a breakup but she was scared of trusting completely, too.

"Caleb, we can't . . . look, we've got to get this business started—"

He interrupted. "I'm not talking about making plans. I'm talking about trust. If whatever that first kiss started is going anywhere, Meri, you're going to have to trust me."

"Did I say that I didn't?"

"No. But I saw it in your face and felt it in everything you said when I got back to the Kitchens yesterday."

She turned and stared out over the peaceful farm, the land rolling away to the gray bluffs to the south and then to the east as far as the road that was turning silver in the light of the coming morning. Over there, the sky was peach and pink with a few lavender clouds floating in long streaks above the first thin crescent of the rising sun.

She didn't want to look away from it. She didn't want to talk about yesterday. She didn't like it when she'd made mistakes and had been in the wrong.

"Meri?"

She glanced back at him. His eyes hadn't left her face.

"I . . . I have a hard time trusting, Cale. You know that. All abandoned children do."

He narrowed his eyes and held her gaze.

"But this is me, babe."

"But no matter what I did yesterday, I couldn't find you. You knew I might need you and it never once occurred to me you might be too far from a cell tower."

"If I had a problem and couldn't take your calls, you'd be the first to know about it."

He looked at her carefully. "Do you believe that?"

"Yes," she said. And she did. At least when she was with him.

The breeze became a sudden gust of wind that whipped her hair around her face. She brushed it away from her mouth and forced her lips apart.

"I hate to say I'm wrong, Caleb, but I owe you an apology. I didn't thank you yesterday and I should have. You saved the day."

He made a wry face. "I admit I was a tad bit disappointed, seeing as how I was expecting to be hailed as the hero, and all."

"I'm sorry. Because if you hadn't brought those boxes in, I'd be sick at heart right now, worrying about the damage to our brand. I want us to be top tier in every area from Day One. Homemade shipping boxes won't quite do that."

"It's okay," he said softly, his blue eyes searching hers as if he were trying to read her heart in her eyes. "I'll give the hero thing another shot sometime. Right now I just need you to believe that I'll always take your calls unless I'm dead or locked up somewhere."

He grinned and reached over to slide his hand up the side of her neck and hold her head to kiss her. Just a light, quick kiss and he was gone.

"Gotta get to work," he said, releasing her.

Then, with a twinkle, "See ya later."

She watched him bound down the steps in spite of the limp in his walk and throw the last of his coffee out across the grass. Then the paper cup into the cab and himself into the driver's seat.

He started the big, rumbling motor, raised a hand in farewell and he was gone.

Maybe she'd see him later today at the Kitchens, maybe not. She needed to be more understanding of the fact he had more than one business and more than one project going.

She needed to be more aware of his needs as well as hers. That's what Tim Montgomery, her last boyfriend, had told her, and he'd been right about that.

Eight

Meri was humming—even though she couldn't really hear herself over the noise of the mixer—and she was also thinking about Caleb, she had to admit—when the machine stopped.

And his voice said, "I think I need to call the law. Do Lilah and Jewel know you've taken over their kitchen?"

She turned around so fast she bumped her hip against the counter.

Caleb was leaning against the doorjamb, silhouetted against the dark alleyway that led to the HGK café, which was closed for the day. And he was gorgeous. As usual. But even more so, because he was all cleaned up and starched and ironed.

"You look good enough to put in the glass case out in the café," she said, returning his mischievous grin. "Except then the women would all be mad at me because I wouldn't let anybody else have you."

He chuckled low and came toward her with purpose, caught her around the waist and kissed her once, quick and hard. Then he looked deep into her eyes. "Right back at'cha, babe," he said. "I see anybody else hangin' around you, he better run for the border."

"I can't think who that might be," she said. "I

haven't had anybody else flirt with me for a long time now."

"That's 'cause they're all scared of me," he said. "They know I'd take 'em off at the knees."

A little thrill ran through her. His protectiveness was one of the things about Caleb that she loved most.

Laughing, she turned away to take the bowl full of batter from the mixer.

"So, explain *yourself,*" he said. "When did you give up managing and start being chief cook around here?"

"When Jewel's grandbaby got sick at day care and her daughter couldn't get off work to go get him. When Lilah went to campaign door-to-door in the north part of the county and we got an order from Maisie Hawthorne for seven dozen brownie cupcakes for her daughter's bridesmaid's luncheon. It's tomorrow."

"Well, then," Caleb drawled. "A cupcake emergency. Hard to believe Lilah'd choose campaigning over cooking. Is she thinking the Judge is down in the polls? Man, I hope not."

Meri looked at him. "I hope not, either. I was thinking today how it'll destroy so many farms and ranches if Missy's people start buying them out for housing developments."

"Yeah." He shook his head. "But when you really think about it, it's a shame for Missy not to have the job. I will never forget how she single-handedly livened up that ice cream social. Man! What a riot! I haven't laughed that hard for a *long* time. She would make the most entertaining public official we have."

He laughed. "Yeah, she'd keep us all in a cheery mood."

Meri shot him a look. "Don't let Lilah hear you say that. She'd be devastated. That might be the one thing that would make her realize you're not perfect."

"But I am!" He scowled playfully. "She's right about that."

"You wish. We don't want Missy, no matter how entertaining she is or how many more customers we might have if Rock County turned into a bedroom community."

"Yeah," he said thoughtfully. "Come to think of it, maybe I oughtta go help Lilah right now."

"Dream on," Meri said, starting to tear open the boxes of little parchment cup liners. "I'm the one who needs the help. Gran doesn't even know about this order. I decided to do it myself."

He raised his eyebrows and twinkled at her. "More skills than just a cowgirl, huh? But if you do it yourself, you can't have any help. I'll just watch you."

She made a face at him as she stirred the batter one more time.

He chuckled and tried to change the subject so she wouldn't be mad at him. She could tell he was going to resist helping, now that he was so cleaned up and starchy. "So you're learning to bake, huh? That'd be a good skill to have in your own home, too, you know."

Your own home. Her heart hit a hard beat. A sharp ache ran through her, body and mind.

It's dangerous to love him. I couldn't bear it if he left. He never wants to be tied down. I've known that all along but . . .

She didn't have time to think about their future now. The only future she would worry about now was this business. That had to get off the ground before they could even think about their relationship.

Besides, hadn't she promised herself to enjoy the moment? Every moment she could? She was trying to learn that she couldn't control the future but she could really live the present.

So she said, "This recipe is easy to make but it takes forever to fill the pans and this time it's even worse because Maisie wants miniature cupcakes. How about if you put on a pair of gloves—right there in the third drawer—" She gestured with a tilt of her head.

He looked at the big bowl full of chocolate batter and frowned. "Well, but this is my only clean shirt, Mer," he said with exaggerated sincerity. "I can do the taste-testing for you and entertain you while you fill the pans and then we can go . . ."

She chuckled. "Not for a long time we can't. They have to bake and we have to wait until they cool out and sift powdered sugar through a doily over the tops."

He looked shocked. "A doily?"

"You know. A lacy paper thing. It'll make a pretty pattern. To use Maisie's own words, 'This is a once-in-a-lifetime event for these girls. We want it to be wonderful and something to remember all their lives.'"

Meri began taking out cup liners and putting them in the pans.

"We make a pattern on something that little? Meri, I can't help you with that."

"After that," she said, ignoring his protest, "we have to put them in airtight containers. And then clean up the kitchen."

His eyes widened. "Where's Bud?"

"No one knows."

Her voice cracked a little on the last word. She was worried about getting it all done but she hated showing it. She was trying hard not to reveal how stressed she was. Even to herself.

Caleb looked at her more closely.

She blurted, "I knew I could do it because the recipe's so easy. And I can. I just don't know if I can do them all while the batter's still fresh."

"Hey, now, Mer. Don't worry."

She began putting the chocolate mixture into the paper cup liners, although she only had them in one pan. Each pan held a dozen cupcakes.

"I want everybody at the luncheon to go all over town raving about how good these are. It's our family recipe, over a hundred and fifty years old, and if I make it a hit, Lilah will be so proud of me."

Caleb smiled. "Oh, honey, she already is proud of you."

"Yes, but you know as well as I do that she plans for me to be the next in a long bloodline of great cooks in our family. I'm the only one who can carry on the reputation."

He cocked his head and looked doubtful. "I dunno, Mer," he teased. "I'm just thinkin' about those steaks you burned the other night. It's not very complicated to cook a piece of meat on a grill . . ."

She smiled at his teasing in spite of her growing irritation that he was wasting time. Not to mention the fact that he'd already teased her unmercifully about the steaks.

"I ate it, didn't I? And so did you. Rare is not the only way to serve a steak. Now come on and help me get this done."

She worked carefully, dipping a tiny measuring cup into the batter and then guiding it into the cup with a narrow, curved spatula. "Lilah told me this is the best way to get the right amount in each one. There's another set of these tools in that drawer underneath the mixer."

"I love brownies," he said thoughtfully. "Do I get paid in mini-cupcakes?"

"I made two dozen extra so we can pick the prettiest ones for the luncheon. You may eat as many as twenty-four of the ugliest."

"Then I'm your man for kitchen helper," he said. "Where's my apron? No, wait. I don't need it. HGK will pay my dry cleaning bill and—"

Meri threw him a sharp look. "Not. Don't forget the apron."

He laughed as he went to suit up in apron and gloves. Then he came to the work counter to help her.

"What's the deal with using all these little paper things? Don't we have any of that spray stuff?"

"That is so typical of you," Meri said. "Looking for the fastest way possible. For your information, I don't trust that spray stuff. We'll just have to do things the slow way this time. And Cale, we can't take all night to do it."

"You need to have more faith." He shot her a sideways grin. "You're always expecting the worst to happen."

"In this case, yes, since you seem to be all hat and no cattle when it comes to the offer of helping me out here."

That made him laugh out loud. "I don't think I offered. I think you pushed me. But what d'you want me to do?"

She demonstrated again how to fill the cups and he began trying to imitate her.

On the very first one, he dripped a string of sticky batter from the spatula onto the pan. He groaned.

"It takes practice," Meri encouraged him. "We'll clean the pan before we put it in the oven. Lilah says this recipe makes the thinnest batter she ever saw for cupcakes. Yet it's so rich it's also thick enough to be really sticky. It takes a little while to get the hang of handling it. Just keep trying."

"I'm not a quitter," he said, gritting his teeth. "I'd never hear the end of it if I did."

"You are so right about that."

"Truth is, my hands are too clumsy for this job," he said, dripping more batter, but on the table this time.

"I don't think your hands are clumsy at all," she said, in a significant tone.

He glanced up and grinned. "Well," he said, "that gives me strength to hang in here until the end of the evenin'."

His big fingers fumbled some more with the tiny papers. "Look. I have to keep batting these little suckers back into the cups. I need a rock to put in each one."

She laughed. "That'd be a great surprise for the wedding party."

"We could use nuts," he said hopefully, chasing

one liner across the table when a gust of air from the fan caught it. "And don't say turn off the fan. Not with these ovens on."

Meri clucked and shook her head. "You're supposed to be tough. I've seen you chasing cows in triple-digit heat and loving every minute of it. Your baking chore here is much cooler than that."

"But a whole lot more frustrating."

"Wait. We'll put the liners in as we go. Don't worry. The first drops of batter will hold them in place."

"Hey, speaking of the batter, when do I get a taste? This whole place smells like chocolate. I can't resist much longer."

He drooped the lids on those bedroom eyes and held her gaze.

"Sorta like the way I feel about you."

Meri laughed as she filled another tiny paper liner.

"That look won't get you out of this job. Neither will your pretty words."

He picked up a spoon, dipped it full of the batter (he was right—it really did have a fabulous aroma) and ate it.

"Mmmm," he said. "Without a doubt, you're a natural-born, prizewinning cook."

"That won't do the trick, either."

"Only one thing I know that's sweeter and better," he said. "I mean it."

"Oh? And what is that? Lilah's batter for this recipe?"

"No, this." He leaned across the muffin pan and kissed her. A long, chocolatey, slow kiss that fired her blood and sent its heat spiraling through her veins.

He meant *that,* too.

Nine

While Meri drove toward town, she went over the day's to-do list in her head. That was her habit because it made her feel uncomfortable not to know what was next at all times. Which, she was learning, wasn't easy when running a business.

And today, it kept her from thinking about Caleb, which would take her mind away from work. Their relationship had already grown deep into her sense of well-being—her reaction to his absence yesterday proved that. If Tim had vanished without explanation, she wouldn't have lost her mind to a clutching stomach full of childhood fears.

Did all this inner turmoil mean she was in love? Real love?

But how scary was that? What if it didn't work out after a few months, a few years? Then she'd be so far in that she couldn't get out.

Her arms went weak on the wheel. She did love

him. It might already be too late to save the walls around her heart.

But the childhood guards around her heart weren't sure whether to buy it. They were still throwing up warning flags right and left. Can we trust him? Really. Can we trust Caleb Burkett, no matter how good it feels to be in his arms?

Those guards were not always logical, but they were faithful. For years, they'd been there, patrolling the even thicker wall she'd thrown up around her fourteen-year-old self on that terrible day when she realized her mother, Edie Jo, was never coming back to claim her.

Worse, she'd known in that same flash of truth that Edie Jo had never *intended* to return. Not even when she looked Meri in the eye while dropping her off at the home of Meri's best friend, promising it'd be "just for the rest of the school year."

Therefore. If that old, cold suspicion of abandonment was still so alive in her, she shouldn't be with an unpredictable man like Caleb Burkett. Honestly, she shouldn't be with any man seriously right now. She was sorting through the pieces of her old life, she was pouring herself into this new business, and she wasn't ready yet to trust any man, since her former almost-fiancé, Tim, had left her to twist in the wind when she lost her old job at the law firm in New York.

• • •

She rounded the curve off Old Briscoe Road onto FM 2317 and drove straight into the gravel parking lot at Leroy's Beer, Bait and Ammo. She had to have more coffee *now.*

She pulled on the brake and got out.

Leroy's was one of the gossip centers in town. When she went in, the usual suspects were gathered at the battered tables near the coffee machine. They looked familiar but she didn't know any of them by name.

They were either deep in conversation or busy eating the enormous breakfast burritos made with "three kinds of peppers guaranteed hot enough to take the hair off your tongue" that Leroy made from scratch and advertised relentlessly. He was at the grill, making more of them, but he looked up when she came through the door, waved the spatula and called good morning.

Meri passed by a table of four hunters dressed in camo just as one of them leaned his chair back on two legs and announced, "I'm tellin' y'all right. Save yourself the trouble of askin'. Jake Burkett don't give permission to hunt on his land 'less he knows you. I can because I used to work for him, but I cain't bring nobody else."

Her attention caught by the name, Meri listened as she took a paper cup from the stack.

"Jake's a mean sumbitch," an older guy said. "Y'all hear about him and Caleb?"

98

The first man laughed. "Ain't that Caleb a pistol? I cain't help but like him, even if he did steal Ronnie Rae from me before he went off up there to Alaska."

The whole group burst out laughing. "Don't even try to tell us that, son."

"No way!"

"You're dreamin' again, Bill John. Ronnie Rae's w-a-ay outta *your* league."

"What I heard," the older man went on, "is Jake told Caleb to stay out of his sight and if he did see him, not to speak to him. That old goat's still mad as hell 'cause Cale outbid him on that Indian River ranch."

"Surely not," the other older man said. "Surely he didn't say that to his own son."

"Yep. Tol Weddle heard it. Yesterday mornin'. That's exactly what he said, right there in the middle of the feed store in front of God and everybody."

They went on gossiping but Meri didn't hear any more. A dark cloud formed in her stomach and spread like fog inside her. The old cloud grown in childhood of very little mothering and no father at all except the one she imagined for herself.

In their ethereal conversations, her father said only loving things to her.

So, in the fantasy of her child's mind, fathers were the source of love and protection. Because, in her experience, mothers were not.

Poor Caleb. Lilah hadn't told her all about his childhood because she said it was his to tell, but she'd remarked more than once that Jake always told Caleb he wouldn't amount to anything.

She stood there until her cup overfilled. While she mopped up the mess with napkins, she hurt for Caleb, as she used to hurt for herself.

Yesterday morning. He'd come straight from the feed store to the office at HGK for her keys so he could put the cat food in her truck—teasing her, as usual, about being the only person in town who ever locked any door. She went out with him so they could steal just a couple of minutes kissing good morning and idly talking, leaning against the truck in the shade out back of the kitchen.

He hadn't said a word about his father or the feed store.

Why not? Usually they told each other pretty much everything.

Or so she'd thought.

He hadn't mentioned J.B. and the second kitchen, either, but that was understandable because they argued all the time about that and he knew she had enough tension right then about the order for Morning Moments. Most of the time, he tried to help her lower her stress level.

Meri put a lid on her cup, grabbed money from her bag and dropped it in the upturned gimme cap Leroy left on the counter for payments on the honor system when he was busy cooking. Then she was out the door.

She had to find Caleb and apologize. Maybe she could comfort him. She didn't know how to comfort people but she was trying to learn.

Her feet stopped working. She stood stock-still in the gravel parking lot, blinded by the warm morning sunlight. Struck by a cold question.

The entire town knew about the encounter between Cale and Jake in the feed store. But she didn't.

So he had no right to complain that she didn't trust him. He didn't trust her, either.

She plunged on toward her car so fast she splashed hot coffee on her hand. She would make a quick call to HGK to see if there was anything urgent going on this morning, and if not she'd go on out to Indian River.

She hated this turmoil going on inside her. She had to get it stopped.

Back in her truck and onto 2317, she checked in with the Kitchens by phone. Jewel's helper answered, of course, because phone calls irritated the cook when she had her mind on the baking. "No problems today," said the retired man called Bud. "Yes, ma'am, the HGK's runnin' smooth as silk."

Meri caught herself speeding twice before she turned off onto the private ranch road that led to Caleb's house from the highway. Then she started scanning the pastures on both sides of it, realizing that she had no idea where he might be. Probably at the barn doing chores, since it was still early, but he could be anywhere.

What was he thinking about her now? Would he be happy to see her?

She saw the tied-up horse first, then the top of the hat on the man bent over one rear hoof. Something deep inside her moved. She would probably know him even in the dark.

As she watched, he straightened up, took off the hat and mopped his face with a bandanna. Early or not, the sun was already hot.

Slowly, Meri backed up, parked and went into the house through the back door. She found the insulated water jug out on the patio table, filled it with ice and water in the kitchen and took it to him, stepping carefully in her high heels on the hard ground.

"You do know your shade's going to move, don't you?" she said, repeating his words to her at the ice cream social.

Caleb grinned up at her sideways, tilting his head to keep sweat out of his eyes. "Why don't you stop the sun for me?"

He went right on working, taking his time to drive a nail exactly straight into the hoof he was holding between his knees. Then he dropped the hammer into a tray, picked up some pliers, bent the end of the nail and snapped it off. He got the file, then, and smoothed it all down.

"Good job," she said.

He dropped the hoof, straightened up out of his crouch and wiped his face again as he tossed the pliers, clattering, into the metal tray of tools. Sweat was pouring off his face and his shirt was wet with it, sticking to his broad chest.

Meri walked to the wooden bench beside the door and poured water into the lid of the jug.

Caleb took his hat off and sent it swirling through the air to land on the other end of the bench. Another bandanna was rolled around his forehead for a sweatband.

"You look like a biker," she said.

You look so good to me. Oh, Cale. What do we have? Is it really love? Please talk to me.

"You first," he said, gesturing toward the cup she was offering.

She shook her head. "I'm not thirsty."

He took it and drank. Up close, he looked a lot more tired than he had down at Honey Grove a couple of hours before. All his responsibilities were wearing on him.

He drank and held out the cup for more.

"Where's your farrier?" she said as she poured again.

"Can't afford 'im. Don't have time to wait, anyhow—too much to do before I catch the plane."

Her heart dipped. "What plane? Oh, no! I forgot all about it. That trip to look at a bull?"

"Yeah."

She almost dropped the cup he was handing back to her. "Honestly, Cale! I'm getting worried. I must've forgotten what day it is. I must be losing my mind."

He grinned reassuringly. "No way. Yesterday just seemed like a week to everybody."

She had to talk to him now. She had to get this settled before he left. Somehow.

"I overheard a conversation in Leroy's," she blurted. Her worry came clear, rising on the sound of her voice.

"Caleb, you talk to me about trust, but now I'm thinking you don't trust me. It worries me."

"You wanna tell me what you're talkin' about?"

"You didn't tell me about you and your father in the feed store yesterday morning. Right before you came to HGK. The whole town knew about it—you had to know that word would get around—yet you didn't confide in me."

Her words just hung out there, naked, and he said nothing.

"I thought we trusted each other with almost everything."

"So did I until I was out of range of your phone for five minutes."

She felt her cheeks burn.

"Oh, babe, I'm sorry," he said. "That wasn't fair."

"I . . . why didn't you tell me, Cale? When we

were out there at the oak tree? It seems like the natural thing to do."

"Yeah," he said, thoughtfully. "But it was embarrassing, I guess."

His cheeks flamed but she didn't let herself look away.

"No man wants to tell a woman a story that hurts his pride. And there's nothing natural about me and Jake. I try not to even think about him."

"But didn't you know I'd hear it from somebody else? Somebody like Doreen would surely mention it to me and when she saw my surprise, there'd be all kinds of speculation about us all over town."

"Well, damn," he said, forcing a grin, trying to make light of it all. "We sure don't want that to happen, do we? Think of the horror—I sure would hate to scandalize Rock Springs."

He paused. "I guess I was just hoping that somehow you'd never hear about it."

She heard the undercurrent of pain he tried to hide. She took a deep breath and reached for his callused, sweaty hands.

"Don't worry about your pride with me," she said. "I've got a lot of stories I could tell you about times I wasn't too proud of myself."

He just looked at her but his gaze was far away, probably seeing Jake.

"Look, Cale. I have so many problems because of my mother. And my father was imaginary. I think that means we should be able to talk to each other about parents anytime, don't you?"

He did a double take. "Imaginary?"

"Edie Jo never gave me a clue about who he was . . . or is," she said. "So I made him up. Perfect, like I wanted him to be."

She felt her face burn. She'd never said that to anyone before.

"So that's why I have so many problems with trust."

The sympathy that came into his eyes then made her blush even more. She hated to be pitied.

"I know I seem as if I'm completely insane," she said, barely loud enough to hear the words herself.

He held her gaze and wouldn't let her look away. His eyes softened to a clear-sky blue.

Shaking his head, he flashed that grin of his. "Aw, come 'ere," he said, and opened his arms to her. "Don't take it so hard. You know what they say—everybody's some kind of crazy."

Ten

Caleb held himself still. It wasn't just that his head would split open if he moved it to sit up and start the truck, it was that he was here to do his duty. He *ached* to fire up the truck, back out of this parking place on the Square and head for home to crash for a couple of hours before he got in the saddle.

But he also wanted to stop Meri's accusations that he didn't care about HGK.

And he had to follow his plan for the first time he saw her after his trip to be where there were lots of other people around. Which was why he parked out front instead of in his spot by the kitchen.

He should never have come by the office to look at those financials on his way out of town. The last thing she'd said to him—again—was, "We need to talk."

Simple truth was he didn't have the juice right now for a rehash of his sins or any kind of personal relationship discussion. No way. He knew women—as well as any man could—and he would bet that expensive bull he just bought in Montana that Meri was primed for exactly that the minute she saw him. It was never good news when a woman said those four little words.

He sighed and even that much movement sent pain shooting through his head. Every shallow breath he took stabbed the spot on his ribs where Bobby Dan hit him. By mistake.

Bottom line: He and Bobby Dan were getting too old for bar fights. Way too old.

Too old for too much to drink. Too old for no sleep. Too old for anything. This must be what it's like to be a hundred years old.

For a couple of seconds, his fuzzy mind let him believe that the pulsing, rattling sound floating in through his truck's open window was nothing but the pain in his own pounding veins.

"Caleb?"

He groaned. God help him. Here was Meri, bright and cheery, all ready to start the day.

His head begged to stay on the headrest, even for just a couple more seconds, but he jerked it upright. He couldn't rest yet. Get up. Work waiting. Get this over with.

Before he turned to look at her, he glanced in the rearview mirror.

Oh, God help him. Major mistake, coming to the Square before he got cleaned up.

He frowned at the mirror and tried to make his hair stop sticking up in all directions while he blinked the red out of his eyes.

Not happening.

Now here she was, leaning in at his window, expecting a kiss at the very instant he noticed his breath smelling worse than a wet dog. He fumbled in the console, feeling for an old mint or something.

"You're back!" she said, happy. "Did you buy the bull or not?"

He grabbed something, which turned out to be an old cough drop stuck to its wrapper, and made himself meet her eyes while he fumbled to open it.

"Yep. He's a winner."

Oh, Meri. She looked so good, standing there

with her eyes sparkling and the sunlight shining on her hair.

Behind her, scattered around the Square, the usual characters were thick on the ground this morning. Or on the benches, he should say. The early-bird Scaly Alligators were all in their places, already spitting tobacco juice into empty Coke cans despite the wind and watching him and Meri like wrinkled old hawks.

"I've missed you," she said, leaning in for a light kiss on the lips.

She drew back and looked him over. "You look a little worse for wear, babe. Have you not been home? I thought you were flying back in last night."

"I did. But I ran into my old friend Bobby Dan at the airport."

She was frowning. He managed to smile, hoping that she would, too.

"We went out for steaks to talk about breeding lines and crosses with my bull. We had a couple of drinks to ol' Enterprise 7457 and—"

"Maybe more than a couple," she said.

"Yeah. It was stupid."

He tried to sound sheepish. Actually, he was desperate. If he didn't get to crash for at least a couple hours here pretty soon, his head would fall off of his body.

He shrugged. "We let the time get away from us . . ."

"You look hungover."

"I feel it, too," he said. The wind was picking up. It held enough cool to be refreshing.

"Well, I've got to get going. Get horseback and let the sun bake the pain away. I just came by to see you for a minute. I missed you, Mer."

He tried to find his grin. "Anything you need me to do around HGK before I head on out to Indian River?"

His big effort to keep the tone light succeeded. Mostly. He thought.

She was still looking him over, her face and eyes solemn. You might even say suspicious.

"That's very thoughtful of you. Come on into the office and let's make plans for the rest of the week. Some coffee will make you feel better."

He bit back a groan. No rest for him yet. He should've gone straight home.

Meri moved back; he opened the door and stepped out of the truck just as a gust of wind blew across the Square. A piece of trash blew out of the floorboard of his truck and fluttered away.

She grabbed for it but the wind was too fast for her. "It's an envelope," she called. "Do you know what . . ."

It kept moving just ahead of her.

"Don't worry about it," he called.

"It looks important," she yelled over her shoulder.

Her words penetrated the fog in his brain and shot straight to his gut. *Oh, God, no!*

He charged, but he was too slow. The envelope lifted like a rocket and pinwheeled through the air.

Meri ran faster, but her high heels slowed her some. Caleb took off running, but he wasn't much faster in his slick-soled boots and with his head pounding worse every time he hit the ground.

He was lost either way. Even if he got to it first, she'd have to know what it was. Meri had to know everything or she couldn't rest.

He was toast. He was hamburger. God help him.

The damned thing stopped, flattened against the sidewalk for an instant. Meri was almost there, but he was only two steps behind her.

That was two too many. She stabbed it in the heart with the tall, skinny heel of one pretty red sandal.

"Thanks," he said, trying not to strangle on the breath caught in his throat. "Don't move." He bent over to get it. The wind picked up again and the full skirt she wore gave him a well-deserved slap in the face.

"Okay, step away, Mer, I got it . . ."

Too late. A hundred years too late. Her heel didn't move and neither did the gaze of those incredulous violet eyes he was craning his neck upwards to see. Definitely, she was reading the bold, black letters, **INTERNAL REVENUE SERVICE**.

He stood up and sucked in a long breath, resigned to taking his whuppin' like a man.

She bent over and picked up the envelope. Then she straightened and met his gaze.

Instead of lashing out, which would've been a thousand times easier to deal with, her face crumpled and her eyes filled with tears. Caleb felt like a sheep-killing dog.

But Meredith Briscoe was no wilting flower. She smoothed out her expression and it hardened. She blinked, but the tears flowed on. She ignored them.

"You couldn't even *mail* it? I had to browbeat you into helping me prepare it and then you couldn't even *mail it?*" He'd never seen her so angry. She was livid. She needed to calm down.

"I . . ."

"You left for vacation in Montana letting me believe that we had met the deadline when all the time, this envelope was sitting in your truck at the San Antonio *airport?*"

Caleb's head was pounding harder as his blood pumped faster. "It was an honest mistake. It must've fallen under the seat. And I was *not* on vacation."

"If you hadn't been putting your ranch first, as always, you'd have looked under the seat for it. You'd have driven to the post office, looked for it beside you on the seat and realized it was missing. You never thought of it again after I put it in your hands, did you? And you *promised.* You offered, so *gallantly,* to take care of mailing it."

Somebody cleared his throat and Cale realized they'd stopped right in front of Suzy's Café. Jimmy Ransford was standing in the doorway. He came on out and took it upon himself to stop and see what the trouble was.

Because he worked for Lilah on the farm, he seemed to think he was Meri's protector.

"Somethin' wrong, Meri? Need some help here?"

He shot Caleb a fighting look and stared at him while he said to her, "Cale, here, giving you a problem of some kind?"

Well, you had to admire that. Caleb had six inches, a hundred pounds and twenty years on him. Surely Jimmy wasn't drunk this early in the day.

"Everything's fine," Caleb said. "But thanks anyway."

"I'd have to hear it from Miss Meri," Jimmy said.

Now it was Mrs. Brassfield and some other lady stopping in their trek down the sidewalk to hover on the other side of Meri. And, oh, Lord, here came Doreen, hobbling out of her dress shop next door on her crutches.

In Rock Springs, it wouldn't take two minutes for a real crowd to gather. He wished he'd never thought of trying to see her with other people around.

"Come on, Meri," he muttered, feeling like the

dumbest guy in the world, "let's go to the office."

She was always one for privacy. Surely she'd cooperate.

Not happening. Right now, Meri was so mad she was blind to everybody but him.

Caleb said again, "Meri, let's go back to the Kitchens."

He tried to take her by the arm but she pulled away.

Jimmy growled, "You don't wanna go, you don't have to, Meri."

She didn't even hear him.

But when Caleb started walking back the way they had come, she stayed with him, matching his pace every step, and began letting him have it with both barrels.

She was starting to sound like a Texas woman. Even used a couple of cusswords. Which he could not dispute.

But there was no point in letting this go on. His head was splitting. His help was hired just until noon today.

He stopped at his truck. "Look, Meri. I'm more sorry than I can say but I've had a lot on my mind. I'll pay it, personally, if there's a penalty."

"Oh, yes. Yes, you will. But that still won't make it right. You may have so much money you don't have to think about it, but Lilah and I both have everything we own invested in HGK. The least you could do is respect that enough to act like a partner and do your job right."

His own temper flared. "You know that's not right. I *have* to put the ranch first because I can't afford for the place to fail."

For the sake of my self-respect.

But he didn't want to talk to her about that.

"Then you can't afford to let HGK fail, either. So you need to stay here and work instead of flying all over the country and going out on the town with your buddies."

"Do you not understand *English?* It was *business.* All business."

He jerked open his truck door. "I'm sorry, Meredith. I am truly sorry I forgot about mailing your tax thing." He got in. "I'll see you later."

"I don't think so," she said, in a voice he didn't recognize. "I need a break."

He stared at her. "You mean from *me?*"

"Yes. I need some space and some time to myself."

She wheeled on her beautiful heel, turned her back on him and walked toward the door of HGK. He fired up the truck and slammed it into gear but he couldn't seem to make himself give it the gas until she disappeared inside.

Eleven

When Shorty Grumbles stepped out of his truck in the VFW parking lot, he stopped for a minute to look at the sunset. It was a dandy—red and purple streaks like a blanket flung down against the coming dark. *And* a little cool in the breeze.

He took off his hat and nodded his appreciation. God bless Texas. How did people survive in places where you couldn't hardly see the sky?

Setting his best straw cowboy hat back onto his head just right, he headed across the gravel toward the rambling old building, light spilling from its windows. He couldn't wait for Lilah to see him all dressed up. He'd polished his boots to a high shine and he was wearing his new blue shirt with the old-time smile pockets. She hadn't even seen it yet.

He and Lilah had been friends all their lives and it was one of those deals where he'd loved her almost that long. But in high school, she'd had eyes only for Ed Briscoe and Shorty could never make her think of him in a romantic way.

But that was gradually changing, he did believe. He'd been best friends and neighbors with her ever since she'd been widowed and lately he thought he felt a little spark between them.

He stopped and looked around at the cars and trucks. Evidently, she wasn't here yet.

Ken Woodard opened the door and loud music

poured out with the light. The band was Lester Mahan and the Re-treads, a bunch of old guys from around Rock County, so that meant some honky-tonk stuff along with the Western swing. Them boys could play. He would request "Waltz Across Texas." That was one of his favorites.

"Hey, Shorty," Ken hollered. "Get in here and show this bunch of clodhoppers how to dance."

Shorty grinned. He and Lilah were pretty good dancers, no two ways about it.

As he reached the door, a pickup came roaring in behind him, throwing gravel everywhere.

He glanced around, but it wasn't Lilah. She didn't like to admit it, but sometimes she drove like a maniac.

"About time," Ken said, welcoming him with a hearty slap on the back. "Ain't been a dance here since the pie contest."

Shorty grinned. "Reckon this one'll be that exciting?"

Both of them laughed. "I swear," Ken said. "I thought for sure Doreen and Lilah'd be in a bawlin', squallin', hair-pullin' fight before that contest was over and done. That little black-headed granddaughter of Lilah's saved the day."

Shorty shook his head at the wonder of it all. Meri had cemented herself into the community that night. "You can say that again. Miss Meri's a pistol, for sure."

"Yep," Ken said, stepping back to let somebody

else in at the door, "this old place's seen a world of fun and good times over the years."

Milt Hazden hollered at Shorty, so he walked over to him and for a minute they talked cattle prices, which, thank God, were on the upswing. Then, before Shorty could get all the way back to the table where he and Lilah always sat with Clem and Flora and some other friends, Billy Hebert flagged him down.

Shorty let him ramble on, but he was keeping an eye on the door, waiting for Lilah to come through it. He couldn't wait for her to see his shirt. She always said he looked good in blue.

Shorty hadn't seen Billy in a coon's age, so he was hard to get away from. Couples started getting out on the dance floor, the excitement level was rising with the beat of the music, and he and Billy agreed that somebody in the back was making some mighty fine enchiladas, if you could judge by the aroma. His mouth watered.

Yep, this was a fine night. Out on the town. No worries.

Finally, he slapped Billy on the shoulder, told him he had to go find a table and started back toward the usual one. He'd talk to Clem and Flora while he waited for Lilah.

But when he turned to go, his eyes flew open wide and locked in place. He couldn't believe them. He looked again at one of the couples out on the dance floor.

Lilah? Was that really Lilah dancing with that old charlatan, the Judge?

It was. How could this *be?* Why wasn't her truck out there in the parking lot? If she needed a ride, why didn't she call *him?*

Just to put the icing on the cake, the song Lester was singing happened to be that old song "Right or Wrong."

Well, by damn, this here situation was nothin' *but* wrong.

Lilah never had, as far as he could recall, danced with somebody else first, before Shorty.

Well, by golly, he'd show *her*.

Shorty turned around and grabbed the first woman he could find, which happened to be Marva Kay Richardson, a wealthy widow-woman neighbor of Barbara Jane's that he usually avoided like the plague. Marva Kay was hunting a man and she stuck like glue with the slightest bit of encouragement.

Well, he'd just have to deal with that later. This here was an emergency.

Marva Kay screamed and squealed a little at the surprise of being dragged away from her friend Tessie Sanders, but then she came right along as soon as she got over the shock. Shorty never once lost sight of Lilah and the Judge as he pushed her ahead of him and headed into the crowd on the dance floor.

Once there, he pulled Marva Kay into his arms

and started trying to move his feet in some semblance of a two-step while he maneuvered to get closer to Lilah and the Judge. What did she think she was *doing?*

Elbert must've taken a sudden notion he wanted to dance and insisted that Lilah be his partner. What else could it be?

He couldn't even think because Marva Kay kept trying to talk to him in her sweet, whispery voice. "Oh, Shorty, I'm *so* glad . . ."

Shorty just shut his ears and kept moving. He had to concentrate on this problem.

He danced her around the considerable combined bulk of Joe Don and Aline Cotton to get close to the Judge and Lilah, who was actually laughing at something the pompous ass was saying. Was she *that* far gone? That old idiot never said anything funny in his life.

Finally, he got close enough for her to see him, and he thought she did, but Shorty actually had to reach around Marva Kay and peck Lilah on the shoulder to get her attention.

When she finally did, he mouthed at her. *What are you thinking?*

She looked at him like she'd never seen him before and then raised her eyebrows, haughty as all get-out, before she turned back to see the Judge's ugly mug.

Shorty messed up the rhythm, but he danced Marva Kay closer to Lilah. He touched her arm.

She twisted her head around just enough to mouth back, *What do you think you're doing?*

He couldn't believe that look. It said he'd made her really mad.

Well, too bad. *He* was the one asking the questions here.

Like, *Are you goin' to let him take you home?*

A cold hand closed around his gut when Marva Kay squeezed his hand and danced closer. He tried not to cough. She must've laid on that perfume with a three-inch paintbrush. Did Lilah actually *come* here with that old codger? Was that why her truck wasn't out there in the parking lot?

The Judge danced Lilah away from him, but Shorty was having none of that. He followed so abruptly that Marva Kay's heels dragged on the floor. She was so surprised she gave out a little yelp.

But that little woman was game, he had to hand her that. She didn't miss a beat, not even when they bumped into the Cottons on the way back by and Joe Don muttered, "Watch where you're goin', Grumbles."

Shorty ignored him and danced faster. This time he got close enough to mutter at Lilah's ear, "He's only got one thing on his mind. You be careful, girl."

Her head whipped around like her neck was on

a swivel. Her eyes bugged out and her cheeks flushed red. She didn't look as surprised, this time. More like she might be *really* getting into being mad.

Well, let her, by golly. He was a little hot under the collar, himself.

She didn't have to act like he was bothering her or something. Come to think of it, she hadn't acted the least bit glad to see him tonight, not any of the time.

Right then, Lester sang out louder on the chorus, "Right or wrong, I'll always love you . . ."

"Oh," Marva said, with a feathery little sigh, "this is such a romantic song. Oh, Shorty, I've always . . ."

"Damn fool wrote that song," Shorty muttered.

He could feel the scowl on his face, it went so deep, but Marva Kay still smiled up at him and kept on going in her little whispery way.

Shorty shut his ears to it, set his sights on Lilah again and whirled Marva in a big circle, trying to stop her talking and cover some ground at the same time.

He was gonna get the message to Lilah if it took him the rest of the evening.

Buster Tremaine and his new girlfriend got right smack-dab in the middle of his way, but Buster never had been very fast on his feet, so Shorty avoided them at the last second and got himself close enough to talk to Lilah again.

"What do you mean, carrying on like this?" he hissed. "Think about your granddaughter. What about your reputation . . ."

If looks could kill, she'd have put him six feet under right then and there.

All because he had her best interests at heart! Why, that glance alone made him mad enough to spit fire. He danced away, but he was coming back. He wasn't about to take that. She could just change her attitude and be grateful somebody cared. Lilah was smart, but sometimes she saw too much good in people.

Shorty made a little half circle and got back around just when the Judge stepped back and away from her to turn. One of the old geezer's big feet splayed right out in front of him and Shorty brought his boot heel down on it faster than you could say Jack Robinson.

He let his weight down and ground it in while he met Lilah's glare with one of his own. He held her eye with a sharp look to let her know this was significant, twirled Marva Kay out to the end of his arm, leaned in and mouthed to Lilah: *The Judge can't see to drive after dark.*

Elbert shoved Shorty off his foot just as Marva Kay came shuffling around to find the next step and crane her neck back at Lilah at the same time, trying to figure out what was going on, but Shorty hung in there. He wouldn't let Lilah break the look between them until he saw to it that she'd understood what he said. He mouthed, *He'll have a wreck and kill you.*

She glared her most disbelieving, disgusted opinion of him and mouthed back: *Get away from here. Now.*

Don't ride with him. I'll take you home.

Lilah rolled her eyes so hard he thought they'd fall out of her head and then threw him another hateful look before she swung back toward the Judge. As she passed Shorty by, she muttered, through clenched teeth, "You hear me? Git gone!"

Only then did Shorty go dancing on off with Marva Kay. At least Lilah was answering him now. Maybe she was about to come to her senses.

Lilah sat in the passenger seat of the Judge's Lincoln Continental and stared out into the night as they tooled along the highway at fifty miles an hour. Sometimes forty-five.

Lord in heaven have mercy, she was worn smooth out. She wanted her home and her shower and her bed.

"Elbert, if you don't kick it up a notch, we're liable to get run over from behind. It's been a long day."

And, oh Lord, if Shorty's prediction came true, she'd never hear the end of it, dead or alive.

The Judge took his eyes off the road to turn and give her a fond smile.

"But the *evenin'* passed in a flash, didn't it, Lilah girl?"

"Watch the road," she said. "No telling who might pull out of Leroy's with one beer too many under his belt."

Passed in a flash, her aunt Fanny. She'd thought it would never end, what with Elbert not even listening to what she had to say about the zoning because he had to try to act all smooth and romantic.

That, combined with Shorty acting like he'd lost his cotton-pickin' mind, had nearly set her free. If it wasn't for the zoning being so important, she would've put a stop to every bit of that foolishness.

If only Elbert knew it, she was on her very last nerve. And if only Shorty knew it, next time she saw him, she was going to tongue-lash him to within an inch of his life.

She sighed. No wonder so many widows chose not to marry again.

Elbert was talking, as usual. When Lilah finally tuned in again, he was saying, ". . . still have to hear your ideas about the zoning change proposal . . ."

"I'll come to your office. One day next week when I get done at the Kitchens. I usually leave in the late morning as soon as whatever new pastry recipe we're trying is out of the oven and tested. The farmwork didn't stop just because we started a business."

"Well, you let me know if you need any help with that testing. I'm hoping you'll keep the Cherokee fry bread on the menu. It'll melt in your mouth and it's better with honey than a sopaipilla because it's not so sweet."

Boss, boss, boss. Get over yourself.

Holding her tongue was making her head hurt.

"Mmm," she said.

"I get really tired of my office," he said. "I spend so much time in there. I need more fresh air. Maybe I could come out to Honey Grove . . ."

"We're so busy now, selling the last of the hay we can spare and buying all the salvage produce we can find from up around Sand Ridge. They had a big storm up there day before yesterday, you know, and . . ."

She rattled on, talking and talking so he couldn't.

They'd turned the Dog Creek corner onto Old Briscoe Road. They'd be at Honey Grove very soon. Just a few more minutes.

She managed to hold the conversation to other topics and keep it off their next meeting until he finally crept down her driveway and rolled to a stop at the gate.

"Well. Thank you for dinner, Elbert," she said, and opened her door.

"Here now. Wait just a minute," he said, shifting into park and turning off the key in a flash. "I was raised right. My mama'd turn over in her grave if

I let you walk yourself to your door, Lilah Briscoe."

If she could ever get into her house again, she was going to throw herself across her bed and not move one muscle or speak a single word until morning. Forget the shower.

And forget Elbert and Shorty. She'd put on some Emmylou and let that crystal sound blow their bossy voices right on out of her head.

Where did either one of them ever get the idea they could tell her what to do?

Elbert came around the front of the car and helped her out. He held her by the elbow and strolled up the brick walk at a snail's pace, commenting on her flowers and her yard and complimenting her right and left.

As they climbed the steps, she thanked him for a nice evening and told him she had to get up early in the morning.

At the door, she said, "Thanks again, El . . ."

"Good night, Lilah . . ."

She turned to face him. Merciful heavens, was he actually puckered up?

Before she could draw breath, he dipped his head and made an awkward dive at her. She jerked away and his lips kissed the screen.

He made a little grunting noise and threw his head up, startled in turn.

"Honestly, Elbert, that serves you right."

She grabbed the handle and stepped inside the

screen door. "I have tried to tell you from the get-go that this was not a date. You should know me well enough to know I mean what I say."

He surprised her again. He chuckled. A deep, sincere, heartfelt chuckle.

"So do I," he said. "And I *do* love it when a woman plays hard to get. There's not nearly enough of that goin' on, these days. Good night, Lilah dear."

He turned and crossed the porch with a jaunty step. By the time he started down the walk, he was actually whistling.

Best Lilah could tell, it was that song they were playing the whole time Shorty was acting the fool, that old Western swing tune, "Right or Wrong."

Well. If only he knew it, *she'd* be the one to say what was right and what was wrong.

She went to her bedroom and threw herself across her bed, all right.

But even frazzled as she felt, she wasn't resting.

She was laughing her head off.

Twelve

Caleb cocked his head, squinted through the fog of exhaustion blurring his vision and swung the hammer again. The nail sank all the way in, up to its head into the trim. Straight. Which was a helluvan accomplishment for his left hand.

The right one was stiff as new jeans from road

rash he got when he dived for that damned letter to the IRS.

Either hand, every blow of the hammer took the top off his head.

He picked another nail from the loose ones in his tool belt and moved on. He needed to get to the fence, but somehow he needed more to work on the house. Every muscle in his body begged for sleep. Or rest. Just to lay his head down for a minute . . .

But that wasn't gonna happen. He couldn't even sit down because his mind was going like a combine driving him.

His temporary help had left a lot of chores undone, too, but right now he couldn't leave the house. If he was just mad he could handle it, but this feeling was way more.

Sick at heart. That was it. What if he'd lost Meri?

Because he forgot to *mail an envelope,* for God's sake?

Surely not. She couldn't be *that* unreasonable. She wanted everything perfect, yes, but usually she didn't go *this* crazy about a small mistake. Not if she loved him.

Well, Hoss, when did she ever tell you she loved you?

But her actions, her violet eyes, the way she looked at him sometimes, had all told him—more than once—that she did. She was always prioritizing. Well, then, how could she make the IRS a higher priority than he was?

It wasn't like they'd be hauled off to prison and put on bread and water if that payment was two days late. Or a week. Or a month.

He hit the nail so hard he could feel the blow all the way up through his shoulder. Even his teeth hurt. He was miserable, skin to gut. He felt like he'd been not only rode hard and put up wet, but kicked in the belly, too.

The sound of a vehicle arriving turned his head around, his eyes snapping wide open on the sneaky hope that it might be Meri. He'd said he was sorry for forgetting the stupid letter. He'd told her that he'd been on the phone about the Montana production sale he was heading for and that made him forget to go by the post office. So maybe she'd come to accept his apology.

She liked fairness. She might even be coming to apologize for overreacting.

But, just to prove once more that a man never knows what's coming down the road, it was Gideon's beloved old black truck.

Gideon had always had a twin's intuition about when Caleb wasn't doing so well. Caleb assumed his brother had come to check on him.

Most of the time, Gid understood how to settle him and help him get his feet back on the ground—Gid's job since they were born—but this time Caleb wasn't so sure Gideon could help.

From the jump, Meri had been special and different from all Cale's other romantic entanglements.

Caleb walked across the porch and down the flagstone path to wait for him. His limp was more pronounced than usual, and his old wound actually pained him a little. Or was it his imagination? He was probably looking for another pain to distract him from the one in his heart.

Gideon parked right in front of his twin. Their eyes met and held.

Gid's were concerned. Caleb hoped his said that he wasn't so sure he wanted company.

He said, "I thought you had a job. Does Jake know you're gone?"

Gideon got out and they stood for a second looking each other over.

"I'd say you look like you just took a whuppin'," Gid said. "I'm too late to help you, man."

Cale tried to grin but couldn't quite make it happen.

Gid slapped him on the back and started walking toward the house with his arm around Cale's shoulders.

"Yep. Word on the street has it that you lost a fight with the wind this mornin'. Let a girl beat you up."

The teasing got a grunt out of Caleb. He said, "Sounds like a good story."

"You okay?"

"Yeah. Just doin' my part to keep the Burkett name in the news."

"Done. The phone lines are burnin' up and the Scaly Alligators who were eyewitnesses are lordin' it over the latecomers like they'd won the lottery."

"Thanks for coming, bro. But there's nothin' you can do."

Gideon opened the screen and ushered Caleb into his own house.

"No intentions of trying," Gideon said. "Your love life is none of my business. I'm here to talk breeding bulls. Heard it on the grapevine you bought Enterprise 7457."

Gideon led the way into the kitchen as if he had a plan. Which, Cale would bet, he did. Gideon thought food would cure anything.

"Where'd you hear that?"

"Trav. He heard it from Roger Stinson. You can imagine how embarrassed I am, what with being the last to know and all."

"Get outta here. You're tickled to death you know it before I got a chance to tell you."

"Sit down before you fall down," Gid ordered, and Caleb dropped into a chair at the kitchen table.

Gideon grabbed the coffeepot, dumped out the old grounds and started making fresh. Cale dropped his head into his hands and massaged his temples.

"I dropped a bundle on him, that's for sure, so I deserve to hold the papers." He felt that little twinge of worry again. Had he bought something he couldn't afford? He surely hoped not. "So, whaddaya think, Gid? Knowing you, you've already researched the hell out of his blood-lines."

"Which you could've asked me to do before you ever went out there," Gid said, shaking his head in despair. "Might be good information to have before you 'drop a bundle' and sign your life away on the dotted line."

Caleb shrugged. "I researched enough. Low birth weights, fast gains. Facts aren't everything. Basically, I had to look 'im over and go by my gut."

Gid cut his head at him. "Make you feel any better, from what I can find out, looks like your gut did good. Ever think about taking a partner on him?"

Caleb looked at him suspiciously. "You wanna get in?"

"I think he'll pay for himself someday," Gid said. "And I always hate for you to be in a project without me. You know how twins are."

"And give me a little financial cushion, too?"

"You're bound to be needing one by now."

They'd inherited equal amounts when their grandmother died and, with HGK and all his ranch expenses, Cale really didn't have a whole lot left.

Jake had never given them anything, in spite of his fortune.

And Gideon would beggar himself before he let Jake be proved right about Indian River Ranch's ultimate failure.

He cooked breakfast and they ate eggs and sausage and gravy while they burned an hour talking breeding cattle and marketing semen before Gid got up and said he had to get back to work. With Cale's belly full and his mind on business, all he wanted right now was to crash. Even a few hours' sleep would help him a lot. He needed some rest because he had to talk things out with Meri, sooner or later.

When Cale walked him out to the truck, Gid said, "Oh, and about Meri . . ."

Cale stiffened and stared at him. "What about her?"

"Thank your lucky stars, man. I hear she coulda run that spike heel right through the palm of your hand."

Caleb grinned a little.

Gideon said, "None of my business—I'm only the one has to scrape you up off the floor every time—but here it is anyway," he said. "Don't let the break go too long, bro. She's a keeper. Y'all are good together. Opposites, but good."

He shouldn't believe it, Caleb thought, because he didn't understand it—or her, sometimes—but it was true. And if ever a man needed to settle down before he burned out, it was him. He was getting too old to feel this bad.

"Yeah," Cale said, "like the little girl with the curl in the middle of her forehead. When we're good we're very, very good but when we're bad, we're horrid."

Cale felt a sudden surge of exhaustion. How could he ever get Meri back? And did he really want to? If he did, he wouldn't know how to handle her, judging by his most recent attempt.

Gid opened the door and climbed into his truck, dropped his elbow out the window and looked at his twin. "I'm just sayin'."

Cale shrugged. "I dunno," he said, trying to sound careless. "We've both got too much on our plates right now to have time for a romance, anyhow. I'm thinkin' this may turn out to be for the best."

"Aw, come on, bro. Buck up. Be brave."

Cale slapped the side of the truck. "Get back to work. Thanks for comin' out."

Meri felt like a fugitive. She slipped out of the post office and ran down the steps to the sidewalk, glancing back over her shoulder to see whether Barbara Jane, who was coming in the other door, had noticed her. Apparently not.

She didn't want to get caught by anyone she knew because she'd lived in Rock Springs long enough to know how it worked. By now, everybody with ears in Rock County would've heard the story of her and Caleb's disgraceful scene on the street and very few of them would be too uninterested or too shy to mention it to her.

Stopping to speak to *anyone* today, while they were the freshest of gossip, would mean a long session of either curious questioning or dispensing of tons of well-meaning advice. Or, perhaps, reminiscences of other public disagreements (probably involving Caleb or some ancient Burkett ancestor of his) down through the years that had also taken place on the Rock Springs Square.

Some, no doubt, going back as far as when Texas was a republic.

Refusing to stand there to listen—and respond, *graciously*—to every word of whatever diatribe simply was not an option for Lilah Briscoe's granddaughter *or* for the owner of a small business in Rock County. Not if she wanted to continue life as she knew it.

No matter which it was, anyone who spoke to her now would mention Caleb. She could not bear it.

Already, she had a hollow of loneliness in her gut. What if she'd made a mistake? His face had looked so terrible it broke her heart to remember it.

But for herself, it took her heart right out of her

body. If she couldn't trust him with the mail, she couldn't trust him with her heart.

She was *furious* with him. But she was even more furious with herself. Always before, she'd kept her guard up. All her life. Since the minute she realized her mother never intended to come back for her, she'd kept the walls around her heart. Letting him get through them was the most stupid thing she'd ever, ever done.

Meri quickened her pace as she got ready to pass in front of Doreen's Dress Shop because Doreen herself, with her famous curiosity shining in her eyes, was the very last person she wanted to see. Maybe she could just rush by, looking down at her armful of letters and packages as if they were urgent.

No luck. The door of the dress shop swung open just as she stepped in front of it.

"Oh, Meri! Hi! Do you have a minute?"

She looked up and blurted, "Where's Doreen?"

It was her employee, Rochelle Bascom, widely known across Rock County as "that pretty young woman who got off the bus."

Rochelle had a mischievous smile. "She's helping her husband show a house to a client right now. Can I give her a message?"Meri shook her head no and the two of them went through the usual routine: How *are* you? Y'all keeping busy at the Kitchens/Dress Shop? How's Miss Lilah today? Doreen still walking better, healing after

137

her wreck? Isn't this weather fine? Oooh, yes! Not quite so hot.

Meri decided Rochelle's accent wasn't Texas, but was from somewhere in the Deep South. "That mysterious girl who got off the bus" was the subject of much speculation. Nobody could figure out why she'd chosen Rock Springs as the place to end her journey and she wasn't giving any clues about that or where her trip had started.

"I know you're busy, Meri," Rochelle drawled, "but I wonder if we could go to lunch someday, or if you don't have time for that, maybe just coffee? I'm lookin' for start-up business advice."

Meri was thinking about Cale again but she forced herself to focus.

"What kind of business?"

"Doreen's going to rent me a corner of her shop to sell my natural cosmetics products that I'm makin' in the kitchen of my apartment."

Meri shifted the armload of catalogs, orders and other mail and adjusted her bag on her shoulder. She wanted to get back to the office where she could escape and be alone for a little while, even though, fifteen minutes ago, she'd desperately had to get out of it.

Maybe she could go back, throw herself into work and check off every item on today's to-do list. *That'd* make her feel better.

"Oh, Rochelle, I don't know anything about business in general," she said. "Not yet. I'm learning on the job, making it up as I go. HGK just grew out of the seed of an idea that fell into my head . . . and Caleb's."

She couldn't keep herself from speaking his name. "He helped me know what to do with it."

The surprising, early success of HGK still shocked Meri every time she thought of it and then fear always followed right on its heels. The whole thing could collapse as fast as it grew.

"Well," Rochelle drawled, "I won't keep you now, but I'd be forever grateful if you'd meet with me sometime. Even if you just recounted your own experiences, I'm sure it'd help me."

Meri forced herself to smile and nod. Lots of people had answered questions for her and she needed to do the same. Rochelle seemed to be a really nice, sincere person, no matter who she was or why she was in Rock Springs.

"I'll look at my calendar and see what I can do," she said, matching the girl's friendly smile. "Good to see you, Rochelle."

Rochelle propped the door open to the fairly cool fall day. "Great to see you, too, Meri. Thanks so much for your time. You take care, now, y'hear?"

As Meri moved on, Rochelle called after her, "Oh, and Meri, when you see Gideon, tell him 'hey' for me, okay?"

"I will."

Gideon! Would her trouble with Caleb damage

her friendship with his twin? She hoped not. There was just something about Gideon that made her feel he was a kindred spirit.

Why did Cale have to be so different from his twin? So difficult?

She walked faster down the east side of the Square, clutching the bundle of mail to her with both arms, her stomach tight with tension, keeping up a brisk pace and thinking about business. Only business.

When she went into the café at HGK, four tables were occupied, three by "regulars." She smiled to herself. Already, this was becoming a hangout in a town where hangout habits were ingrained.

Mrs. Gardenhire was at one table alone and a man reading a newspaper at another. The other two occupied tables held working men, one group of them already dirty from working all night on an oil spill and the other in clean shirts and jeans, plus cowboy hats. All had coffee cups.

Maybe they were all here only because it was someplace new, but maybe not. Lilah and Jewel made the best pastries in town. The dried peach pies, chocolate covered twists and pecan cinnamon rolls were nothing short of fabulous. Meri was pushing them to make a new pastry every week and then let people vote for favorites to be added to the every-day list.

Her eye fell on the coffeepot. Empty. That wasn't good and it wasn't typical of Hadley. So far, the new girl hired to be Thelma's helper had done an excellent job, therefore something was wrong.

Meri dumped the mail into a chair and changed direction to go pick up the pot to refill it.

Hadley wasn't behind the glass pastry-display counter, either. Meri sighed. It'd be a pain to try and find a replacement already.

"Thanks for coming in, everyone, and good morning," she said as she headed for the kitchen. "Let me go find some more coffee for you . . ."

"Oh, honey, I hate to tell you, but it's worse than an empty coffeepot," Mrs. Gardenhire said, a note of pain in her wispy voice. She was president of a group that had chosen HGK for their weekly meetings, the Ladies' Light Reading Book Club.

(Formed, Mrs. Gardenhire had explained at the first meeting, because its members had experienced all of the serious and dark in life that they could stand, therefore, they were not going to spend their remaining time on earth and their eyesight reading about anything bad or troubling, scary or low-down.)

They had the same philosophy about music. Meri stopped and turned to look at her.

"Oh, Mrs. Gardenhire, has someone been playing heartbreak songs again?"

Her own heart *hurt* when those words came out of her mouth. Literally.

It wasn't a sad song playing now on the "sound

141

system," the old CD player that Lilah had insisted should be put to good use. She'd asked for donations of CDs, since so many people used digital players nowadays, and there was a huge basket of all kinds of music beside the table holding the player.

"Don't you think Asleep at the Wheel is cheerful enough?"

She wished for Lilah to be here instead of at the farm. All Meri wanted was to get to the office and close the door and be alone.

Sometimes these disagreements among customers got out of hand.

Last week, at the same time as the book club meeting, the Scaly Alligators had been in the café playing dominoes and they insisted on playing honky-tonk cheating songs. The ladies almost rioted. Lilah had to come out from the kitchen and settle the dispute.

Meri had no idea how to do that. Only Lilah could talk so straight and sharp to the Scaly Alligators and get them to cooperate with no hurt feelings.

But no Scaly Alligators here today. They were all out on the Square, whittling and chewing tobacco and making the story about Meri and Caleb grow bigger and bigger.

"Oh, yes, I love Asleep at the Wheel and always have," Mrs. Gardenhire said. "It's a larger problem of mixed-up orders today, dear."

Meri's heart sank. She could forget privacy and time to pull herself together. She'd have to fire Hadley and start all over again.

Banker Buford Quisenberry rattled his newspaper and came out from behind it. "If you're going to try to run a business, you need to hire good help. My omelet had not one pepper in it."

Oh, no! He was here on his first visit to the café, as far as Meri knew, and they had empty coffeepots and mixed-up orders! When she and Caleb had saved Honey Grove Farm from Buford's foreclosure threat, he'd been so furious that he'd predicted HGK would fail. Clearly, he was loving this.

"You should've said something right away, Buford," Mrs. Gardenhire said. "If you hadn't gobbled it so fast you'd have realized there were no peppers in mine before I began eating yours. You're the one who should've said something about them switching our orders if you didn't like mine."

She smiled at Meri. "It was wonderful. Next time I'm ordering the Texas Hot Special to begin with."

That made Meri blink. Delicate Mrs. Gardenhire happily eating an omelet that had made more than one tough man cry was a scene hard to imagine.

"I knew it immediately," the banker said. "I simply didn't have time to wait for them to cook another one."

"But yet you're still here," Mrs. Gardenhire said. "Reading the paper for more than half an hour."

He pretended not to hear. "I can tell you right now that this business will fail, Miss Meredith. I said it before and I'll say it again—getting into this salvage business is the most foolish mistake Lilah Briscoe ever made."

Meri bit back the words *Oh, get over it.* He still held so much animosity about the foreclosure that never happened that he would talk about this omelet confusion all over town. No sense giving him more reason to talk by being rude to him.

Well, Lilah would say look on the bright side. This would mean the gossip wouldn't be *all* about Caleb and Meri.

"I'm so sorry for the mix-up," she said, going to his table. "My apologies, Mr. Quisenberry. Your breakfast is complimentary."

Before he could answer, she went to the lady's table. "I'm so sorry for the mix-up. Your breakfast is also complimentary, Mrs. Gardenhire."

"Well, it most certainly is *not,*" the good woman said. "Y'all are just getting started and times are bad. I loved your habañeros. I must talk to Lilah and see if she grew them out at Honey Grove."

Meri made small talk with her, then looked around the room, which seemed peaceful at the moment, and headed for the kitchen. "I'll be right back with coffee for everyone."

Her frustration with Hadley was growing by the second, twisting into a knot in her stomach. She and Lilah couldn't be here every second. What would happen if they couldn't keep good help?

In the kitchen, Jewel turned from the oven to say, "I just sent Hadley home. She can't work for having to run to the restroom and throw up."

Meri went to the big standing pot of coffee to refill the small one. "Oh, I hope it's not contagious. The customers . . ."

"It's not. She just found out yesterday she's pregnant."

Meri's hand froze on the lever. She couldn't fire Hadley. Not only did she have a reason for poor performance today, her husband was in the National Guard unit just deployed to Afghanistan. The girl's only resource was her family and her father recently lost his job at a car dealership that went out of business.

But Hadley couldn't work today.

And there was no one to take her place but Meri.

No, wait. Dallas Fremont always wanted to work. Maybe she could come as soon as school was out for the day and take care of the café while Meri got to her paperwork.

Meri sent a text because Dallas was probably in class. Almost immediately, the girl called. She was between classes. She'd love to work in the café. She'd be there at three.

Just before she ended the call, she said, "Oh, and

Meri! We're all so excited about you and Caleb chaperoning the Youth Rodeo Association dance. I can't wait!"

Meri stood in the middle of the kitchen with the phone to her ear and her mouth open. Chaperone? She and Caleb?

No. That wasn't happening.

Thirteen

"I drove too fast," Lilah said as she came in Dulcie's back door. "But Hector and his crew could *not* seem to get all the crates loaded and I just *had* to talk to you for a minute. I'm so glad B.J. and Parmalee aren't here yet."

Dulcie nearly dropped the cookie sheet she was taking out of one of her wall ovens. She peered over her shoulder.

"Do you know something? Did Meri talk to you?"

Lilah waved that away. "No. Oh, no. Sorry I got your hopes up. I was hurrying to see if Cale by some miracle confided in his mama."

Dulcie pulled the pan out and closed the oven door.

"No, from what I hear on the grapevine, if he's confided in anybody, it's Ronnie Rae. Gossip is they ran into each other at the Dairy Queen last night and sat in her car in the parking lot for a long time, talking. A long time. Hours."

Lilah's eyes went wide. "Don't tell me that!"

"They've always been friends. Especially after she shot him. You know that."

Lilah laid her Bible and her bag on the breakfast table and went to wash her hands. She sighed. "Yes. I think they're too much alike to pair up *and* too much alike to leave each other alone."

Dulcie plopped the cookie sheet onto the Mexican tiled bar. "I tell you, Lilah, I'm scared witless that Caleb's going to mess this up with Meri."

Lilah dried her hands and went to help take up the cookies.

"You've mothered him nearly as much as I have and you know as well as I do that he can be completely impossible!"

She handed a spatula to Lilah and put the black wire cooling rack between them. They both began to work taking cookies off the sheet.

"Listen, if Meri hears about him and Ronnie Rae . . ."

"How can she not?" Lilah said. "This is Rock Springs you're talking about."

". . . *please* tell her it doesn't mean there's anything romantic going on between them. If they were going to make a go of it, it would've happened a long time ago."

Dulcie looked so anxious Lilah could've cried. She felt the same way.

"I'll tell you what, Dulcie. Being the parent—or

grandparent—of an adult is the hardest thing in the whole world."

"I believe it. We think we're not wise enough to parent when they're little, but at least *they* think we know what we're doing. When they're grown it's *much* harder. They think we don't have a clue and we don't."

They laughed. "I don't know why but that makes me feel a little better," Lilah said.

"Might as well laugh," Dulcie said. "I've been thinking about Meri constantly because I know what a handful Caleb can be. I just hope she won't give up on him.

"Oh, I forgot to make the coffee! Finish these, will you? I don't know why I didn't do that first."

Lilah nodded. "All I know is Meri's gonna lose the few pounds I finally managed to put on her bones if she doesn't start eating. And I hear her up at all times of the night again, but if I try to get her to talk, she gives me the skunk eye."

"I talked to Cale for a minute yesterday, but he didn't mention her. Gid said he's working on his house like a madman and talking about his new bull, nothing else."

They made identical tsking sounds.

"Meri doesn't know much about how to handle men," Lilah said.

"Caleb doesn't know one thing about staying with a woman and working things out," Dulcie said. "Whenever it hits a real rough patch, he's outta there. That's my main prayer—that he won't run this time. Meri's his only hope, as far as I can see."

Lilah nodded. "You know what? Praying's all we can do."

She helped herself to a warm cookie, took a bite and then swooned. "I do declare, Dulcie Burkett, nobody can make a chocolate chip cookie like you can."

It was the absolute truth and it didn't even rankle Lilah to admit she was one of the nobodies in that arena. Mostly because Dulcie had never been as good as Lilah at making cowboy cookies, which she thoughtfully didn't mention right then, like the good friend she was.

"Mm *hmmm,*" B.J. called as she opened the back door. "It smells so good in here I'm off my diet for the whole afternoon."

Parmalee was with her and they came in talking and exclaiming about the fragrant cookies, plus the fact that it was cool enough to sit on the porch for the meeting.

So, they left the coffee to perk and walked through the sprawling old ranch house with its Indian rugs and antique saddles and worn leather furniture to the front porch where Dulcie turned on the ceiling fans and they all settled into the woven-leather rockers with their Bibles and notes in their laps. Dulcie took a deep breath.

"Let's just start with a prayer for us to know

how to listen for the Spirit and go from there."

After that, as they went around the circle, Lilah was ashamed to realize she wasn't in it with her whole heart. In the back of her mind, no matter who was the subject of their group prayer, she was selfishly throwing in thoughts of Meri and Caleb, and even of HGK and what a permanent break between them might do to the business. Her cheeks burned, she was so mortified.

When they'd finished praying and started visiting, Dulcie and Lilah served the coffee and cookies.

They planned a party their Sunday school class was going to give for the old folks at the nursing home up on the hill and discussed the schedule for the Sunday afternoon singings that all the churches in town held there in rotation.

"Dulcie, tell your Presbyterian singers not to sing any more of those contemporary Christian songs that drag on and on and say the same thing over and over," Lilah said. "Maudie Hewitt told me that in all her 106 years she never heard such mournful music about a comforting subject."

B.J. said, "Yes, and Old Man Deere wants that young men's gospel bluegrass group from Lufkin to come back. You know what? I thought we might hire them to do a fund-raiser for the Judge. We could go pick up Mr. Deere and take him to the picnic to hear them."

As soon as the words "the Judge" left B.J.'s lips, all eyes turned to Lilah.

"Don't look at me! I'm not raising a penny for the Judge until he says how he'll vote on the zoning question."

Dulcie raised her eyebrows. "From what I hear, you've got him wrapped around your little finger," she said. "He'll vote whichever way you want."

Lilah scowled at her. "That was not a *date,* no matter what anybody says. It was a political meeting—one where I never got a promise, however."

"But he's the better choice," B.J. said. "Common sense tells you that Missy Lambert will vote for it."

Lilah said, "No doubt about that. We'd be a bedroom community in a heartbeat. Forget 'quaint' Rock Springs."

Parmalee said, in her soft, sweet voice, "Well, now, Lilah, we don't want to jump to conclusions here."

Lilah's head whipped around. She gave Parmalee a hard, incredulous look and opened her mouth to set her straight, but Dulcie got ahead of her and tried to change the subject.

"Oh, girls, it's too pretty a morning to waste talking politics. If y'all won't stay for a walk along the river, I'm going down there by myself and work on the watercolor I started yesterday."

B.J. said, "I'll lead us in our closing prayer."

But Lilah couldn't let it go. She said, "B.J., please pray that we can hold the line right here and stop that zoning change from happening."

Parmalee's little voice came out just a shade louder than usual.

"No, don't, B.J. I don't think the Good Lord would be at all pleased to hear that."

Lilah turned and stared at her slack-jawed. "*What* do you mean?"

Parmalee never did like confrontations, but she bowed up like a natural fighter and stared right back. She rarely showed it but Lilah knew from long experience that she did have a lot of backbone. She'd never be in this group in the first place if she didn't.

"What I mean is that praying something like that is abusing God's name," Parmalee said. "He's got much more important things to tend to than changing the zoning on Jones Orchards."

Lilah had to play that back in her memory to make sure she'd heard it right.

"It's trivializing the whole concept of prayer," Parmalee said.

"*What?* When He tells us that He notices every sparrow that falls? When He counts the hairs on your head? What are you *talking* about, Parmalee Parsons?"

"I just told you. And I also have to say that I think the zoning *should* be changed."

Lilah literally could not breathe. "You can't mean that!"

Parmalee narrowed her eyes at Lilah. "I know you think you're right, Lilah. You always think you're right, even when you know you're wrong. But you are *wrong* this time."

Lilah came up out of her chair before she even knew she was going to move.

"Have you lost your mind?"

"The zoning *should* be changed. I've thought about it a lot."

"Surely you can't believe that."

Lilah racked her brain to make sense of this heresy. She felt like Parmalee had kicked her in the gut. How could her dear friend she'd loved for so long feel this way?

Parmalee held up one hand in a stop sign. It was a totally unnecessary gesture. Lilah was too hurt to speak.

She dropped back down into her chair. Thank the Lord, it was still there behind her. (*If* that wasn't too trivial of a thing to thank the Lord for.)

"Parmalee, you cannot—surely you can*not* mean what you're saying."

What could she do? Parmalee was one of her heart-sisters! Lilah never dreamed that any of them would want the zoning changed, of all things!

"Parmalee," she said, in her best ex-schoolteacher

voice. "Think for a minute. We all know how precious our community is just the way we have it. And I'm not saying we couldn't benefit from some new blood in here, I don't mean that."

"So what do you mean?"

"That we shouldn't destroy the land and our own way of life. The 4-H horse club and the rodeos and mutton-bustings and even the ice cream social! All that'll die, because once the dam is broken, housing developments will pour all over the little farms and ranches and drown them."

With infuriating calm, Parmalee said, "It's not like you to be such a doomsayer, Lilah."

"I'm telling the truth, that's all. It'll kill the way of life that small farms and ranches create. *Our* way of life. Parmalee, remember how the funeral dinners are dwindling and people don't bring home-cooked dishes much at all?"

"Yes, and without a housing development in sight. It's just changing times, Lilah. It's *life*. Everything changes."

"Well, we don't have to put it on a fast train."

Lilah was gasping like a fish out of water. She forced herself to breathe normally. But she couldn't. She couldn't speak, either.

"Girls," Dulcie the hostess said firmly, "we were about to have the closing prayer."

B.J. prayed for love and patience and under-standing for them all.

Lilah's eyes filled with tears. She was so frozen

on the outside that she couldn't even close them to pray. On the inside, she was breaking into pieces.

No matter what she thought politically, a true friend would be on Lilah's side. If Parmalee were a true friend, she would want what was best for Lilah. The zoning change would affect Lilah *personally.* And professionally.

Her whole life would change against her will and Parmalee was for that.

Oh, Lord! What would she do?

She couldn't live without her prayer group.

Fourteen

Meri walked fast into the kitchen and went straight to the coffeepot to pour a cup so she wouldn't have to meet Lilah's eyes. Sometimes Lilah could just look at her and read her thoughts.

"I've gotta run," she said. "I need to finish that paperwork tonight and I forgot to bring it home."

Lilah was at the butcher block, cutting out biscuits and putting them in the pans.

"Not before you eat at least two biscuits. I'm making breakfast for supper just to tempt your appetite. Meri, you're skinny as a stick."

"I can't, Gran. I have to get going. But first I need to ask you a favor."

She turned around, leaned against the counter and held her coffee with both hands. She'd thought about this ever since she talked to Dallas. There was no reason it wouldn't work if she could just keep Lilah from drawing her into really talking about it.

That was another thing. Lilah could make just the right remark and cause Meri to start spilling way too many feelings that she didn't want to look at. She hadn't quite decided yet if that was an advantage or another disadvantage, like the mind reading, to having a grandmother. She had to admit that sometimes it did make her feel stronger.

"Could you and Shorty chaperone the youth rodeo dance? It's next Saturday night."

Lilah kept cutting biscuits as she gave Meri a long look.

"Since when did they put you in charge of the Youth Rodeo Association?"

Meri shrugged. "Dallas mentioned today that Caleb volunteered the two of us to do it. That won't work now, since we're no longer a couple . . ."

Lilah turned a biscuit in the glass pie plate of sizzling oil on a corner of the butcher block. "Neither are Shorty and me, last time I looked. Couplehood's not a requirement to chaperone, I don't think."

"He didn't even tell me he agreed for us to do it."

Lilah cut another round of dough. Her mouth turned down in that grim look.

To try and lighten things up, Meri teased, "If not Shorty, how about you and the Judge?"

"How about you doing what you're committed to do?"

The tone of Lilah's voice brought an argumentative "Yowrr" from Henry, who stopped twining himself around Meri's ankles to sit and glare up at Lilah.

Meri squatted down to pet him and noticed her hand was trembling. This was ridiculous. Just because she was going to confront Caleb.

"You stay out of this," Lilah told Henry.

"I didn't commit. Cale spoke for me. Without asking me."

Lilah dropped her biscuit cutter and looked at Meri.

"He thought you'd support him. He thought you'd be with him on a Saturday night anyway."

Meri's quick anger surged. "He had no right to speak for me—"

"Now you listen here to me, Meredith Kathleen."

Lilah stopped for a moment and when she spoke again, it was in a lower tone. "You and Caleb can be a couple or not. Y'all can fight or not. Y'all can speak or not in your private lives. But none of your shenanigans had better have the slightest effect on Honey Grove Kitchens. Partners getting crossways personally can kill a successful business. None of us can afford that."

Lilah's calm vehemence trembled in the air

between them. They stared at each other. Meri's blood pounded against her eardrums, she was so angry.

Mostly because she knew Lilah was exactly right.

"Do you hear me?"

"Yes!" She reached for a softer tone and took a deep breath. "But Caleb needs to hear you, too. The beginning of this trouble was his neglect of the *business* . . ."

"This chaperone role is about the business, too, Meri. Not something to use in a personal fight."

Meri thought about that. "I still forget sometimes how intertwined a small town is," she admitted. "But, Gran, Cale can't speak for me."

"Too late. He did it. And those kids and their parents are expecting you and Caleb to be at that dance. They love to be with y'all, not me and some old codger. HGK is a rodeo sponsor. You can't back out now."

"I can't *not* back out. We'll have to think of someone to take my place. How can I possibly go anywhere with Caleb? I just can't."

"In your personal life. But this is business. Y'all must get *that* separation worked out right now."

Meri's nerves snapped. "Please don't use that tone with me. I feel as if I'm being lectured like a child."

"Then stop acting like one. You're making a mountain out of a molehill."

Meri's shoulders slumped in defeat. "I wish I could find a substitute . . ."

"That won't work and you know it. Those kids want you."

Meri sighed. "You're right. I'll have to do it, no matter how hard it may be."

She went to the coatrack, picked up her bag and walked out the back door, not giving in to the temptation to let the screen door slam.

"Be careful," Lilah called after her. "They're working on the road out by Indian River."

Meri gritted her teeth as she ran down the back steps. Definitely, for sure, without a *doubt,* being in a family and having a grandmother wasn't always the bed of roses she'd dreamed it was during her childhood. It was so frustrating that Lilah was always right.

How had Lilah known where she was going?

This sundress. Caleb liked it. But she hadn't chosen to wear it because of that. Not at all. She was just tired of businesswear and jeans and this evening was as hot as if summer had never wavered.

The very *last* thing she wanted to do right now was please Caleb.

As Meri drove, her anger dissipated and all the doubts came back. Was Lilah right? Had Meri made a mountain out of the molehill of one forgotten letter?

She might not be brokenhearted, but she missed Caleb every minute. Had she made a terrible mistake? Everything about her life was different when he was around.

But he didn't care if they were together or not. He'd agreed to the break in a millisecond.

And *that* fact stabbed her in the heart. Even as she'd given in to her anger and blurted those words, even as they left her lips, on some level she'd been expecting him to be shocked by the idea. To refuse it out of hand. To reach for her and hold her and whisper apologies in her ear.

Maybe even, by some miracle, to say that he loved her.

Only that one time, had he ever told her that. What had that all been about, anyway?

Should she have been more patient? He'd been even more exhausted than hungover that morning on the Square. For days and days, he'd been going nonstop, nerves wound tight, working at proving his father wrong about him and his ranch and helping with HGK at the same time he was trying to decide whether to risk a lot of money on a new bull. He'd been stressed beyond belief.

Even so, he'd had no right to say she would chaperone the dance with him. He had no right to speak for her on *any* subject.

The sun was going down behind her when she turned off the highway onto the ranch road at

Indian River but she forgot all about her live-in-the-moment resolutions and barely noticed the way the red and gold light fell across the grass and the water of the river. All she could see was Caleb. She had to make him understand that their personal life was over and they'd better talk about how to handle their professional one now.

As she drove across the low-water bridge, she remembered the first time she ever came to his place and how surprised at herself she'd been when she laid her hand in his out on the patio that day. Something about him had always made her feel slightly crazed.

She should've known then not to believe that he loved her. She simply wasn't the type people fell in love with when they first knew her.

Or even later, to be brutally honest.

People described her as reserved, distant, private, businesslike, independent, but never lovable.

Yet, early on, Caleb had said he did. Too soon.

He was an impulsive person. And the day he'd said that was the day that she sent her old boyfriend, Tim, away. He'd surprised her with his arrival on the Square in Rock Springs, and Caleb had offered to run him off for her.

So, that declaration had been Caleb's male ego speaking. What he'd really meant, instead of "I love you," was "I won."

Really, if this relationship were perfect, this break wouldn't be happening now at the most stressful time for both of them.

She accelerated slightly when she left the bridge for the gravel road, watching for cows on each side of it. Sometimes they stood in the middle of the road as if they were waiting to direct traffic and that made her smile.

She could use a smile right now but her face felt so stiff she probably wouldn't be able to summon one.

There were no cows nearby, anyway. She pulled up and parked in front of the house, saw that there was a light on in the kitchen, got out and went up the walk without letting herself think. Get this over with and get out. Go home and try to get some rest.

The wooden door stood open to the cooling evening. She knocked.

"Come in." His voice sounded flat. And tired.

She walked through the dim house that was so familiar to her now. In the doorway between the empty dining room and the kitchen, she stopped.

"How'd you know I wasn't a crazed killer at your door?"

Caleb was at the stove with his back to her and he didn't so much as glance her way. The heavenly scent of sautéing onions and peppers, sausage and eggs filled the room. He finished stirring the contents of the skillet, slid it all onto a platter, turned off the burners and forked two sizzling slices of Texas toast off the griddle next to the skillet. It was like watching a dance.

"The sound of your truck. A crazed killer would've stolen something better." His voice was raspy with fatigue.

Insults to her truck was a game between them but she couldn't even think of a comeback. Caleb looked awful—completely drained.

But he didn't forget his mannerly upbringing. "Wanna split this with me? Sorry, but it's all I have in the house."

"No, thanks," she said. "I've been eating all day."

He gave a skeptical grunt.

He knew she was lying. But he didn't follow up with his usual lecture about her needing fuel.

"Coffee?"

"No, thanks."

He poured a cup, then walked to the little table with both hands full, his limp more pronounced than ever, and gestured with his head for her to sit down on the other side. She did. He sat and began to eat. His arm trembled, he was so tired. His hands had new cuts and nicks and scars that she hadn't seen. Hadn't touched.

She wanted to feel his skin underneath her fingertips. She wanted to reach for him so much that she had to clasp her hands in her lap.

He smelled like horse and dirt and sunbaked

skin. His worn chambray shirt was stiff with drying sweat. His farmer's tan was deeper and his hair was wet. To cool off he'd, no doubt, held his head under the hose at the barn.

"Sorry I haven't showered," he said, reading her mind, as usual. "Wasn't expecting company."

He concentrated on the food as if she'd disappeared. Her hopes of getting some kind of parameters set for a new all-business relationship drained away. He was so miserably tired.

"I'm not here for company," she said, trying to hold the sympathy out of her voice. "It's business, really. I talked to Dallas today. Why didn't you ask me before you committed us to chaperone the rodeo dance? We're not a couple anymore, remember?"

He took a big bite of toast and chewed it while he looked at her with a hard blue stare, a look that held her at arm's length.

"That's an example of why I came out here. It made me realize we should talk about how to run a business together when we no longer have a personal life together. But you're too tired. We'll do it another time."

"Well," he drawled, "call me a dirty coyote. I agreed to chaperone back when we were a couple."

Those words were a cold blade slicing through her hot, mixed feelings of love and anger. Her hand wanted to reach out and touch his, her whole body wanted to just hold him. Hold his head and let him rest while she stroked his hair—in spite of the fact it was salt-caked from sweat.

She hated it when her feelings ran riot against her will. And she also hated to be wrong. She hadn't even thought of that possibility.

Such a sadness for what they'd lost spiraled through her that she slumped in her chair.

He flicked a blue marble glance at her.

"Don't worry, it'll be all business relationship at the dance. HGK's a popular sponsor for the rodeo and we'll get a lot of word-of-mouth about the food that way. People will be there from all the counties around and they'll look us up when they come to Rock Springs."

He took a drink of coffee and set the cup down.

"Hear me, now," he said, his steady gaze locking with hers. "Those kids like you a lot. Their parents trust you. And I trust you to be all business and not come on to me, even once."

Meri did a double take, then gave a startled laugh. His wicked humor glinted in his eyes.

Some insane part of her was disappointed that he went back to the topic at hand.

"Don't worry," he said. "I know how you like rules and order. We can get our business relationship all lined out while we dance."

She hadn't even thought of that. Better not go into his arms at all.

He pushed back his chair and got up. "Now, if

you'll excuse me, Meri, I'm about to drop in my tracks and I have to get up early tomorrow."

He held her chair. "I'll walk you to your truck."

"No, I—"

"In the most businesslike way, of course. Otherwise, my mama would have my hide."

She thought she'd choke on all the words she couldn't get organized in her head. She should've eaten something. All the emotions roiling in her were making her dizzy.

They walked back through the house that smelled of fried potatoes, onions, coffee and fresh-cut wood with just a hint of new paint.

Across the porch and down the walk.

As he opened her truck door, he said, "Six o'clock Saturday night. Rodeo first to hand out the HGK trophies and then the dance. Your best boots and jeans required."

She got in, fired it up, pulled around in a hard circle and peeled out down the gravel road like a high school boy. It made her feel a release, some-how, even if it did destroy the last of her dignity.

Fifteen

Lilah made too sharp a turn coming out of the kitchen at HGK, so she had to lift up Doreen's wheelchair a bit to get it around into the hallway.

"Don't do that," Doreen said. "Tell me and I'll stand on one foot while you move the chair."

"You're not that heavy," Lilah said, before she thought. Big mistake. Now that'd make Doreen even worse with her occasional hints about how she'd kept her figure so much better than Lilah had done. Doreen was vain as a peacock.

"Well, thanks," her old frenemy said, "but you're not getting any younger and I don't want you to hurt yourself helping me. I owe you enough already."

"*I'm* not getting any younger? Are you forgetting you're the same age I am?"

She tried to bite back the words—she *had* forgiven Doreen, she must remember that—but they popped out anyway, "And let's not even get into what all you owe me."

Lilah snapped her lips shut. She had to be careful or Doreen would drive her crazy enough to start up their old troubles again.

They were past all that.

She hoped.

But, Lord help her, she could not wait until Doreen was completely healed and past all the drama. How *long,* Lord, was she going to milk that accident? Yes, it had been awful and she'd been seriously hurt, but this latest thing of backsliding into the wheelchair from using just the crutches was fake, in Lilah's considered opinion.

Nothing in the world but an insecure ploy to get more of Lawrence's attention because he was spending too much time with Missy Lambert. But Lilah wasn't going to bring that up, either. At least, not if Doreen would behave herself.

Lilah glanced down at the stack of rainbow-colored flyers in Doreen's lap, all of them printed with the message she wanted every voter to see.

We, the People, must take responsibility for the future of Rock County. Do you want our good farmland turned into half-acre mini-ranches that hold the summer heat with their paved streets and use up water on their lawns? Our farms help feed Texas and the world.

Why is there a proposal on the table to change the zoning of Jones Orchards from agricultural to residential? Ask that question of every candidate for county office, especially those running for County Judge.

"You did a good job of printing these, Doreen. Thank you."

The election was the important thing today. She pushed the wheelchair rapidly into the café and through it, so they wouldn't get caught in conversation and waste time. Each table in there already had flyers on it. Lilah had a lot of other urgent things to do, but she'd decided to let them go this morning so she could get the word out and there was no sense stopping to argue with any naysayers that might be in the bunch.

Jeb Stinson jumped up and held the door for them. They were going so fast that Doreen's hair blew back and they had to holler thanks to Jeb back over their shoulders. Every minute counted.

"My goodness," Doreen complained. "Slow down. You're gonna completely ruin my hair."

"I've got to get this done and get back to test a couple of recipes," Lilah said. "Pecan tassies and pumpkin muffins, both sweetened only with organic honey."

"Use my pecan tassies as your starting point," Doreen said.

"You're a more-than-decent general cook, Doreen, but baking's not your strong suit."

"Well!" Doreen huffed. "I might remind you that it's my recipe for pecan cinnamon rolls that you are using in this very café."

"It is not your recipe," Lilah snapped. "It was Dear Old Thing Sophronie Warner's, in her family since the War Between the States."

"Well, but I'm the one used it first and I'm the one gave it to you."

"She left copies of it to half the women in town. Give it up. And besides, I've tweaked it some. Don't you go around town saying it's your cinnamon rolls I'm serving."

And then, to change the subject so they wouldn't get into a full-blown fuss-fight, Lilah complimented her. Doreen loved compliments.

"I couldn't have done those flyers on a computer if somebody paid me a million dollars," she said. "I admire that you know how."

Doreen took the bait.

"I was getting Lawrence's secretary, Miranda, to do it," Doreen said. "But he caught us red-handed and told her to get back to business. I tell you what, Lilah, Lawrence and I are having *more* trouble." She sighed.

"I'm sorry," Lilah said.

She didn't ask a single question because she knew Doreen wouldn't want to tell her any more than that. Doreen was free with other people's intimate information but not her own.

But she did go on to say, "This zoning deal is one of our disagreements. He can't see past the idea of selling houses in developments to how they would change things."

"Well, his realty business has been in a slump lately," Lilah said. "And you really like money, Doreen. I'm surprised you don't agree with him."

"I want to keep this town 'quaint,' as the tourists always say."

"And the farms bring them in, too. Have you noticed how many outsiders there are at the farmers markets lately? Of course, the pumpkins always attract them in the fall, but that was true all summer, too."

"Yes. Mostly, they come to my shop because I

carry such unique things, but everything else is a draw, too, like the farm produce and y'all's bakery and the peace and quiet they always mention on the Square. Wouldn't it be horrible if we ended up with an outlet mall and a bunch of fast-food places?"

"Lord help us all."

"That's what I say, too." Doreen paused. "You know what?" she said, crooking her neck to look up at Lilah. "It scares me bad when we agree on something big like this."

Lilah laughed. "Me, too. But don't worry. It'll still be a long, cold day in July when we don't have our differences."

"Well, that's *some* comfort."

They rolled into Betty's Beauty Shop.

"Come in, girls!" Betty called from her station where she was cutting hair.

It was Verna Carl in the chair, getting her usual bob. Really, she could use a little color, too. Her hair wasn't a very pretty shade of gray, but then Lilah had suggested that before. Verna was too tightfisted to pay for color.

She said hello and B.J. waved at them from under the dryer.

"I see y'all are campaigning," Betty said. "Put some of your flyers on that table over by the window. I'll paste one on the glass, too."

The nail stylist, Twila Langford, was working on Charlene Polston, painting some tiny somethings on the big, long, bloodred nails she'd just put on her.

Lilah shook her head. That was one of the more insane wastes of time the young people had come up with lately and she'd told them that before.

Charlene grinned at her. She couldn't care less what Lilah thought, of course. She wasn't old enough to know better.

"Charlene," Lilah said, "how many times do I have to tell you that you'll never be able to run the cash register right with all that mess stuck on your fingers."

"Well, so far, so good, Miss Lilah. I haven't had any trouble with them yet."

Lilah returned the grin. "Then more power to you."

Twila said innocently, "Doreen, I hear Lawrence is campaigning against the Judge. Is he as crazy about that Missy Lambert as all the rest of the men? I swear, that county judge race is going to be the main one in this whole election."

Charlene said, "At the Grab It 'n' Go, when anybody mentions the election, every man in the place starts talking about Missy and how she's so great. So pretty. Such a hottie. How we need a new judge."

"Hmph," Doreen said. "Lawrence isn't thinking like *that*. He's just campaigning for her because of his realty business."

"Well, I hope so," Charlene said. "You know

how it is when a celebrity is in a race—everybody thinks they're glamorous just because they're famous. I mean, really, you can't be grand marshal of the Christmas parade for four years running and a TV star without attracting some attention."

Doreen gave her a hard look. "Lawrence isn't impressed with any of that. He's all business."

But now Charlene was on a roll down memory lane. "Wasn't that a riot? When he drove her up into the middle of the ice cream social and she nearly fell out of his Jeep and her dog got away from her? That was the most exciting election kickoff we ever had."

Betty joined in. "Yes! And funny! I don't think I ever saw Lawrence in such a fizz as when he was tryin' to catch that yappin' little dog. I hear she takes it everywhere she campaigns, even into people's houses in her purse."

"Lilah," Doreen said as she slapped some of the flyers onto Betty's table, "let's go. We've got to get moving if we're going to every business on the Square."

Lilah felt a twinge of sympathy for Doreen as she turned the wheelchair and started for the door. She really didn't believe there was anything untoward going on between Lawrence and Missy. She'd known the man all her life.

But he was getting a lot more independent, disagreeing with Doreen politically and all. Poor

Doreen. She'd have a hard time learning how to handle that, but learn she would have to.

Once the balance of power in a marriage started shifting like that, it was likely to keep right on going. Well, that'd be good for Doreen.

Lilah smiled to herself.

And, by extension for the whole town.

But then her smile vanished. It sure as shooting wouldn't be good for *anybody* if Lawrence's new independence got Missy elected.

Oh, Lord! He needed to listen to Doreen. She had more sense than he did.

Sixteen

Meri stood beside the table full of trophies set up at the side of the arena and watched Dallas and Denton getting their horses settled into the chutes. She would think about them, not about herself and how everything was so weird between her and Caleb.

She couldn't let herself think like that. They had a huge investment together, they had to work together every day, so she could just tamp her feelings down and do whatever had to be done.

However, that small bit of teasing about her behavior at the dance should give her hope that they'd be able to keep their senses of humor and treat each other less distantly.

Tonight she'd be pleasant and professional and

do her job perfectly. She would hand out the trophies for the events HGK sponsored and chaperone the dance, and be cordial to everyone, including him. They were adults. They could do this.

She took a couple of steps toward the chutes to try and see Dallas' face right before the run. Dallas could be so natural, so openly excited or sad or mad or whatever. Meri wished she could be like that, too. It would be wonderful to know what she was feeling instead of always being tied up in knots of contradiction.

The two Fremont kids had been telling her about their team-roping exploits since they met but this was only the third time she'd seen them compete. She smiled to herself. It still seemed strange and warm—at the same time—for them to care whether or not she came to see them compete. Those two were all about competition.

Right now, what Dallas was, was determined. She pulled her cowboy hat down tight onto her head and she and her horse waited for the calf to be released with a whole-being, confident expectation. They were winners and they knew it.

The calf burst out of its chute and both horses burst into a run from a standing stop, working on their own while Dallas and Denton rode with their eyes on the calf and their ropes spinning in the air. Meri couldn't see either the head or the heel catch because both happened so fast and in the cloud of dust, but the calf was stretched out on the ground after only a very few seconds.

"And they did it again!" the teenaged announcer yelled. "It's a 4.39 seconds score, everybody! The fastest yet! Let's hear it for the Fremonts! They're liable to be our winning team tonight. As usual. But before we know that for sure, we have five more fast, strong teams to go. And one of them might just beat their time!"

Meri joined in the applause, then turned to walk back to the table, but Caleb crossed her line of vision. He was loading a calf into the chute for the next team of ropers. They were already in the boxes.

She looked away. She couldn't even think about him. She realized she was somehow disappointed that all day he'd adhered so strictly to the business-only rule. Forget that. She had to get better control of her feelings.

As her business partner, he'd done the right thing in bringing them here tonight, even if he'd done it in a high-handed way. This was business.

And it showed her that, in her personal life, he wasn't the perfect one, because he wouldn't hesitate to take the lead, therefore she wouldn't always be in control. She already knew, from his victory in sending Henry home with her wrapped in a towel that time, that Caleb's will was stronger than hers and that he could outlast her in a battle.

That was a scary thought she'd been forgetting these past few months.

Her stomach clutched. Would she ever find a man who really loved her and would give her a family?

Should she call Tim, perhaps? He said he still loved her, and he had moved to Texas to be closer to her, whether she would see him or not. He continued to call to check in with her.

In contrast, everything about Caleb's behavior told her he was fine with this break in their romance becoming permanent. According to the latest word on the street this afternoon, he'd been seen with Ronnie Rae Hardesty again.

And that was just fine. Without him, Meri could recover her identity and her real sense of herself. She didn't need him. She'd already been abandoned enough times in her life.

The boyish announcer's voice cracked as he said over the PA system that there'd be a slight delay to reset the time clock. Caleb relaxed and leaned back against the boards of the chute to wait, one knee bent to hook his boot heel onto the bottom one. He was so comfortable in his own skin, just like Dallas was in hers.

Meri could only try to imagine how that might feel.

A woman was walking toward Cale from behind, her attention intent on him. She, too, had an eye-catching way of moving.

Ronnie Rae. The woman's intuition that Lilah was always talking about whispered that name in Meri's ear.

She'd heard several descriptions of the red-headed owner of Hardesty Ranches and they'd always included the word *beautiful*. This woman was that.

Ronnie Rae walked up to the outside of the chute, reached through and laid her hand on Caleb's shoulder.

He startled, turned and, Meri could see, even from that distance, grinned his famous grin. He looked delighted. He reached for her, arms between the boards and squeezed her shoulders. They were already laughing and talking.

Ronnie Rae was about Meri's height, but bigger in the bust. She was dressed in the very best Western style, complete with a big belt buckle on a tiny waist. Silky, draped-just-right retro shirt, embroidered yoke and smile pockets, a line of fringe swinging. But no hat. That would hide the hair. It was thick and glossy, the most gorgeous shade of red hair Meri had ever seen. It was even more alluring than Edie Jo's natural color had been.

Meri turned away. He'd moved on as quickly as he'd agreed to the break with Meri.

Finally, the time clock was fixed and the announcer called out the names of the pair of team ropers who were up. Caleb went back to work with the calf and Ronnie Rae turned away from the chutes to start walking toward Meri, the wind blowing her hair so gently that it glimmered like a halo under the lights.

"Brent and Brock Muchmore!" the boy announcer shouted, trying to sound like a professional. "A team of brothers from Rock Springs, Texas. Brent's the header and Brock's the heeler. They've won a lot of ropings, folks, but not as many as Dallas and Denton Fremont. We've got a battle of the best, here. Let's see who comes out on top tonight!"

Meri stepped closer to the arena fence, pretending to be interested in nothing but the rodeo event. The knot had vanished from her stomach. In its place bloomed an empty space. A live space that was spreading to hollow out her arms and legs. Her fingers and toes.

This team of brothers came thundering out of the chutes, racing after the calf, loops in the air, but the heeler couldn't seem to find the right moment to throw his rope. They chased the calf to the end of the arena where it turned and started back again. The crowd began to laugh.

"You must be Meredith Briscoe." Underneath the noise of the crowd in the grandstand, the low, smooth voice sounded like a song.

Meri turned and looked into the big brown eyes of Caleb's friend. She *was* beautiful. Her skin was perfect or else she used some kind of magic makeup.

And she had that air about her—that unmistakable attitude which comes from knowing whatever you want or need will come straight into your hand and wherever you are is where you belong. As a homeless orphan, Meri had envied girls who possessed that aura.

Evidently, she still did.

"Yes," she said. "I am."

"I'm Ronnie Rae Hardesty," the beautiful creature said, in a sweet Texas drawl. She offered her hand. Meri took it.

"Cale pointed you out for me," she said. "I guess he's told you Hardesty Ranches is your cosponsor for this event."

"No," Meri said, "he must've forgotten to mention that."

Stunned, she tried to absorb that information at the same time she recognized the question that'd been pulling at her subconscious since her first glimpse of Ronnie Rae: *This* is the woman who shot Caleb in the leg and gave him a limp for life? Theirs had to have been the most memorable breakup that Rock Springs had ever seen.

Not some honky-tonk queen wearing tons of eyeshadow and a spandex top that shows her cleavage while it covers the pistol stuck in the waistband of her jeans?

"We breed a lot of roping horses," Ronnie Rae confided, "and we want to encourage all the young ropers we can. I just got back into town this minute or I would've come by your bakery to meet you sooner."

She sounded sincere. She seemed likeable. She wore a fine turquoise bangle bracelet mixed with slender silver ones and, on the other arm, one woven horsehair cuff. Diamond stud earrings, not too large. All in the very best of taste.

No rings on her left hand.

"So," she said with a smile, "looks like the two of us are a team, here at the Team-roping Championship Finals."

She had a great smile. Of course. She had everything.

Probably she'd always had Caleb's heart.

It wasn't easy to look at her and imagine her shooting him. And yet . . . there was an edge to her, somewhere in there, almost concealed by her looks and charm. Meri could sense it.

Caleb liked adventure. He'd told her he rode bulls early on in his adult life because of the danger. Loving Ronnie Rae must be quite an interesting venture for him.

Ronnie Rae glanced down at the trophies. "These are the ones? I'd like to present Denton's if you don't mind. He works for me sometimes at the barn and he's one of my faves."

"Perfect," Meri said. "Dallas is a friend of mine. But if they happen not to . . ."

Ronnie Rae interrupted with a wave of her graceful, perfectly French-manicured hand. "Oh, even if they don't win, let's give 'em the trophies anyway for being such good kids. Sure, we might make some enemies, but we'd be fast enough to outrun 'em, don't you think?"

Ronnie Rae had a devilish grin. Of course. In addition to that irresistible smile. The grin reminded Meri of Cale's.

Ronnie Rae had everything.

Meri's stomach tightened. Maybe Ronnie Rae was the reason Caleb had agreed to the break so quickly. And the reason he hadn't objected to it since.

Which was perfectly fine. It fit right in with Meri's plans for the future and left her free to be herself. Just seeing him out at Indian River had unsettled her so much he had turned out to be the one with the poise and humor.

Every argument they had, Caleb won it by rousing her emotions. She couldn't live her life like that.

After all, her stubborn, mental competitiveness was her strong suit. It was what had saved her as a child. And as an abandoned teenager. And a penniless college student. And a fledgling attorney.

Caleb weakened that aspect of her and caused her to lose control. More proof he wasn't perfect for her. His decision to share the sponsorship of the team-roping event with Ronnie Rae without mentioning that, either, to Meri was just the icing on the cake of his disregard of her.

Oh, God. Could they even be successful business partners? They had to be, for Lilah's sake. Not one of them, at least according to what Caleb said about his finances, could afford to buy the others out now. She would have to *make* it work.

Seventeen

As Caleb drove Meri across the fairgrounds to the old Women's Building where the Youth Rodeo Association was holding the dance, he was whistling softly under his breath. Meri didn't say it, but she found it charming. Even soothing.

The tune was something she'd heard in her continuing explorations of different kinds of roots music, but she couldn't quite name it and she didn't ask. It was a peaceful moment. They both needed that.

Oh, how was she ever going to do this? She wanted to touch him right now. There were four or five more hours coming up that she'd be looking at him, talking to him, even dancing with him. If she refused, it would start all kinds of rumors to add to the ones already circulating all over town.

That wouldn't be good for the business, either. She had to do it for the sake of HGK and not because the thought of being in his arms filled her with longing.

He stopped whistling, turned to look at her with a sparkle in his eye, and said, "Ronnie Rae might drop by the dance. She'd love to get to know you better, she said, but she's got a production sale at her Wyoming ranch pretty soon and she may go home to start working on that."

Ronnie Rae. So that explained the twinkle in his eye. Meri's teeth clenched.

Ridiculous, Mer. You've already decided it's all over with Caleb.

But he should be told that he'd been wrong to involve Ronnie Rae at all. Dallas and Denton as winners and HGK as sponsor should've had all the attention for the team roping at the arena tonight. Ronnie Rae had been gracious in pushing her way into the spotlight, Meri had to admit, but she'd held on to the mike way too long, raving about her famous roping-horse sires of the Hardesty Ranches.

But Meri would not say that. Actually, if she and Caleb were no longer a couple, Ronnie Rae was none of her business. She wouldn't make a big deal about her. But when they talked about how to be business partners only, she would casually mention the trophy presentation.

No matter. Her mouth opened and words pushed their way out.

"Caleb, even if we're only business partners . . ." She bit her lip. She hadn't meant to imply the personal relationship was more important. She tried again. "I would appreciate it if you'd keep me informed about arrangements you make."

There. That was good. Maybe she wasn't losing her mind after all.

He shot her a fast, slanting glance. "What're you talkin' about?"

"I had no idea your friend was cosponsoring the roping trophies with us. She just appeared out of the blue to help me do my job."

He shrugged and shot her a quick glance, in which she thought she glimpsed amusement. "It's no big deal. I saw her this afternoon, she offered to pay half on our sponsorship so she could get out there and mention her production sale, and I didn't care. Why would I? It's no big deal."

He saw her this afternoon. For a minute, that was all Meri could hear.

He threw her that quick glance again. "You're not jealous, are you?"

"Of course not." She couldn't say the words fast enough. "I'm talking to you as your business partner. Sponsorships are to advertise the business."

He looked at her longer this time. "Okay, good." Then he used that grin, which was an illegal weapon. "I just got my hopes up there for a minute."

Do not get sucked in. Do not do it, Meri.

She tried to keep lecturing herself in her head and she deliberately turned her head away and stared straight ahead.

She'd made the right decision. They could not be romantic partners and business partners both. They could not. They should not.

He smiled at her. "You just make too big a deal out of little things, Meri," he said, his tone more solemn than his look.

"And we both know that *you* don't make a big enough deal out of anything. Not even the most important things."

"We just established that you're no judge of that."

"No, we didn't. Anything to do with the finances or the arrangements for anything concerning HGK is a big deal. If we don't both think of it that way, we could fail."

"I do think you're jealous. Even though we're not together anymore."

That hit her in the gut. Sounded like he wanted them apart.

Well, she did, too. And this would work out so much better for the sake of the whole partnership in HGK. Perfect.

"We're not," she said. "And you've got it all wrong. I'm not jealous."

"Hey, Meri. This is Cale you're talking to. Don't try to lie to me."

"Don't try to distract me. We're talking about your behavior as my business partner. Stop making unilateral decisions. That's bad enough, but not informing me and Gran of what you've done is worse. HGK can't function this way."

"That's not the problem. You're jealous. That's the reason why you don't like Ronnie Rae."

She tried to stick to her guns and control the topic but just hearing him say Ronnie Rae's name tied another knot in her gut. She should never have gotten into this relationship in the first place. He had too much influence on her feelings. She hated not having control.

"Did I *say* I don't like her?"

He slowed to a crawl, watching two kids leading their horses across the road from one barn to another.

"No, but your whole body was stiff as a post while y'all were talking and doing the presentations."

She leaned around to stare into his face. "Why were you watching us? And I always stand up straight. It's a habit of mine."

"Oh, yeah."

"I like her," Meri said, realizing against her will that it was true. "What's not to like? She's a charmer. Any businesswoman has to be assertive if she wants to succeed."

"Oh, so now she's assertive."

"She insisted on becoming an event sponsor at the last minute, didn't she?"

He reached the end of the road, turned the wheel to the right and drove into a gravel parking lot surrounding a frame, tree-shaded building at the end of the fairgrounds. He shifted into park and turned to her with his most infuriating smile.

"Matter of fact, she didn't have to," he drawled. "I thought it was a fine idea, right from the start."

He glanced at her to see how she was taking that. "Team roping," he said. "There's two trophies to be presented, so why not?"

He turned off the motor. "Don't worry, she's good for her half. She'll pay us."

Frustration choked her. "As if all I ever worry about is money! Caleb, it is impossible to talk to you."

The grin again. "Then don't. Just dance with me tonight."

"Don't even ask!"

"I didn't say you're all about money. Mostly what you worry about, Mer, is crossing all the t's and dotting all the i's. When I take care of the small stuff I'm just tryin' to save you some energy, that's all."

He sounded so sincere. But she wasn't falling for it.

"No, you're just being you. Doing what you want when you want.

"Think. Save me from frustration by not causing it. First you volunteer me to chaperone this evening, then you solicit a cosponsor for our event and don't bother to mention either to me, much less ask my opinion. Give me a break!"

She sensed him pull back but his body didn't move. His smile didn't waver, but in the glow of the security light she saw the expression change in his eyes. Now she'd made him mad.

"I already did."

He shrugged as if it didn't matter, turned away and opened his door.

Meri sat very still for a minute and looked the other way.

She had to get *control.* She had to realize what she'd done when she broke up with him and come to terms with it. She wasn't in love with him. She had only thought that she might be.

When had she ever thought she loved anybody after such a short time? She hadn't known Caleb long enough to even know him. She didn't even know herself anymore.

He turned around and looked into the truck. She felt his gaze but she refused to turn and meet it. She couldn't deal with it right this second. She had a whole evening to buttress her heart for.

At this moment, she could not look at his obnoxiously handsome face. With its gorgeous mouth. And its sky-blue eyes.

His beautiful eyes that had always been able to see right to the very heart of her and read what it was feeling.

Then her head turned against her will and she did exactly what she'd sworn not to do. He was waiting for her gaze to meet his.

"You'd better be careful," she blurted. "Around Ronnie Rae."

"Oh?" he said. "And how did you get to know her so well?"

Her brain was in a knot, what with her little voices trying to get through to her.

Shut up.

You shouldn't've said all that.

You're digging yourself into a hole.

She managed to think fast. "She shot you, didn't she?"

He laughed. That sexy, low chuckle that was like a touch of his hand.

A restless, dissatisfied, prickling feeling stabbed into her gut. It was torturing her. It was driving her. She did not like to be driven by her feelings.

So she jerked open her own door and got out before he could come around and help her, which always irritated him. He was raised to open doors for women. He might lose his temper and he might lose his focus but he never lost his gallantry, no matter what the situation.

He walked around the truck to escort her, in spite of her rudeness. They stood for a minute to take in the event they were here to chaperone.

The lights were already on inside the old building and they could see through the big windows that the band was busy setting up in the far corner of a huge room. Outside, a group of boys were congregating at the far end of the porch. Several trucks were already parked and others were coming in.

"Let's get in there and see what needs to be organized," he said, and started for the steps, his hand lightly touching her elbow, not resting in the small of her back as it always used to do.

She walked a little faster toward the porch steps, looking around to distract herself. She was here to do a job. She would concentrate on that. Live in the present. Don't think about the past. Don't think about Caleb. Just deal with him, one moment at a time when they had to be together.

The truck parked under the largest tree, over by the fence, looked familiar. It was Bobby Kyle Allbritton's. She stared at it.

"I hate to sound like one of the old ladies but I agree Bobby Kyle's too old for Addison," she said. "Maybe I should go over there and ask them to help us unload."

Caleb laughed. "You're not her mama. Leave them alone."

"But, thanks to you, I am the chaperone."

"Not in the job description. Parking lot's neutral territory unless there's blood or explosives."

"Hey, boys," he yelled to the ones on the porch, "how about y'all get out here and help me offload the food?

"Bobby and Addison'll do what they want, no matter where they are. Remember when you were a teenager?"

"Yes," she said tightly. "I didn't even *have* a boyfriend. I was busy working to save money so I could get an education, then a good job and never have to live in a friend's house again or depend on anybody's charity ever."

She glanced at him. "Maybe I'm extra-cautious because I wasn't drinking and causing havoc and running wild all over the country in fast cars with faster women."

He stood still. She met his eyes but couldn't read them. "Sorry," he said. "I shouldn't've brought up the past."

His tone said he was talking about both their stories. They held the look.

"Right back at'cha," she said.

She went on in to look around while he and the group of boys carried things in. The wide door opened into a big, square room with a creaky wood floor.

Besides the band, there were kids in setting up tables and folding chairs here and there around the edges of the room. The floor was worn smooth in the middle from dancing. Lilah had told her she and Ed had been in a square dance club that danced here for many years.

Meri stood just inside the door for a moment, trying to imagine them dancing to a fiddle tune, the grandfather she could barely remember twirling a young Lilah wearing a bright red flowered skirt with lots of crinolines under it. Had

Edie Jo sat on the side and watched them, too?

She did not want to imagine Edie Jo. Not now. So she started telling the kids where to put the tables and began arranging chairs in the corner that would be best for refreshments.

"This place must be fifty years old or more," Caleb said, coming up behind her with both arms full of HGK boxes. "It looked just like this when I was a kid."

Startled, she whirled around to look at him and that brought her back to the present in an instant. He'd brought enough sweets for an army.

The fiddler struck up a fast tune and the very young band began to play some very old Western swing as Caleb went to the longest table with his load.

He set the boxes down. The boys behind him added two more stacks of them to the table.

She stared at them.

"How many cookies did you *bring?*"

He started opening the boxes, folding back the lids to prop them up. "I don't know. I just didn't want to run short."

"But, Cale, we have enough here for the whole county!"

She began opening the ones on the second stack.

Pecan tassies, lemon bars, honey-nut drops, cream cheese brownies. The next box she opened held double-chocolate cherry blossoms.

Oh my! He'd brought the most expensive ones that were the most time-consuming to make.

But she bit her tongue. It would do no good to point that out now. She'd make a note to mention it at the next management meeting.

"I asked Jewel to whip me out a few extras."

She shook her head and smiled in spite of her worry. He was so happy with his cookies to give away. She couldn't bear to begrudge him (and the kids) that pleasure but she couldn't resist saying, "I could've told you . . . or Lilah could've told you . . . how many to bring. Why didn't you ask us?"

"Don't wanna nickel-and-dime it," he said, happily opening more boxes. "Gotta keep up HGK's reputation."

Meri's stomach tied into a knot. Could be, it would take a miracle for HGK to make a profit. She'd have to ask Gran to help keep an eye on him whenever he was taking free food somewhere.

Teenagers were gravitating toward them. Two boys came in carrying the tub full of chilling cola cans that had been in the back of Caleb's truck.

He opened a box of coconut-almond macaroons as Addison arrived at the table, thank goodness, with Bobby Kyle in tow.

"Meri! Hi! Oooh, this looks wonderful. Hey, look, Bobby Kyle, there's the cherry chocolate ones you like . . ."

Other hungry kids buzzed around the table, too.

Dallas and Denton came in, both over the moon about winning yet another event. They thanked Meri and Caleb for buying the trophies (better and bigger than any the Youth Rodeo Association had ever awarded before) and looked around for Ronnie Rae so they could thank her again, too.

They chatted about the roping and then about the band when one of its members stepped up to sing, but inside, Meri's mind was racing. What could she do, what could she say, what tactic could she take to keep Caleb doing only what he did well as an HGK partner? How could she get control?

She kept busy organizing the refreshments and encouraging kids to help themselves, she discussed the winning run with Dallas and listened to Addison talk about the last performance of the horseback drill team, then, finally, everything was done and most kids were dancing. This was her chance to take a deep breath and try to calm down.

She drifted toward the door, hoping no one would notice her step out onto the porch of the old building. She needed to be alone and try to think. About her life.

Halfway there, Caleb caught her.

He put his arm around her waist, and his lips close to her ear.

"Let's dance. I need to talk to you."

She wanted to resist, she needed to think before

they talked, but it was too late now. He was already dancing her out onto the floor. She *couldn't* make a scene. She was becoming fodder for the gossips of the town, just as Caleb told her his family had always been.

"Right back at'cha," she said, her voice tight. Every muscle in her body tightened, too. "But maybe tonight's not the best time for talking."

"I think you're right," he said, his breath warm, tickling her hair against her ear. "They're playing our song."

"We don't have a song. Even if we did, we're not a couple anymore."

"It's 'The West Texas Waltz,'" he said, totally unperturbed. "Really, Meri, don't you remember the first night we went out? This is the first song we ever danced to."

"So what? Even if we were still a couple, it couldn't be our song because you stopped dancing in the middle of it and went back to the table."

"Don't worry, Mer. This time we'll dance it all the way through. My favorite verse is the one where he teaches his dog to do the West Texas waltz."

He sighed and pulled her a little closer to dance her around Dallas and some boy Meri didn't know.

"We had a double date with Lilah and Shorty and we went to Taylor's Inn," Caleb said.

"Try to pull yourself out of the throes of

reminiscence, Caleb. You sound like a very old man. That was not a date."

"Well, maybe not. Probably not. Probably you just didn't want to let me out of your sight in case there was another scary garden snake running away from you and you'd need to climb my frame again to get away from it."

She thumped her fist against his shoulder before she knew what she was doing. Heat filled her face, but she couldn't keep back a smile.

"Stop it. When are you ever going to let me live that down?"

The feeling of being in his arms for the first time, there in the middle of the tomato patch, came back to her in a rush. It'd been such an enlightening sensation—a sudden knowledge that she *could* feel safe, after all the years she'd lived without it.

But that gut instinct had been wrong. There was no safety. The circle of his arms around her wasn't a haven, it was a trap.

She pulled back and looked into his blue, blue eyes.

"I was a greenhorn then," she said, pointedly. "I didn't know which snakes were dangerous and which weren't."

Swift lightning flashed in his eyes, pain so deep Meri could feel its burn.

Eighteen

She heard her before she got to the barn, but when Lilah stood in the doorway, she couldn't see her in the dim aisle. "Meri?"

Lilah flipped on the lights. The girl was collapsed on the hay bales stacked against the wall of the second stall, her face buried in her arms crossed on an old saddle blanket. She didn't even lift her head—she was too busy sobbing her heart out.

Oh, Lord. It's finally caught up with her.

Her sweet girl. It hurt Lilah's heart to see her in such agony. She shook her head as she started walking to her. If only love could ever be easy.

"Now look here," she said, standing over her. "You'll make yourself sick, carrying on like that."

The wholehearted weeping was even worse in her granddaughter because Meri was usually so contained. Lilah stood over her and started rubbing her shaking shoulders.

"Meri. That's enough. It's not the end of the world."

Meri shook her head and kept on crying.

"You're ruining your pretty face on that scratchy old blanket. Do you want it to be all rubbed raw when you go into work tomorrow?"

That did the trick. Meri sat up and leaned back against the wall, letting both her hands drop into her lap, open in a gesture so hopeless that Lilah could hardly bear to see it. A crumpled photo fell to the floor.

Lilah picked it up. It was a picture Gideon took at the ice cream social that day of the election campaign kickoff. Caleb and Meri, gazing at each other, totally in love.

"Look at me."

Meri did. Her eyes were so full of pain she looked awful. As bad as that terrible night when she appeared in this very barn doorway, come back from New York with her life in ruins.

"Oh, Gran," she wailed, "what have I done?"

Lilah lifted her apron and used it to dab the tears off her granddaughter's cheeks, reddened, sure enough, by the rough wool. That gave her an instant to pray for wisdom. Meri's tears were lessening. She was slowing down to occasional, but regular, sobs.

"Darlin', no man on earth's worth all this misery. You could destroy your health, grieving so hard. This isn't like you."

"I shouldn't've broken up with him. Or maybe I should've." Her voice rose to a wail. "*I* don't know! Maybe I lost my temper and overreacted when he didn't mail the tax form."

Lilah smoothed her hair. "Don't be so hard on yourself."

Meri shook her head.

"Really, I didn't take time to think, I was so

furious. Deep inside, though, I think I thought he'd refuse and talk me out of it. Calm me down. And then last night, I . . ."

She stopped to swallow hard. ". . . well, anyway, now he's gotten back with Ronnie Rae. And I've hurt his feelings so much he'll never even be friends with me again."

She looked at Lilah with those tragic eyes, their violet color gone to purple with grief. "Ooh, Gran! This is going to affect HGK, and not in a good way. You warned me."

Tears rolling down her face, Meri looked as forlorn as a lost little girl. Lilah sat down on the bale beside her granddaughter and started rubbing her back. Meri leaned on Lilah's shoulder. Just for a moment. The child could never let herself rest.

Lilah smoothed her hair back from her face. "Well, if you doubt you did the right thing, shouldn't y'all talk it over? And if you hurt his feelings, shouldn't you apologize?"

"I . . . tried to call him. He doesn't answer. I hurt him, Gran. Really deep."

"What'd you do?"

Meri shook her head. She wasn't going to tell that.

"I am just so mad at him because he keeps making decisions like bringing way too many high-end cookies from HGK without asking you or me what would be appropriate and how many and then letting Ronnie Rae share our sponsor-ship . . ."

A hiccup interrupted. She was getting down to dry sobs now, the kind that were as hard to stop once they got started.

"Honey, is any of that—*any* of it—important enough for all this suffering you're doing?"

"I was so mad. And then he dragged me out onto the dance floor. Then I was mad *and* scared. Oh, Gran, it felt so good to be in his arms and then so horrible when I remembered I can't trust him."

"You talkin' about *Caleb?*"

"Well, yes. He didn't mail the tax . . ."

Lilah shook her head. "Well, there's trust and then there's trust. Think about it. There's fancy cookies and letters to mail on the one hand.

"On the other, well, life and death for example. Help in times of trouble. Doing the right thing for no other reason than it's right. You can trust him on those."

Meri pouted. "I can't trust him to include me in his decisions."

Lilah leaned back against the stall wall. So did Meri. They sat side by side for a few heartbeats.

Lilah prayed for wisdom, but nothing fell into her head.

She sighed. "Right now, only the Good Lord knows how this will all turn out for y'all."

Meri blurted. "I hurt him so much I just can't

bear it when I remember the look in his eyes. It's torturing me."

Lilah threw up her hands. "Well, tell him you're sorry."

"I should've *thought* before I spoke."

"Nobody in love can think. That's been scientifically proven, but I could've told 'em that and saved all those research dollars."

That brought fierce words as Meri wiped her eyes. "I'm not in love with him!"

The words hung in the air for a minute.

"Well," Lilah said. "Then I wonder what all this cryin's about."

Meri sniffed.

"Time will tell," Lilah said. "Stop thinking about it. You can't think up love and you can't think it away."

Meri hiccupped. "I'm his business partner for years and years to come and how am I going to deal with that?"

Lilah reached over and started rubbing her back.

"Come on, Meredith Kathleen, take ahold. You come from a long line of strong women and we stand together, no matter what. Together, we can handle anything from fire to famine."

She smiled. "You know that. We've already survived the fire at Raul's Restaurant."

Meri's reply was a little hiccupping giggle but then she burst into tears again and dropped her face into her hands.

"I'll never have a family of my own and it's all my fault. I'll never find a man who truly loves me. I'm not lovable. Everybody leaves me."

Tears rushed into Lilah's eyes, too, although most of the time nowadays she couldn't cry if she tried.

Talk about something that'll rip your heart out: If she'd kept on looking and found Meri when she was little, the child would never have felt unloved and unlovable.

Lilah willed her words to come out slow and even but they gushed out with her tears.

"Listen to your Granny," she said, and she hugged Meri tight. "I've lived a long time and I know what I'm talking about. You *are* lovable. I love you way beyond what words can tell. Lots of other people love you, too."

Shocked, Meri pulled back and looked at her.

"*Gran?* You're crying? About me?" She stared. "I thought you never cried."

She looked so bewildered Lilah had to laugh through her tears. "Oh, honey. If . . . you . . . only . . . knew . . ."

Meri gave Lilah an awkward pat on the back. "Except only that one afternoon you thought you were certain to lose Honey Grove."

Lilah shook her head in wonder. "Oh, no, sugar. I've wept many a tear. Other times, I held them back for fear if I ever got started crying, I'd wash away the world."

She caught her breath fast and it came out sounding like a sob.

Meri hugged her again. "Oh, Gran. Don't cry. I love you, too . . ."

But she couldn't talk anymore with her throat so full. Neither could Lilah.

She tightened her arms around her darling granddaughter, Meri hugged her back hard, and they held on to each other for a long, long time.

"Grandma knows best," Lilah said. "Don't do anything. Let go and let things work out the way the Good Lord intends them to."

She looked at Meri's beautiful profile. "How do you know what he wants?"

"He hasn't called me. He hasn't tried to get together and talk about us. He finally picked up when I called and said he didn't want to talk to me now."

Meri still didn't look at her. "So he's probably with Ronnie Rae again."

Lilah shrugged. "You can't know how he feels. Caleb's a complicated one."

"Well, then, I'm too simple to understand him."

Lilah didn't answer. No sense feeding the negativity and Meri wasn't in the mood to hear anything positive.

Anything could happen with Meri and Caleb. Lilah couldn't think about that now.

And, even though she was hurting for them,

both of whom had already had enough hurt in their lives, she couldn't think about that, either. And she shouldn't pray for them to get back together because only God knew if that was right, too.

Nineteen

Lilah had her window down in the truck, trying to enjoy the almost-brisk afternoon and the fact that she didn't have to drive while she did it. There was actually some traffic on the Lake Road.

"Big doin's in Rock County today," she said to Meri, who was driving. "I love it that this many people are turning out for the election debate. I think that bodes well for our zoning question. It surely gives me a lot of fresh people to campaign."

Meri glanced at her and just rolled her eyes— Lilah was talking about the zoning yet again— then she went back to watching Terry Smith's battered tailgate on that disgrace of a pickup he insisted on driving, even though everybody knew he had more money than Buford Quisenberry.

"Don't try to pass now," Lilah said. "It's a double yellow line and that hill up there can hide an eighteen-wheeler coming at you."

For once, Meri didn't complain about Lilah telling her how to drive.

Instead, she blurted, "I've thought about it until

I can't think anymore. I'm going to tell Caleb that this personal break is definitely permanent."

She made a funny little noise. "He wants that, too."

She glanced at Lilah over the tall drink dispenser full of sweet tea. To Meri's dismay, Lilah had put it there so it'd keep cooler, smack in the front seat, directly in front of the air conditioner vent.

"Stop saying that," Lilah said. "You can't know how he feels."

Meri didn't say another word until they turned off the road into the park. "What's the latest on who'll introduce the candidates?"

She was trying for a change of subject *and* her perky tone.

"Sue Ann asked me that this morning when I was in Brenham, trying to get our jams and jellies into Lagniappe. She said everybody's talking about the Great Debate."

"Did she say anything about the zoning question?"

"No."

Lilah frowned. Maybe Sue Ann would be here tonight and she could talk to her. She leaned forward to set her tote bag straight so her flyers wouldn't spill. She hoped to get one into the hands of everybody there.

"But she mentioned that Doreen is in a fit to find out. She wants to be first with the news, Sue Ann said, but she also wants to know because all the men, including Lawrence, are brazenly campaigning for Missy."

"Yes, and if that little cotton-brained TV star wins and changes the zoning out here, they'll all live to regret it," Lilah said. "Sue Ann's Doreen's cousin twice removed. On her mama's side. Did you know that?"

"No."

"Well, she is. And she's just as big a gossip as Doreen, too, so be careful what you say to her. Carrying the news, accurate or not, runs in that family."

They drove across the parking lot with Lilah gesturing which direction they should go and where Meri should park.

"This is fine," Lilah said when Meri pulled into an open spot. "As close as we can get to our table. See? Up the slope under those post oaks? B.J.'s saving it for us."

She looked again, holding her hand up against the glare of the sun.

"Isn't that Dallas up there, too?"

Meri ducked her head and looked through the windshield. "Yes. And Addison's with her."

"Great!" Lilah said, picking up her tote bag as she opened the door. "You and those girls can carry this cooler and the food up there. Don't wait for me. Y'all go ahead and eat and feed whoever drops by. I'm going to campaign."

Meri gave her an indulgent smile, as if Lilah

were a little kid excited about a picnic.

Lilah didn't care. Before she got out, she looked around the lake's picnic grounds, where there were people everywhere. Some at the shady concrete picnic tables, others already sitting in their folding chairs set up in front of the "stage," which was a flatbed truck, as usual. Pud Rigley's bluegrass band was already on it, tuning up. There was a big knot of people under the giant live-oak tree, too. She glimpsed Shorty's nephew, Tucker's, trick pony, a neatly made little paint that loved to perform. Some children were watching him, others were playing on the swing sets and slides. There were a couple of the Scaly Alligators fishing off the dock.

She scanned everything again, trying to decide where to start with her flyers.

"Well, will you look at that," she said, doing a double take at a bunch of men standing not too far from the stage. Missy Lambert was in the middle of the group, smiling and laughing like she was having a real good time.

"Well, there's a bunch of husbands'll be going without any home cooking," Lilah said. "They'd better be moving along."

"Sue Ann said Doreen told her that Bessie Quisenberry hasn't cooked for Buford since he came out for Missy," Meri said.

"I heard that, too, and I don't doubt it for a minute. Okay, let's get going."

Lilah stepped out of the truck and motioned for Addison and Dallas to come help unload everything.

Meri got out, too, and went to let down the tailgate. Lilah called to her, "If the Judge comes by our table, be sure and tell him I made a peach pie—used the last of the ones I froze this year. Cut him a slice to eat right then and let him take the rest of it home. That oughtta put him in the mood to stop this zoning nonsense in its tracks."

Her last words were drowned out by the roar of a diesel motor. She and Meri both turned to see the vehicle.

It was Caleb's big white truck.

"Oh, Lord," Lilah said, and clutched her tote bag tighter in her hand. "I hope the Kitchens hasn't caught on fire."

Meri caught her breath, hard. "Surely he wouldn't be the one to bring the news if it had. I sincerely doubt he was there working, when there's always so much to be done on the ranch."

"Be fair," Lilah said. "He got that deal done for the new freezers."

Meri raised her eyebrows and nodded reluctantly. One thing about it, the girl did value fairness. "Yeah," she said. "I have to admit that's true."

Caleb screeched to a stop right behind their truck, slammed his into park, opened the door and left it open as he threw himself out and limped around the front of the cab toward them. He nodded a greeting.

"Miss Lilah, Meri." His eyes met Meri's, but only as a passing glance.

He looked like death warmed-over.

"Have y'all seen Gid? He was supposed to be here but I can't get him on his phone. He must've laid it down somewhere and walked off and left it."

"Maybe he doesn't want to talk to you," Meri said.

A trace of sarcasm, an attempt to get a rise out of him. It wasn't like Meri to vie for attention.

Lilah looked at her granddaughter but Meri had eyes only for Caleb.

He was disheveled and dirty, with his thick hair sticking up in every direction as if he'd been running his hands through it. That had been his habit in times of stress ever since he was a little kid.

His shirttail hung out and his jeans were splashed with mud.

No, it was worse than that. There was a distinct odor of cow manure about him.

"Or have y'all seen Dr. Vincent anywhere?"

His eyes were haunted. Every inch of him screamed exhaustion. And desperation.

Lilah clapped her hand over her heart. "Oh, Lordy," she said. "What's wrong? It's not your mama . . . ?"

His teasing grin was barely there. "No," he drawled, patting her on the shoulder. "Dr. *Vincent*. So far, we're not quite down to callin' the veterinarian for people."

Lilah patted his back, even if he did reek. She felt her face heat. These kids'd be thinking she was going senile or deaf, one or the other.

"What's wrong with me? I don't even know why I thought that when Dulcie's not even sick. She just flashed into my mind when I saw your face."

He nodded absently, hardly hearing her. "I've got an outbreak in my calves," he said. "That new virus, I think. Doc's out of pocket—probably gone to the Coast to fish. I've gotta have help to work the gate so I can inject 'em with amoxicillin and hope it stops the diarrhea until he gets back."

"How many of 'em are sick?" Lilah said.

"Three head, so far. I've got 'em quarantined but likely it's too late for that."

"Are they bad?"

"Bad enough. They may not make it. I can't afford to lose even one of those high-dollar babies.

"My so-called help quit yesterday and—"

"Well, let's get you somebody," Lilah said, fumbling in her jeans pocket for her phone. "I'll call Shorty."

The whole time Caleb was talking to Lilah. Looking at Lilah. But the tension between him and Meri was a live thing in the air.

Meri hadn't been able to see anything but him since the second he roared into the parking lot.

Lilah scrolled her phone. "Hang on, Cale. I'll get Shorty."

Caleb nodded his thanks. He was already turning, heading back to the driver's seat. "I gotta get back. He'll need his own truck anyhow. I'll be too wiped out to take him home by the time we're done."

He lifted his hand in good-bye, got around the truck, climbed in and closed the door. Shifted gears.

Meri blurted, "Don't send Shorty."

She ran to the passenger side of Caleb's truck, opened the door and jumped in.

Twenty

Lilah watched Caleb's truck out of sight. This might be good. Maybe Meri would change her mind.

She did love him or she wouldn't have been so touched by his distress.

Lilah sighed to herself. Anything could happen with those two. And now there was HGK in the mix . . .

But this wasn't the time to worry about any of that. She'd better get her mind on the fact HGK would be in for a world of hurt if Rock County went from farming country to a bedroom community.

212

This minute, she had to get to handing out these flyers and talking to people. Once the debate was over, the evening was over and lots of them would leave here in a hurry.

"Miss Lilah! What else do you want us to take up to your picnic table?"

She turned to see Dallas and Addison with their heads in her truck, working together to pull out the tall container of sweet tea.

"You're doing right," she told them. "Everything else is in the backseat. Just carry it all up there and make a pretty table. Y'all know how."

She repeated the instructions she'd given Meri about the peach pie and the Judge, then double-checked the number of flyers in her bag.

"Did you bring snickerdoodles, Miss Lilah?" Dallas called.

"Yes, honey, I made them just for you. They're in one of the HGK boxes."

She pulled a short stack of the colorful papers out of her bag and laid them on the front seat as the two girls left the truck carrying the cooler between them. "Next trip, lay these flyers out on the table, too, please, girls. Don't forget to be friendly—y'all never do—and hand one of these to everyone who doesn't pick one up."

"Yes, ma'am," they chorused.

Lilah waved at B.J., up at the table, and pointed at the bag in her hand. B.J. gave her a thumbs-up and went back to talking to her cousin, Gloria, visiting from San Antonio, so Lilah headed out to campaign as many people as possible before everybody got settled down to listen to the speeches and debate.

She scoped out the crowd and spotted the Judge, head and shoulders taller than anybody else, in the crowd gathered around the trick pony. Before he spoke, she wanted to try one more time to get a promise from him about the zoning, or, at best, ask him to hint at his likely decision during the debate.

She had told him and told him that most of the voters were on her side about that question but he didn't entirely believe her.

She handed a flyer to Terence Burton and kept moving, giving them out right and left while she tried to stop obsessing about what the Judge would do. Her energy had to go to talking to as many people as possible and praying that the election would prove her right.

She had a good feeling that it would.

Surely hardly anybody wanted housing developments in here and they knew no way would Missy Lambert vote against them.

Lilah spoke to everyone she could and gave them one of the ads on her way to campaign in the pony-watching crowd. She even gave two to Clem and Flora who were already on her side and told them to pass them on. One to Hugh Brown and a little visit with him, then she moved to the next group. Hugh's support was probably iffy at best because he owned the one lumberyard in Rock Springs.

As she worked her way closer to her quarry, she realized that newcomers were coming from all directions to join the group. Excited voices coming from it. Trouble was brewing.

She heard the word *fight* in the buzz of onlookers as she arrived.

Shorty's voice was loud, saying, "Just because you're the Judge . . ."

Lilah's blood chilled. If they started fussing again, the Judge would be angry as a wasp and in no mood to promise her anything.

"Excuse me," she said, tugging on Jimsy Bledsoe's elbow because he was hard of hearing. He was one of the oldest of the Scaly Alligators. "Jimsy, I need to get through here . . ."

Reluctantly, he stepped back to let her through. He hollered, "You be careful not to git between 'em, Miss Lilah. They's liable to start throwin' punches any minute now."

He was grinning all over his face.

Somebody else yelled, "You tell 'em, Shorty!"

Jimsy's friend, Boliver Simmons, had to put in his two cents' worth.

"You're just in time, Miss Lilah. I reckon yore two boyfriends is about to have a leetle dustup, here."

She ignored the word *boyfriends* and pushed on

through. She came up right behind Shorty, who was aware of nothing but his opponent.

"Hush up!" she whispered, right behind him. "Don't push Elbert the wrong way."

Shorty jumped a little, so she knew he heard her, but he gave no sign.

"You can stop this actin' so all-fired high and mighty," Shorty said. "You're playin' with fire here, Elbert. You been Judge so long you think you're king, so it's about time we throwed you outta office."

Somebody else hollered, "Yeah! Git a job. See what it's like to work for a livin'."

Oh, Lordy mercy! Surely Shorty wouldn't start campaigning against the Judge!

Her heart just sank right through her shoes and into the ground. This right here could be the ruination of them all. When Shorty got mad, he lost all reason.

She stiffened her spine and stepped into the fray.

"What's wrong, you two? What are y'all arguing . . ."

Shorty took her by the arm and set her aside, and none too gently at that.

"Lilah, stay out of this.

"You're way outta line, Elbert. You're pickin' on Tucker 'cause he's my nephew. Use your eyes, man! He's got this pony fat and slick as a whistle. Nobody in their right mind would say he's abusin' this animal."

"You overestimate your own importance, Grumbles. This has nothing to do with you. People are complaining and the next thing we know we're liable to have a bunch of tree huggers coming in here, camping in the park and marching and carrying on, making Rock Springs look bad on the television news!"

"Prove it," Shorty said.

"You calling me a liar?"

"I'm sayin' you've got a grudge against me and Tucker's my nephew. Nobody treats their animals better than he does. So surely there's a reason for you losin' your mind like this."

Tucker and the pony, whose name was Judy, stood behind the Judge, both listening intently. Neither looked very worried. Tucker had had a hard life. The threat of tree huggers didn't seem to move him at all.

"I'm telling you, I've heard complaints. I'm trying to put out a fire before it starts," the Judge said.

Shorty shot back, "Who complained?"

"None of your business."

Shorty stepped closer, his neck crooked to look up at the Judge.

"You've made it my business. You've insulted my family. Spit out a name or I'll pound it out of you."

Elbert drew himself up and tried to gather his dignity. "That's private information—"

"Spit it out."

"Yes!" somebody called. "Or else we'll all think you're lyin'."

"What about that transparency idea?" another voice said. "Is this one o' them secret, under-the-table deals?"

"Maybe there's money changin' hands here. Likely he's been Judge too long."

"Yeah! Ain't that right, folks?"

"It's all right, Judge," came a sweet voice. "I'll be happy to own up to making the complaint."

Marva Kay Richardson stepped out of the crowd.

She was looking at Shorty. (With what—for Marva Kay, whose face was always practically frozen in a pleasant expression—was a hard look.)

"I just think it's animal abuse to ask this little pony to stand on a bucket," she said. "It's not good for her because she has to put her tiny hooves too close together. I could tell it is not easy for her to do that and—"

Shorty interrupted, "Well, Marva Kay, how long did she stand there? Ten seconds? Why . . ."

Lilah saw it before he did, of course. So she recognized the look that came over his face when he realized his suspicions had been right in the first place. He *was* the target of all this uproar. *Marva Kay's* target, not the Judge's.

A few seconds of silence, and everybody there caught on.

"I'm thinkin' yore women're jist about to swarm on ya, Shorty," Jimsy announced in his bullhorn voice to a now-laughing crowd. "You need any help with 'em, just gimme a holler."

By the time everybody settled down, the speeches were done and it was time for the formal debate to start. Lilah dropped into the lawn chair beside Shorty's and accepted the lemonade he brought her. She was so exhausted from sorting everybody out she could hardly say a thank-you to him, much less give him the stern talking-to he'd earned by going after the Judge in public like that.

Marva Kay formally withdrew her complaint after Tucker flattered her a bit for her powers of observation and paid her a lot of attention, demonstrating how much Judy liked doing her tricks and explaining how he'd trained her. While all that had been going on, Lilah talked to Elbert. He was all right now but she didn't push him hard on the zoning since he was already so worked up over it all. Now she had to get through to Shorty.

"I understand how you were feeling," she told him, keeping her voice down so none of the folk sitting near them could hear, "but Shorty, if you still feel bad at the Judge, I beg you to keep it to yourself. If you talk him down everywhere, it could lose him the election."

He shot her a slanting look. "I doubt it."

Sometimes he was so stubborn she could just wring his neck.

"You listen here to me, Shorty Grumbles. You've gotta just let that go. At least until after the election."

He pretended not to understand.

"It wasn't the Judge being jealous of you. It was Marva Kay. Let it go."

His only answer was a shrug.

Finally, she gave up and tried to put all that out of her mind so she could really listen to the debate to come. That was such a struggle that she could hardly sing "The Star-Spangled Banner." Standing there with her hand over her heart, she felt it beating just as fast as her brain was whirling. At this rate, she was liable to have a sinking spell.

Get a grip, girl. Take a deep breath. Concentrate or you won't know enough to advise the Judge after you hear him and Missy.

She did manage to listen to the invocation. It was the Pentecostal preacher, Brother Castleberry's, turn to give it and he was as heartfelt a man as she had ever heard pray over a county election.

When she and Shorty sat down, she took a deep breath and looked for her funeral-home fan in her bag of flyers. She had to get her mind on something else.

So, when he asked where Meri was, she told him about her jumping in the truck with Caleb.

"What do you think," she said, starting to fan

away the heat in her face that had been there ever since she heard Shorty going at the Judge, "reckon the two of them will make a go of it?"

"I don't know how to break it to you, Lilah, but the news is that's none of your beeswax."

He was still mad at her for interfering in his argument with the Judge.

She bristled. "Well, I guess it *is!* They're my business partners and basically my children, to boot!"

Shorty shook his head. "Well, they're the most opposite male and female that ever stumbled into each other's arms."

He cut her that look of his—the one that put a hard period at the end of what he'd just said, marking it wisdom irrefutable.

"I don't wanna hear it," she said. "You're making my heart sink again. I can't afford to get down now. Just when I think maybe life's about to settle around here and smooth out to normal, something else happens to rock it."

"Well, 'smooth out' don't have much chance during election season," Shorty said, "especially if normal's what you're after."

"You know what I mean—everything's changing so fast everywhere that we need something to stay solid, like love, for example. And I know those kids love each other."

Shorty raised his eyebrows and that teasing glint came into his brown eyes. "Well, then, settle down and concentrate on your boyfriend," he said. "He's about to get up there on the stage here in a minute and make a further ass of himself."

That just flew all over her.

"You think you're so smart, Shorty Grumbles," she said. "And he is *not* my boyfriend."

He chuckled in that knowing way of his that never failed to irritate her even more than the look. She turned away and looked at the stage where the young Rock Springs mayor and hobbyist goat farmer, Derek Hornbuckle (he lived in town and worked as an accountant), was presiding.

But what she saw was Doreen, dressed in a cute (*almost* too young for her) outfit of capri pants and ruffly top, getting around much better and barely using her crutches since she was finally healing fast. Following her came the youngest Williams boy carrying two folded lawn chairs. Clearly, they were headed straight for Lilah and Shorty.

"I swear to my time," Lilah said to him, "here comes Doreen to sit with us. Where's Lawrence?"

"Up there by the stage with Missy Lambert," Shorty said. "I hear she's looking at the Sessions' house now."

"I cannot believe she's so confident she'll win."

"Maybe she just wants to move to Rock Springs no matter what," Shorty drawled. "It *is* damn near irresistible."

"Shorty. Listen to me. Don't say one word to Doreen about Meri jumping in the truck with Caleb. I'm not ready to deal with her speculations about them."

He turned around to look at her full-faced and drawled, "I understand how you feel." His tone was so dry and mischievous she had to laugh.

He always knew how to get around her when she was mad at him.

She slapped his arm. "All right, now, I mean it. Help me entertain her. Maybe you can get some news out of her for *your* gossip mill."

He squinted at her. "You callin' me a gossip? Call me Tol Weddle and them's fightin' words."

They were both laughing when Doreen and her chairs arrived, so they had to explain the reason why while Shorty and the Williams boy set up her chairs and Doreen settled in.

"Lawrence will be here in a few minutes," she said, after thanking the Williams boy for his help. "He's got a couple of pieces of business to take care of first."

As usual, then Doreen had to look all around to spot the scenes to keep watch of while she was in that vicinity.

"Your nephew's doing a fine job with that pony," she said, after watching Tucker for a minute. "I don't care what that silly Marva Kay says. He should put out a tip jar for the parents for entertaining their kids. They're all into that."

Shorty scowled at her. "Tuck wouldn't take no pay. He'd be insulted. He's practicing to perform at the fair."

"Oh," she said, "sorry."

"Just because *you* would put out a big tip jar, Doreen," Lilah said. "That's one of your problems getting along with people—you always think what you would do is the only way to do something."

"Don't pick on me tonight," Doreen blurted. "I've got a bad feeling."

"About what?"

"Wait and see if it happens."

Then, to deflect Lilah's sharp look, she changed the subject.

"Verna Carl's going to introduce the Judge because she's president of the League of Women Voters."

"What about Missy?"

Doreen shrugged. "Still a mystery. Nobody seems to know. Lawrence and everybody on the committee says they don't know yet."

Lilah said, "I still think there's something funny going on, making such a big deal of those introductions. Lord have mercy! Time was, the mayor would've done it and that would've been that."

Doreen said, "I noticed Meri jumping into Caleb's truck awhile ago. Did they get back together and I missed it?"

Lilah rolled her eyes. "Merciful heavens," she

said. "Do you know what time I brushed my teeth this morning?"

Doreen smiled. She took that as a compliment. "Probably around six A.M.," she said. "Knowing you get up with the sun."

She speculated about Meri and Caleb a little bit, and quizzed Lilah some more, but she couldn't quite get into her speculations to her usual extent for fretting about her husband. She kept looking and craning her neck trying to see him.

The next minute he appeared climbing up onto the back of the stage escorting Missy Lambert. They went over to the row of four chairs where Verna Carl sat beside the Judge and took their seats.

Doreen gasped and muttered under her breath. "That's what I thought. Lawrence is the one who's going to introduce her. Yet he wouldn't admit it when I asked him."

"Keep cool," Lilah said. "It's business. Maybe he'll sell her the Sessions' house and make a lot of money. Which can't be easy in this real estate market."

That didn't pacify Doreen. She fidgeted all the time Verna Carl was introducing the Judge—she did a fine job of it, of course, although everybody there already knew every fact she told about him.

Then Elbert came to the microphone to make his case for why he should be reelected for the umpteenth time.

Well, not exactly. To Lilah's horror, mostly he just mouthed platitudes.

"I've lived in Rock County all my life and I've served y'all in a variety of offices and, before that, as a private attorney and . . ." blah, blah, blah, yammer, yammer, yammer, ending up with, ". . . you all know me and you all know I'll take care of you. I'm humbly asking for your vote on Election Day."

He used his big smile and waved to the crowd, then ambled over to his chair and sat down.

"He didn't talk five minutes!" Lilah said, horrified. "And he didn't say a blessed thing, much less give a hint of what he thinks about the future of the county! What is he *thinking?*"

"That he's already got it all sewed up," Shorty said.

"He's overconfident," Doreen said. "He thinks Missy's not serious enough to have a ghost of a chance."

Lilah just sat there and tried to pick up her jaw. "Why, Elbert did a better job than that even when he didn't have an opponent last time around!"

"I told you he'd make a further ass of himself," Shorty said. "He's too damn lazy to bother working up a speech. He thinks he's got it won already."

Doreen was still staring at Lawrence, but she said, in an absentminded tone, "Don't worry, Lilah. He didn't need to do any better to come out the winner. Missy'll be a giggling, flirtatious, featherbrained mess. How could she not be? Look, she's got that aggravating little dog with her again."

Her voice cracked. "Lawrence will look so stupid. He'll have to take care of it while she speaks."

Lilah thought she was actually going to cry. "Doreen . . ."

She leaned over to put her head together with Lilah's so Shorty couldn't hear. "Here lately, Lawrence can't talk about anything without saying 'Missy this' and 'Missy that.' Lilah, he makes me so mad . . ."

Which was what Lilah would expect from her old frenemy, but truth to tell, Doreen sounded more sad and scared than mad. It hit her then that Doreen had come to sit beside her for comfort.

That was a strange feeling. A result of their forgiving each other.

The sound of Lawrence's voice in the microphone made them jerk apart and gape at the stage.

"It's my privilege and honor tonight to introduce the Judge's opponent, the lovely Missy Lambert." He mimed applause and got it, plus whistles of admiration from some of the men.

"We all feel like we know and love Missy because she came into our homes for the past few years on our television screens. Now our favorite newscaster is here among us in person and we want to welcome her to Rock Springs . . ."

"How corny can he be?" Doreen demanded of Lilah. "And what did I ever see in such a susceptible idiot?"

Lilah tried to calm her down before she made a scene.

"Now, Doreen. Remember he's trying to sell her a house."

"I don't care," Doreen said, which made Lilah's head whip around to look at her. And not just because Doreen sounded near tears. Doreen *always* cared about getting more money.

But Doreen's jealous bone had always been her downfall.

This was more than that, though. It was like Doreen thought she was whipped, which Lilah had never seen before. She watched her from the corner of her eye. Bless her heart. This was no stage in life to be scared of losing your husband to another woman.

Lilah felt sympathy tears burn behind her eyes.

Lawrence went on praising Missy, including the thought that it'd be nice to have a beautiful woman on the bench for a change. Laughter from the crowd as he apologized to the Judge.

Lord help! When would he ever shut up?

Whistles and catcalls from the crowd just made it all worse for Doreen when he made his final flourishes with yet another reference to Missy's looks.

"Cheesy and politically incorrect," she whispered to Lilah, trying to sound as if she didn't care. "Sexual harassment. She's an attorney. He's liable to cause her to sue him instead of buying a house from him. And how did *he* get this job of introducing her, anyway?"

Finally, Lawrence shut up and Missy pranced up to the podium in her fancy five-inch heels. He reached for the little dog she carried and received a blinding smile of thanks as he took it. As she began to speak, he left the stage with the feisty dog in his arms.

"I am going to kill him dead and tell God he died," Doreen muttered.

"Now, Doreen. When he gets here, don't say anything to cause a scene. Give yourself time to cool off and wait 'til y'all get home."

She looked at her pointedly. "You know how this town loves a scene and a scandal and it could affect both y'all's businesses because most people would think where there's smoke, there's fire."

Doreen looked back at her defiantly, then sullenly. She nodded. Those really were tears shining in her eyes. "I know that's good advice."

"Yes, and you'd best take it."

When Lawrence arrived with the dog, Doreen looked at him once, then ignored him. He pulled his chair a little closer to hers.

They all settled in and started listening to Missy. Lilah's jaw dropped. The first couple of sentences out of her mouth said far more than Elbert had done in his entire three or four minutes. She didn't say a word about herself, except to say that she was a native of Rock County who'd always maintained a home near her family, sixth-generation farmers and businesspeople up near Pleasant Hill. After that, she was all business, talking about the county and its future and its possibilities of attracting more citizens.

Lilah could hardly keep from wringing her hands. Missy was preparing everyone for the zoning change. The businesspeople she mentioned in her family were builders, that's what. And Missy was presenting herself and her views so much better than the Judge had done that it wasn't even funny.

She was smart. She was talking about new blood in the county offices and new ideas for crime prevention and punishment and more money from sales and property taxes.

Oh! Lilah, would have to get to work immediately—campaigning for the Judge, yes, but also working on *him*. Somebody had to make him realize that this campaign was not a done deal in his favor. Elbert had to wake up!

But she couldn't half think or hear what else Missy had to say for Doreen stirring things up with Lawrence. Lilah should've known that her sage advice wouldn't stop Doreen from jumping in the middle of him and stomping him down right here and right now. That would take a miracle.

Lilah reached over and touched Doreen's arm lightly, as a reminder of where they were, but Doreen ignored her completely.

Loud enough for Lilah and Shorty—and probably the Davisons and Moffetts, who had placed their chairs not too far away—to hear, Doreen said, "How much did you have to give to get the job of introducing that hussy?"

"Doreen! Hush," he said. "What are you talking about?"

"The great mystery of who will introduce *'beautiful'* Missy. You've been telling me for two weeks that you didn't know."

Lilah had the thought that Doreen was probably angrier about not knowing ahead of time than all the rest of it.

She had married Lawrence one month to the day after Lilah married Ed. From childhood, Doreen had loved Ed (or thought she did) and once he was married, she'd started a whirlwind romance with Lawrence, who'd always been as crazy about her as she was about Ed. She'd dated him and others all through high school, but she'd always held out the hope that Ed would love her, too.

Poor Lawrence really loved her and he usually tried to please her and cringed when he didn't.

But not tonight.

He smiled and petted the dog. "I *didn't* know. We had a betting pool—winner introduces Missy and the money goes to the repairs at the Fairgrounds."

She gaped at him.

"*What?* Who all was in this pool?"

He shrugged. "Most of the men in town."

"And y'all managed to keep that a *secret?*"

Lilah sighed and tried to close her ears. She didn't want to hear any more.

Nothing was the same, not even Doreen and Lawrence.

Nothing ever stayed the same and she knew that. Nothing. Maybe not even the county judge.

Which meant neither would the county.

Talk about the ground shifting under your feet.

She leaned over to Shorty and said, "You know what? It may be that we ain't seen nothin' yet."

Twenty-one

Meri slid the bar into place behind the calf and closed the gate to keep the animal in the chute, breathing a sigh of relief that this was the last one. Standing there for seventeen of them to pass through and be inoculated had coated her hair and her clothes with the essences of cow, manure and dust, so she was desperate to get home and into the shower.

And even more desperate to get away from

Caleb. She hated being with him when he wasn't really *with* her at all. The difference between the magic they used to have between them and this humming, hurting tension was awful.

Now she knew what Lilah meant by the expression "sick at heart."

"Last one," he said. His voice sounded rusty. And rightly so, since he'd hardly spoken this whole time, except to give orders.

He'd asked her what she was doing when she jumped into his truck and he'd told her how to work the gate. Yet every time he'd turned to check on the next calf, his eyes had gone to exactly where she was.

"I'm glad," she said. "I need to get back to Honey Grove."

He shrugged and started the process of getting the shot ready for the calf. She couldn't resist watching his every move and that made her furious with herself.

Yet, she couldn't stop watching him. His big, sure hands went through the ritual of lifting the bottle of serum and filling the syringe with the same sure movements every time. It made her think of how his callused palms felt against her skin.

And how surely he always escorted her with one big hand warming the very same spot in the small of her back.

But all that was gone. She was done. The only thing remaining was to tell him.

So why did you jump into the truck with him? Why didn't you think about what you were doing?

Her critical voices were nattering at her every minute. She hated them.

I did think. I had to tell him my decision about us.

She didn't want to admit, even to herself, that the desperate way he had looked and spoken had seized her heart. He needed help. Her instinct had been that she couldn't let him leave without it.

You are not the kind of person to follow instinct. You use your head, remember?

He still had that weary, desperate air about him.

Yes, and I've thought it through. Caleb and I are not meant for each other.

Even if there's this . . . tension or whatever it is between us.

He gave the shot to the calf and stepped forward to slam open the chute's front gate. The calf ran through the opening and across the grassy space to join the ones who'd gone before it.

Meri began cleaning up the temporary table he'd set up as a work space.

Caleb watched the calves for a moment, then turned and walked back to her.

"Thanks," he said. "This would've taken a lot longer alone."

He stopped near her, close enough to touch. Close enough for her to smell his sweat.

Oh! If that old saw was true, he was the man for

her. How could she walk away from him? But they would probably make each other miserable.

He'd been able to read her feelings since the day they met. Even when she was trying to hide them. And right now, she wasn't trying.

"I'll take you home," he said, his voice rough with weariness.

Only then did she know how weary she was inside. As tired as he was in body.

She didn't want to talk, after all. She didn't want to be in his truck with him for the long drive to Honey Grove. Not with this vibration between them.

It made her want to grab him by the front of his filthy shirt and pull his mouth down to hers. It made her literally weak in the knees.

He felt it, too, she knew that, but he wasn't going to do anything about it. He was keeping the distance. And who could blame him? She'd said a terrible, mean thing to him and now she knew it was because she was scared out of her mind at falling in love with him completely. That would leave her helplessly out of control in every way.

She wanted to go somewhere cool and sit down and just stare into space. She felt drained to the core. She couldn't think. She just could not bear to think.

But she opened her mouth and said, "Caleb, I need to apologize for that snake comparison the other night. It was over the top."

He did that one-shouldered shrug again. "Forget it."

He started gathering up the trash on the table.

She had to touch him *somehow*. Right now it felt like what they used to have had never existed.

"I still remember your lecture about the power of the insult in the word *liar,*" she said, trying for a light tone. "I don't know for sure if it's the same for *snake* but . . ."

He threw the trash into the barrel behind him, turned, slapped both hands palms down on the table and leaned toward her across it.

"Call me a snake or a liar or a low-down lazy hound dog for forgetting to mail a letter, I don't care," he said, his eyes a blue so hot it burned her.

"Our problem, Meri, is that you don't trust me. Nothin's any good without trust."

"But I—"

"No," he said, stepping back to pick up the old door serving as the top of the makeshift table. "Excuses won't change a thing."

He carried the door into the barn.

She followed. "Caleb, I've been thinking a lot about us. I've decided that we should . . ."

But then she couldn't finish the sentence. It was too final. She was too much in turmoil to.

That brought only the briefest glance from him.

"We're opposites," she said. "We don't have the

same priorities. We're not perfect for each other, after all."

He stood the door up against the barn wall and turned to face her.

He smiled but there was no humor in it. "And perfect's what we're after, right?"

His gaze wouldn't let hers go.

"Good luck with that, Mer."

It tore the heart out of her when he called her Mer. In fact, the look on his face made her want to take it into her hands and kiss him senseless.

But her emotions were roiling like waves in a storm and that always scared her more than any danger. She had to think first. She had to figure out what was best for them.

If she went into his arms this minute and promised to trust him forever, she'd lose all control of her life.

"We can still be friends," she said, her mouth so dry the words would hardly come off her tongue. "And we're business partners forever. So . . ."

"Gimme a minute here," he said, his arm trembling slightly with fatigue as he brushed back the hair from his forehead. "I'll check on the sick ones back here and then I'll take you home."

A strange desperation grabbed her in the gut. She had to do something. She had to say something. She had to get control of this. Everything was spinning out into space.

But she didn't know what to do or say.

And she had to do *something*. She had to get away before she said something she couldn't take back.

"I'll drive myself," she said, almost choking on the words. "Can I take your old truck?"

He held her gaze for two long heartbeats.

Then he said, "Key's in it."

Twenty-two

Well, if anybody asked her, Lilah could tell them right now, this very minute, that a daughter or a granddaughter was bound to bring a big plenty of worries along with the joys. Ever since she got home from the debate last night to find Caleb's old truck in the driveway, a good-night note on the kitchen table and the girl in her room with the lights off, she'd been in a swivet about Meri.

Lilah hadn't pushed it after she knocked on the door and got no answer. It was possible Meri really was asleep at 10:00 P.M., but if she was, she must be coming down with something. Always, it was nearly midnight before she gave it up and went to bed.

Something was wrong. It wasn't like Caleb to let her drive herself home after dark. He was old-fashioned in so many ways.

Then, this morning early, the child had blown through the kitchen like a high wind without taking time to eat her breakfast, and now here she was, shut up in the office with only a cup of yogurt and an oat bran muffin (which, Lilah knew, she probably wouldn't finish, if she ate any of it) to counteract the gallons of coffee she would consume during the day.

And she'd rushed through this HGK kitchen, too, with not one word to her Gran about why she went jumping into the truck with Caleb or how they did doctoring his calves or if she and Cale had kissed and made up or what. All she'd have to do for privacy was call Lilah into the office and close the door.

Lilah tasted, then stirred just a dab more maple into the icing for the cinnamon rolls that Jewel was pulling out of the oven. Then the good vanilla she always ordered.

"I think we should use two icings every morning," she said to Jewel, trying to get her mind off Meri and what some people would say was none of her business. (Of course, any grandmother knew her girl's heart *was* her business.)

"Give customers a choice. Plain butter or maple. Next day, orange or lemon. Near Christmas, peppermint or pecan."

Jewel thought about it as she carried the big pan of fresh rolls over to Lilah's worktable.

Finally, she nodded her agreement and added, "Chocolate?"

Lilah considered it. "Somehow, I don't think so.

Anything chocolate needs a thicker coating of it. A *serious* frosting, not a glaze."

"Makes sense," Jewel said. They both got busy pouring the topping over the hot rolls. Jewel never was one to waste words.

"That's why I said 'no' from the beginning to chocolate long johns and doughnuts," Lilah said as they worked. "Anybody who wants them can go to the Grab It 'n' Go for store-bought."

When they finished and Jewel went to put the new supply of rolls in the café display case, Lilah was still so antsy to question Meri that she knew she couldn't hang around HGK any longer without barging into the office and saying something.

No matter what it might turn out to be, it'd be wrong.

She looked at the clock. She'd arranged to meet the Judge at noon. If he didn't commit to doing the right thing about the Jones Orchards zoning pretty soon, she didn't know what she was going to do. Maybe bribe him with a peach pie a week for a year.

But that was a bit much to mention now. After his poor showing last night, he might not even win the election and get on the zoning board. She'd overheard talk in the café this morning saying that he didn't care whether he won or not. Somebody else chimed in to say he'd gotten so arrogant and felt so entitled to be the county judge that he was taking winning for granted.

And even a peach pie a week wouldn't move tight-dress Missy to go against the zoning change. Not with her people all in the building business. So the Judge was it and Lilah was the only one who could set him on the straight and narrow.

She glanced at the clock. It was almost eleven. She might as well start campaigning some other people, too, about the zoning change. That'd get her warmed up to pressure stubborn Elbert.

That evening Meri had the meltdown in the barn, she'd finally talked to her grandma about her feelings for Caleb. Surely she would again, good news or bad.

It's not your place to say what's good news or bad, Lilah Briscoe. Not on that subject. You don't know those two belong together. Leave that up to the Good Lord. Your business with Meri's heart is to help her protect it, that's all.

Lilah held that bit of truth in the front of her mind as she went to the office to get her purse and her zoning flyers. Meri was on the phone, so she just nodded hello and wiggled her fingers good-bye. From the few words Lilah heard her say, it sounded like she was talking business, and not with Cale.

Outside on the Square, Lilah looked both ways and tried to decide where to start. She'd heard that Lester was pushing *for* the zoning change, talking to everybody who came into the saddle shop about growing the town's businesses, raving that Rock

Springs' sales taxes would go through the roof if only some shady developer could turn Jones Orchards into Peach Valley Estates or Falcon Ridge Ranchettes or some other such ridiculous mess of houses to ruin good farmland.

Of course, those last words were Lilah's and not Lester's, but no matter how he might say it, she was right.

Before she met with the Judge, she had time to help Lester see the light, so she started walking toward the saddle shop. Lester was a pretty level-headed businessman and saddle-maker. What was he *thinking?* How many of those newcomers, estate and ranchette owners alike, did he think would be in his shop buying saddles, anyhow? They'd be after lawn sprinklers to use up all the water in the aquifer and tofu and running shoes and fitness gyms.

Why didn't the Judge declare to her privately that he'd be against the zoning change so she could get busy and campaign for him?

He was right in saying that Lilah had a lot of influence. And he should be feeling a little threatened now because Missy's popularity was exploding. After last night, even some of the women were admitting she was more than just a pretty face.

Except for some of the really jealous wives, of course. The news of the husbands' betting pool for introducing Missy at the debate was going to create more business for the cafés and restaurants in town.

Especially at breakfast time. She needed to remind Jewel there'd probably be more business for the café at HGK for a while, now.

Lilah was lost in thought, trotting along just on the other side of Treva's Fine Nails and Tanning Salon, which was next door to HGK, when she spotted the Judge driving around the Square toward her in his new pearl-white Cadillac Escalade. He pulled into one of the slanted spaces in front of the Rock Springs Fitness Center and, ever the gentleman, instead of calling to her from the car, he got out and walked to meet her.

She sighed. Now what was this change of plans?

Elbert's smile was at its most charming. "Good to see you, Miss Lilah," he said, tipping his hat as they met. "Beautiful day. Just enough cool in the air."

"I'm not late, am I?" she said, although she knew she wasn't.

"No, no," he said, grinning from ear to ear he was so pleased with himself. "I'm thinking we should take a little drive."

Oh, Good Lord! Will you give it up?

She should never have gone out with him the first time. But she must be careful not to offend him, since he was her—and the county's—only hope.

"Elbert, thank you so much, but I just don't

have that kind of time. I've got a million things to do . . ."

"I need to see what you're talking about out there around Honey Grove and Jones Orchards," he said, in syrupy tones, escorting her toward his car by the elbow. "I have to scope out the neighborhood with that zoning change in mind. I haven't been out that way for a coon's age except when I took you home the other night and it was too dark to see anything then."

Oh, well. What else could she do? This was her chance to nail him down.

"I need you, Lilah. You know that," he purred as he opened the passenger door for her. It was his "date" voice. "You can make or break me in this election. We've been friends for a long time and you've probably heard people saying that Missy skunked me in the debate."

"I have heard that said," she informed him. "But I'm not going to campaign against her, not one step will I take, until you give me your sacred word that you'll vote to keep my neighborhood just the way it is and always has been."

He handed her up into the fancy SUV. "Well," he drawled, "that's what we're going to research on our little country drive."

She let out a sigh. "Research won't do it . . ." she said, settling in while he went around to the driver's side. He got in. ". . . I've got to have a decision."

Treva waved from the window of her salon as they drove away.

So, forget escaping the gossips. Traipsing all over the countryside with Elbert would set tongues wagging all over everywhere and Shorty'd be sure to get his nose out of joint again. However, she couldn't very well put a little aggravation like that ahead of something as important as saving the county.

"This is a thrill for me, being seen with the Queen of Rock County driving around in my new car."

Lilah looked out the window and rolled her eyes. "Well, it's all up to you whether I'll ever step foot into it again," she said tartly.

He raised his bushy brows. "Sounds like the possibility of a third date to me." She whipped her head around to see him smiling to himself like a mule eating peas off the vine.

"No," she said. "It'd be the *first* date. These are political meetings, Elbert. If you could get through law school, you can get *that* through your thick head."

"I *am* known as stubborn," he said pleasantly.

She threw up her hands. "I swear you *are!* Now watch your driving going around corners. You nearly sideswiped the sheriff's car right there. How would that look with Missy telling it in the campaign? She'd say you're too old to drive, so you're too old to be the Judge."

He shot her a shocked sideways glance. "How could she . . . ?"

"Elbert! You're gettin' on toward seventy! That sounds old to the young people and they're not too polite to say so."

"Hmph. She's no spring chicken herself."

"Well, she's a far cry from seventy, I can tell you that."

As they left the Square and headed out FM 2317, he asked her what she'd been hearing about the Judge's race this morning and she told him.

"You didn't say anything with any substance to it, Elbert. Missy talked about the 'issues' as they say on TV. She was all business. She surprised the people who'd thought she was nothin' but a sexy woman with a little-girl name."

He bristled. "Well, I shouldn't *have* to talk about the 'issues.' Everybody in the county knows me and knows what I'll do."

"Not on the zoning, we don't. You don't have to tell the world, Elbert, or compromise your judicial neutrality, but you do have to promise *me* that you'll stop that zoning change or you're sunk."

"You'll *have* to take a chance on me," he shot back, "or you'll be the one sunk. Missy said enough in her *issues* remarks for you to know she'll vote for it."

That just flew all over her. "So then, we need to come to an agreement, don't we?" She hated that she sounded mad because that verse, "He who angers you, conquers you," was really true. But she was about to slap him upside the head with her purse.

Instead of snapping back, Elbert apologized for being sharp with her. "I didn't mean that, Lilah. Let's just enjoy the day. Two old friends out for a drive. I couldn't be happier."

He turned and flashed her his politician's smile.

"I hope you're not counting on flirting with me to shut me up," she said.

He gave her his sweetest smile.

He drove on for a while. Then, when they were crossing Dog Creek, he said, "Remember when us boys used to dare each other to jump off that bluff?"

She sighed. "Yes. There wasn't a brain in the bunch. That must be where the joke comes from about the four famous last words of so many young Texas men: 'Hey, y'all! Watch this!'"

He chuckled as he followed the S-curve on around onto Old Briscoe Road.

"It's a wonder any of us lived to be twenty-one."

They chatted a little more about high school—he'd been a senior when she was a sophomore—and in the middle of all that reminiscing, he pulled off into the little roadside park where three ancient live oaks stood guard over an historical marker from the War for Texas Independence. He parked, cut off the motor and turned to her.

"Elbert! What are you *doing?*" Lilah said.

He gave her a twinkly grin. "Speaking of high school . . ."

She had to laugh but she was aggravated, too. "We're a little bit old to go parking," she said. "Especially when we're *not* on a date. Now, you start this car this minute."

Good Lord! Didn't he remember kissing her screen door?

He laughed. "Calm down. We're right out here in plain sight of the road," he said. "I brought a picnic so we can have lunch while we talk about politics and zoning laws and all that stuff."

"But, I don't have time . . ."

He'd already unbuckled his seat belt. "Ah," he said, "a pity how we rush through life. Come on, Lilah. Let's enjoy."

He got out and came around to open her door.

Well, after all, the reason she'd come with him was to talk about "politics and zoning laws and all that stuff."

She let him help her out and went with him to open the hatchback.

He handed her a bouquet of flowers in a sturdy vase.

"Lilies for Lilah," he said, giving her that smile again. "Here, let me spread the blanket out over there under that tree and you sit down and relax. Take time to smell the flowers. I'll bring everything else."

"Everything else" turned out to be a basket of

food that included truffles! of all things, and he even had a cooler holding a bottle of champagne.

Lilah sat, astounded, while he unpacked it all.

"Elbert! You've put a great deal of thought—and expense—into this. My goodness gracious! *Why?*"

"I'll be honest—I need your considerable influence thrown to me, you know that. But you are a remarkable woman and a dear friend and I thought you needed a surprise," he said. "A *good* surprise. Don't we all?"

"Well," she said. "I'm purely flabbergasted."

"I can be thoughtful sometimes," he said as he filled a plate for her.

The chicken salad finger sandwiches smelled heavenly. She picked one up and took a bite, moaning with pleasure at the delicate flavor.

It caused a flash of insanity when she wondered if she really would like to take him seriously and have a real romance. Lord help her, no!

"I had Callie's Catering in Brenham make this up for us," he said, clearly pleased as punch with himself. "Because word was bound to leak out ahead of time if I used HGK."

"Well, Callie's great. We'll have to go some to compete with her if and when we get serious about growing our catering service . . ."

He waved that away. "No work talk, now. Let's just enjoy this wonderful day." He opened the champagne and poured it into the glass flutes from the fancy picnic set.

"Try the truffles," he said. "Just a nibble will make you swoon again."

She did and hummed with pleasure at the nutty flavor on her tongue.

As they ate and drank, with the flowers so bright and gorgeous in the center of the blanket, Lilah began to relax. He even took out his phone and used the iPod in it to play some Mozart.

She chuckled. "Merciful heavens, Elbert, you've thought of everything!"

He beamed with pleasure and reached over to touch her hand. She hoped that remark wouldn't cause him to think she was willing to be his date but it had to be said. He'd gone to a whole lot of trouble to please her, whatever his motives.

The road wasn't very busy but from time to time a vehicle passed and the driver honked and waved. Somebody yelled something they didn't quite catch.

Lilah began to tense up again. Lord, the whole town was probably already talking and Shorty would be beyond impossible to deal with.

Why hadn't she refused to get out of the car? Why hadn't she refused to get *in* the car? How silly did this look to everyone, anyhow?

Having a picnic out in public—and before the weather even turned very cool—made them look foolish. People would be talking about them dating, yes, but they'd also be saying that she and the Judge were both getting senile.

She'd never live long enough to live this down. Not if she lived to be a hundred and ten.

But there was nothing she could do about it now.

So she kept her head turned away from the road and let him pour her a little more champagne. Elbert was just starting to tell her about the camping mishaps from his latest trip to hunt elk in Colorado and they were laughing when brakes screeched and tires squealed and the gravel in the turnaround snapped and crunched and flew through the air in all directions.

Lilah stared. Shorty's battered, ancient pickup truck slammed to a stop beside Elbert's shiny new SUV, and the dust swirled over them both like fog.

Mr. Grumbles was out and headed straight for them in a New York minute.

"Hey!" he hollered. "What's goin' on here? How come I'm about to miss the picnic? Lilah, you never told me you had another date with the Judge."

Lilah scrambled up to give him a piece of her mind. This whole stupid dates-and-jealousy thing was beginning to make her fighting mad. First Elbert pushing her into a public spectacle and then Shorty arriving to pitch a fit about it.

Visions of how he'd acted when she was dancing with the Judge ran through her head in a steady stream. That right there proved the man did not have a lick of sense when the old green-eyed monster jealousy got ahold of him.

"Can a person not have five minutes of privacy around here?" she hollered back at him, hands on her hips.

"Well, not if she's making a public spectacle of herself! And five minutes is plenty of time for her to step into some serious trouble."

"I'm here to save the county, you hardheaded hillbilly . . ."

"Ugh! Uh. Oomph, uh, *oh my* . . ." came from behind her.

Lilah whirled around to see the Judge half-up and half-down, frozen all spraddled out falling over on his face, holding up with one hand and reaching in vain for something to pull up on with the other. She ran around the blanket full of food and flowers to grab his arm but he was way too heavy for her to lift.

"Shorty!" she yelled. "Get over here and help me. Oh, Elbert, how did you get in such a fix so fast?"

". . . foot hung up," he grunted. "Tangled in the other one . . ."

Shorty got to them and he and Lilah together managed to hold the Judge until he could get one knee under him and they steadied him until he could get the other leg out. Then he straightened up, Shorty turned loose and Elbert sat flat down with a plop.

"Shorty!" he said. "Thanks, old buddy. Sit down, sit down. Here, have some sandwiches. Have some truffles."

He reached for the big picnic basket and pulled out another plate and a glass. "It's good this thing came equipped with four of everything," he said. "Shorty, here's some champagne, too."

Shorty said, "Why, Elbert. Looks like Lilah's got you drunk. That's what tangled your feet up, is what I'm thinkin'. Am I right or what?"

"You are! That woman's a caution. I never know what she'll do next."

"Me neither, buddy. She's knocked my socks right off me more times than I can tell you. Even with my shoes on!"

Both men guffawed while Shorty held the glass and Elbert poured. They smiled at each other and then at her, neither one paying one bit of attention to her most ferocious glare.

"Hey, well, *all right,*" Shorty said, sitting down where Lilah had been. "Thanks. I'd love nothin' better than to join y'all.

"This is *nice,*" he said, inhaling a finger sandwich in one bite. "Why, looky here. Flowers and chocolates both."

Shorty took a big swig of champagne and slapped his knee. "Hot dog! I got here just in time." He looked at the truffles. "And what's this here?"

"Have one," Elbert said, "they're truffles."

"Like what them pigs digs up like acorns? In France or one o' them countries over there across the pond?"

"That's it," said the Judge. "Have one."

Shorty picked one up and tossed it into his mouth. "Umm," he said, chewing. "Not bad. Not bad at all."

"Most times you sorta nibble 'em," Elbert said, demonstrating.

"No!" Shorty roared. "No. Look, try it this way, Judge."

He popped the whole thing in like he did the first one and smiled like a possum as he ate it.

Elbert did the same thing and laughed so loud that Lilah realized Shorty might be right that the Judge'd had too much to drink. She just stood there, shaking her head in disgust. Men.

If she ever again, *ever,* had even the faintest glimmer of a thought that she'd like to have a real romance with either one of these clod-hopping morons, she'd tell Meri to go ahead and send her to the old folks' home that very day.

And Shorty didn't even have the excuse of too much to drink. He was just acting the fool.

"You know," he mumbled with his mouth full— as if he had the manners of a goat, which he did not—"javelinas're thick on the ground around here. Reckon they could dig us up any of these things?"

The Judge threw back his head and guffawed.

Lilah lifted her eyes to heaven.

Oh, Ed, why did you have to go? Just look at these clowns I'm left with down here!

How could these two act like this when she'd come out here to talk about something as important as the zoning?

She turned on her heel and headed for Shorty's truck.

She got in, fired it up and threw gravel all over the world on her way out onto the road.

She could only hope it flew far enough to shower the two yahoos sitting on the blanket.

Twenty-three

The road was empty right then, except for him, and Gideon Burkett drove slowly for once, enjoying the slightly cooler air on his way to town to pick up feed. Passing Honey Grove Farm had started him thinking about Meri and Caleb again, which he did a lot, lately. When his twin had trouble, so did he.

It'd always been like that. When they were little, if one of them got sick, the other did, too, in sympathy. But what could he do to help his brother now?

Usually, Cale was ready to move on after one of his romances fell apart but the whole time since Meri'd made the break with him, he'd been miserable, whether he admitted it or not. Maybe he and Gid were destined never to marry.

Their parents' marriage made the whole idea look unappealing. Their two older brothers, who lived in other counties managing other Burkett business enterprises, hadn't done much better with theirs than Jake and Dulcie. Aaron had stayed married to his first wife for the children's sake, but he was a philanderer like Jake. Tate had been married so many times Gid had lost count.

He shook his head to clear it and tried to concentrate on driving. Because his speed was 50 mph instead of his customary 70, he noticed the SUV parked at the historical monument. No one ever stopped there, so, as any Rock County citizen would do, he looked past the car to see if it belonged to anyone he knew and what that person was doing here. He slowed to get a good look.

The *Judge?* Yes, this was his new vehicle.

And there he was. With . . . *Shorty Grumbles?*

What the hell? The first thing that crossed his mind was some kind of a fight, a let's-step-outside-to-settle-our-differences kind of a meeting because, the way Gid heard it, lately they'd been crossways with each other.

But there was no other vehicle there. Where was Shorty's truck? They must've come out here together.

For a *picnic?*

He slowed to a crawl, aware that he was craning

his neck out the window gaping like Doreen Semples would've done, but he didn't even care.

What? Champagne flutes and them making a toast? A bouquet of flowers, for God's sake? A whole spread of food? Picnicking like a pair of lovers.

Gideon stared, blinked, looked again. He was losing either his eyesight or his mind.

He stepped on the brake. The whole world had gone crazy.

There was no mistaking what he was seeing. They had a big, two-handled woven basket for the food—like you see in the movies—and a silver cooler for the champagne. This could be Hollywood, but not Rock County.

He tried to think he was hallucinating. But their loud laughter came floating to him on the wind and it was as real as the steering wheel in his hands.

There was a bottle in front of the Judge and another one sticking up out of the cooler. Those two old coots were drunk as skunks.

He'd never heard anything about either of them drinking too much, not that he could recall in the shock of the moment.

Gideon was no kind of gossip. Anyone who knew him would tell you he was naturally tight-lipped with his own news and everybody else's.

But, to his own surprise, he took one long look back over his shoulder and floored the old flatbed ranch truck. It roared on up the road with a mind of its own. As he came off the S-curve at Dog Creek, he made a hard right into the parking lot at Leroy's Beer, Bait and Ammo, braked fast and jammed it into park.

He still could not believe the images seared on his eyeballs. Maybe somebody else had come up Old Briscoe Road, too, and could confirm what he'd seen.

He jumped out of the truck, strode to the door and pushed his way through it into the roomful of thirsty, sweaty men who were grateful to get a sandwich and a drink and thirty minutes in the cool before they went back to work in the sun.

"Hey, boys," Gid hollered. "Y'all won't believe what I've just seen."

Ten minutes later, Lilah parked Shorty's truck on the Square and got out. Her feet had no more than hit the ground when the HGK café door swung open and Doreen hollered at her, even though she was hobbling out to meet her. The bouquet of lilies had become two dozen red roses.

Caleb heard it from Gideon, of course, so he wasn't surprised when he walked into Pete Suggs' diner the next morning to get some breakfast and found all the regulars having a high old time giving Shorty hell about his "date" with the Judge. One of them was Jake.

Well, damn. All Caleb wanted was to wake up

and get some coffee and a decent breakfast in him before the hardware store opened. He didn't want to think, not about anything emotional, not for one millisecond, and he didn't have time for it, anyhow. He had to do the errands fast and get back because they were building fence today and the help that was supposed to show up was lazy as hell. If he was five minutes late getting home, those two boys would be long gone.

If they'd showed up in the first place. Plus he had to check all the cattle again to make sure there were no more sick ones. Thank God, the ones he'd doctored were still getting better, so, most likely, none of them would die.

Cale headed for the booth farthest away from the groups clustered around the tables in the middle of the room. If he could get Sandy Lee over here pretty quick to take his order, at least maybe he wouldn't have to deal with Jake on an empty stomach. He prayed Jake was still too mad to speak to him.

It hit him then, like a fist to the gut: he was aching to leave town. His whole body, mind and soul was screaming to take off and leave Rock County in the dust like he usually did after a breakup with a woman or a major fight with Jake.

Drive fast on the open road. See all new country. Head up to Wyoming and find that outfitter . . . he had the guy's name and number written down someplace . . . and go deep into the high country if there wasn't too much snow already.

Bubba Watson's loud voice shattered that fantasy as Caleb slid into an empty booth.

"I think Miss Lilah's a whole lot prettier than the Judge. I don't see why you'd trade her in for him."

"Me, neither," his cousin Junior chimed in. "Shorty, have you had your eyes checked lately?"

"Why don't you two loudmouths mind your own business?"

Shorty sounded pretty irritated. This'd probably been going on ever since he came into the place and Shorty usually got here around the time Pete opened up.

Caleb grinned to himself, visualizing Shorty and the Judge picnicking on the side of the road. He hadn't seen Gid laugh that much for a long time as when he came out to Indian River to tell Caleb what he'd seen.

They both had laughed. Cale had to admit he'd felt quite a bit better afterward. Maybe there was hope for him yet. Maybe he wasn't going to fall apart over Meri, after all.

The conversation seemed to be general. From another table, Tol Weddle, who stopped by Pete's every day to catch the gossip there bcfore he moved on to hang out at the Dairy Queen for the rest of the morning, piped up with, "I jist cain't wait to talk to Miss Lilah. I'm wondering how she feels about bein' thrown over for ol' Elbert. I'm bettin' she has hurt feelin's over it and that's a cryin' shame."

He twisted around in his chair to look at Caleb. "I wager she's jealous, ain't she, Cale? She said anything to you yet about how broke her heart is?"

Caleb could pretend not to hear that, since Sandy Lee had just appeared at his booth with the coffeepot and her order pad. He didn't want to get into this if he could help it. It was nothing but a lot of hot air—the question was whether poor ol' Shorty could take it. He was looking pretty aggravated right now.

"Hey, sugar. You want the usual?"

Caleb nodded. "Heavy on the jalapeños."

Sandy shook her head. "Gotta wake up somehow. This coffee'll help you, too, 'til I can get back with the peppers."

She patted him on the shoulder and trotted off to give the order to Pete. You had to hand it to her. She must be seventy years old but she still worked as hard and fast as she ever did.

Caleb sipped his coffee. He'd always liked Sandy Lee and she'd always liked him, too. Sometimes a little town was nice.

But sometimes not so much. Once there ever was a good joke, like this with Shorty and the Judge, it lived forever and in the beginning everybody had to get in on the fun. In Rock Springs you could keep on breathing until you were a hundred and never live down anything you did since birth. Caleb could speak from experience on that.

"That's enough," Shorty growled. "None of you comedians is funny enough to be on TV, so shut your traps."

Maybe Shorty would get up and punch Tol in the nose and that'd give all the gossiping bums something new to jaw about.

Whatever happened to talk about the county fair? Usually, this time of year, it was the news. Hadn't anybody brought in a one-hundred-pound watermelon or an albino calf or a champion steer that was so fine everybody was talking bulls and bloodlines? Why weren't they talking about Indian River's new bull and his bloodlines?

Cale picked up a folded newspaper somebody had left on the table and started flipping through it.

"Well. If it isn't my do-nothing son," Jake said. "Never done a damn thing in his life, never made anything of himself. No initiative, no git-up-and-go, no work ethic. No rancher, that's for sure."

He slid into the other side of the booth.

"I shoulda *named* you Do-Nothing. I knew when your mother named you twins from the Bible that *you* wouldn't turn out to be no Old Testament hero."

This was good. This was *great. Perfect.* He needed to be reminded of the most powerful reason he wasn't already gone to the cool mountains of Wyoming. He was in Texas and he would be here until Indian River was established as a self-sustaining, working ranch or he died. One or the other.

And it was good that the wounds from those old, familiar words of Jake's had grown scars so thick they didn't hurt anymore.

Caleb dropped the paper and gave him a blank look. "What can I help you with this time, Jake?"

Jake snorted. "As if you *ever* helped me or did what I told you."

Sandy Lee brought Jake a fresh coffee cup and poured. Refilled Caleb's.

"Whatsa matter, Grumbles?" Jim was saying. "You can't take a little razzin'? You can dish it out but you can't take it. Ain't that right?"

"Leave Lilah out of this," Shorty said, his voice trembling with anger. "Or we're gonna step outside."

Cale would keep an ear open in that direction just in case Shorty needed his help.

"Can't run a ranch from a booth in a café," Jake said. "And you must be spread pretty thin what with the Kitchens and all. I'm lookin' for Indian River to come up bankrupt any day now. Might get it cheap at auction."

Caleb couldn't resist taunting him in return. "Since you couldn't do it the first time?"

"Because my own sneaking, underhanded *son*

bought it out from under me," Jake growled. "Such a tree-huggin', save-the-earth, anti-progress hippie that you'd knife your own dad in the back."

Cale let Jake see his disdain. "What do you want this time, *Dad?*"

"For you to do one small thing to help your mother."

He hit Caleb with his hardest look.

"It's the least you can do for me since you robbed me of big money."

Cale wanted to say it was a pleasure, but he'd promised himself that he was *not* going to get into this with Jake again. He wasn't proud of what he'd done in an impulsive strike of revenge—it *had* been sneaky and underhanded to outbid his father for the land he wanted—but Caleb was still glad that he'd saved the historic ranch from development.

He shrugged. "People oughtta save a few places from the past."

"So you owe me," Jake said. "Dulcie's quit cooking. Talk to her, will you?"

Caleb stared at him. "Now that's a stretch, even for you, Jake. How's that a small thing to help my mother? You want her cooking *your* meals again, but it's for *her* good? How d'you figure that?"

"It's always better for her when things are on an even keel. The usual routine. Everything normal. All this hanging out down at the river doing nothing but messing with those paints or watercolors or whatever the hell they are is making her weird."

"How so?"

"She doesn't want to talk to me. She acts like she forgets when it's mealtime. She's sad. Maybe depressed, I'm thinking."

Caleb stared at him. "Hel-lo! *You're* the one I need to talk to. When I see her, she's fine. She just doesn't want to talk to you. Or cook for you. You're reaping what you've sowed, my man."

Jake's eyes widened in surprise. He glared. "You shut your mouth. It's *my* marriage. You don't know a damn thing about it."

I know a hell of a lot more about it than I ever wanted to know.

It nearly choked him, but Caleb held the words back. He said, in the softest voice he could muster, "For now, how about you heading on out so I can have my breakfast in peace? You are absolutely right. It's your marriage and you'll have to be the one to fix it. If you can."

He went back to the newspaper.

Jake got up and left, banging the door as he went. A short silence fell and Caleb felt eyes flick to him.

But then the noise started up and it was all about Shorty again.

Sandy Lee served Caleb's omelet and he began to eat.

"Who bought the roses?" Bubba wanted to know. "You bring 'em to the Judge or did he bring 'em to you?"

Shorty stood up so fast he knocked over his chair. "You wanna watch what you say, Bubba boy," he said. "Come on. Let's take it outside."

Caleb laid down his fork. Bubba was actually getting up, although he had thirty years and probably sixty pounds on Shorty. And not enough decency to refuse to fight an old man.

But Cale didn't have to worry. Sandy Lee signaled Pete and he put down his spatula and came out of the kitchen to settle them all down.

Bubba and Junior left. Right after that, Shorty did, too, lifting a hand to Caleb as he went out the door. Evidently, he didn't want to talk to anybody right then, and Caleb could understand that.

He felt the same way. He forced himself to shovel the fuel into his body because he had a long, grueling day ahead but there was a rock in his gut as big as Dallas.

He'd been wrong. The scars on the old wounds weren't quite as healed as he'd thought.

He finished eating and took out his cell phone as he downed another cup of coffee. He had to talk to Gideon. He had to get this out of his system.

But the phone rang and rang. No telling where Gid was or what he was doing. There were parts of the ranch where the cell tower signal didn't reach.

Caleb finished the coffee, got up and threw some bills on the table. It wasn't until he was walking out the door, lifting a hand to acknowledge Pete's calling to him to have a good day, that the truth hit him.

He didn't care if he could get ahold of Gid or not. It was Meri he wanted.

He couldn't talk to anyone but Meri.

Meri paced the tiny office at HGK and pondered the taste of the apple she'd just sliced. She took another bite. It was pleasant enough, but not strong and definitely *not* tart.

She sent Lilah a text.

She tried another piece, chewed, swallowed and sighed. They couldn't use these. It'd be a huge mess, but the supplier would have to take them back. Meri had told them *tart*. These were not.

Through the open door she heard Jewel's voice out in the kitchen.

"Hey, there, Caleb. Long time no see."

Meri's breath caught in her chest. *Oh. Caleb.*

Just hearing his name, just *thinking* his name, shook her composure. She hated that. She should be stronger than this.

"Hey, Jewel. How's it going?"

The silky, low sound of his voice was worse, much worse, than hearing his name. It made her forget about everything but him.

What was she ever going to do? Somehow,

weirdly, waiting for him to come into the room was as hard as walking away from him and driving herself home.

You should've kept your guard up. You should never have felt such sympathy and wanted to help him so much that you jumped into his truck. You should control your emotions.

She tried to put her mind in control of her body while she waited for him to appear.

But I'm not waiting for him. Really, I'm not.

She had work to do. This wasn't Indian River or Honey Grove. This was business at HGK with urgent decisions to be made. This was the perfect time to prove they could have a business relationship that wasn't affected by the personal one.

It was great timing, actually, since the partners needed to know that she was going to return these apples.

When Caleb appeared in the doorway, Meri kept her mind on the apples. Almost entirely.

She'd forgotten how he could fill up a room just by walking into it. Today, in addition to that, he brought a tension to match her own.

And he didn't even know about the apples. Oh! What was wrong? He certainly didn't need any more troubles on top of his sick calves.

"Hey, Mer."

She tried for a businesslike half-smile, but it didn't work. He was holding in some kind of strong emotion. It wasn't about her. She wanted to know what was wrong.

But his greeting had been in a distant tone, so she wasn't going to ask. He was trying to keep it all business, as she'd asked him to do, and they did have business to attend to.

"Caleb. Good timing. I was just going to call you."

She offered the plate of apple slices and held it between them. "Have a piece, please, and describe the taste in one word."

"You writin' a poem? Makin' an ad?"

"I wish. I think we're going to have to send them back."

"Oh, no!" he teased. "You saying we got something here that's not perfect?"

She rolled her eyes, but she couldn't help smiling a little in spite of her worry. "One word, Caleb. Please."

He took a bite and savored it. Raised his eyebrows with a half-shrug.

"Sweet."

"Right! That's why I'm thinking we should send them back."

He swallowed. When he spoke, his tone was shocked. "All those crates out there?"

"Yes. I specifically ordered tart. These turnovers need tart."

He reached for another slice. Her eyes betrayed her by lingering on his tanned, work-worn hand.

His hands were almost as beautiful as his mouth.

He ate that slice, too. "No, they're fine. Most people like sweet."

"Not in this recipe, they don't. Really, Cale, any apple dessert needs tart apples to balance the sugar. Otherwise, they're too sweet."

"That's Lilah and Jewel's territory. I came by to talk to you. Let's take a little drive."

Her heart whirled in a circle.

She wanted to know what was upsetting him, didn't she? She wanted to comfort him.

"Oh, I wish I could, Caleb. I really do. But right now we have a crisis here.

"I have to find some tart apples with a taste that'll balance with the honey glaze."

"Leave it off."

"The customer specifically asked for it."

She tried to make her tone very firm, but somewhere, deep inside, the sensual Meri was throwing the plate of apple slices over her shoulder and running out to throw herself into his truck yet again.

Because his tone when he asked her was so natural, so right, so . . . like it all used to be between them.

The businesswoman Meri screamed: *Get this work done.*

"They ordered honey glaze, Cale. All we need is tart apples. We have to get these turnovers into production."

He gave her a long look. "Meri, get real. These are apples. They're firm and healthy and sweet, plenty good enough to put in any apple pastry."

Her whole weak body was leaning toward him. She was losing her mind.

"Morning Moments is our pathway to growth when we're ready to expand. They're our biggest client. The products we make for them need to be perfect."

He grunted. "Let me clue you in, babe. That's a lost cause. Nothin's perfect. You should know that by now."

She ignored that. "Oh, I know! If we could haul them back to Winthrop's Farm ourselves, that'll save the shipping fee and . . ."

He made a disgusted face. "Don't start a big ruckus. You'll build up a lot of bad will because they won't want to take them back. They'd have a right to sue us, even, because there's nothing wrong with these apples."

Her phone beeped in her hand. She looked at it.

"Lilah," she said, "answering my text. She thinks we can add lemon zest and lemon juice to the recipe . . ."

"Great!" Caleb said. "*Perfect,* as you yourself would say. Now. Why don't you give Jewel that message and let's go somewhere we can talk. I need—"

"But I don't agree. Lemon might help but it wouldn't be the same as the samples we sent to make this sale. Oh, Cale, we have so much invested here! We can't afford to . . ."

His blue eyes turned stormy.

"You're always telling me to get more involved in HGK. Well, here I am. We can't afford to buy more and waste these," he said, his tone flat with authority. "And we can't afford to offend our suppliers. Sending these back could cause bad blood we'd never get past."

"Well, I don't know about that . . ."

"You don't know is exactly right. There are people out there who'll vote against a candidate whose family had trouble with their family four generations ago. We can't afford to start a feud. It would not only lose customers for us but suppliers, too."

Meri shook her head.

He tried again. "We'd have to keep these and buy more. We can't freeze them, obviously. And we don't have the personnel lined up right now to process them for drying."

"I want these pastries to be perfect."

"They will be. Listen to me and Lilah."

When she didn't respond, he went on, his tone getting angrier and angrier.

"If you're gonna be this picky you oughtta drive around all over the country sampling apples in person before you order them. And even then, you wouldn't know if all of any variety would taste exactly like the one you sampled."

He shook his head at her as if she should know better.

"I can't believe this," he lectured. "Not when every time I talk to you, you're all worked up about expenses and how much salaries cost and can we possibly keep on doing as well as our amazing start-up."

She stared at him stubbornly. "Don't patronize me."

He shook his head in disgust. "You're the one supposed to have the head for business around here."

"How can you be so dense?"

"*Me?* You're the mule."

They glared at each other. For two long heartbeats.

Then Caleb leaned back and stuck two fingers into the coin pocket of his jeans. He pulled out a quarter and held it up as he took a step toward her.

Meri drew in a ragged breath that carried the heady scent of him into her blood and spread it through her body.

"Here's your only chance. As you might recall, Attorney Briscoe, the contract for partnership in Honey Grove Kitchens reads that when two partners out of three agree on a decision, then that's what we'll do. Me and Lilah are all about a dab of lemon juice and a sprinkle of lemon zest on the apples we have."

Meri gritted her teeth and tried to keep a

confident face. But a coin toss was her only hope.

There was no way Lilah would change her mind. Not only had Meri spent hours worrying about extra expenses to her grandmother, Lilah always thought she was the last word about any recipe. She had the solution and she expected them to use it.

Thoroughly thwarted, anger surged through Meri. Along with a dozen other, more complicated feelings forming a whirlpool, pulling her in.

"Call it," he said.

"Heads."

He flipped the coin but before it even hit the floor, he took her face in his hands and kissed her.

Twenty-four

The shock of it stunned her. The heat, his scent, the strength of his hands, the feel of his mouth on hers. Her Morning Moments worry hung on for a nanosecond more and a sharp awareness of the rift between them touched her mind in the first instant he touched her, but his mouth was so sweet and intense that they melted away and the rest of her mind with them. Nothing was left of her but her body which had been deprived of this for far too long.

She was starving for this. She'd been waiting for this and didn't know it.

One step forward to take hold of her and she

was off the ground, lost in a whole new world where she was safe in his arms. Every inch of her drank him in. All that mattered was holding on to him. Her arms wrapped themselves around his neck and she kissed him back with a matching passion.

His kiss felt so intense, almost angry. Her blood pulsed hard underneath her skin and set her heart beating twice as fast.

When they had no more breath and he tore his mouth away, he still held her wrapped in his arms. She clung there, his heart pounding deep inside, his wide, warm chest in rhythm with his slowing breath.

Caleb. He rested his chin on the top of her head and held her, rocking slightly back and forth. She wouldn't open her eyes. She couldn't bear to see the real world. Already, the guards of her heart were rousing to natter at her.

Be careful. You two are supposed to be on break. You've thought this through, over and over again. He's not perfect for you, remember?

Her legs wouldn't move enough to step out of his embrace and her arms wouldn't drop away from his solid warmth, but she pulled back enough to look at him. His eyes were as stormy as she'd ever seen them.

"Meri?"

Jewel's raspy voice brought her back to reality. The kitchen manager, blushing, stood in the doorway but only for a second. "Sorry," she said, and vanished.

Meri blinked as her mind began to work again. "The apples! I have to tell Jewel what to do about the apples."

"Tell her and let's get out of here."

Her stomach clutched. "But the pastries . . . it's for Morning Moments . . . I need to be here . . . these apples aren't tart . . ."

"We settled that," he said. "Where's the quarter?"

They began looking for the coin. "Maybe I won," she said. "Maybe—"

"We've fixed that."

Standing up from looking under the desk to scan the rest of the floor, he sent her a straight look.

"No," she said. "If I won the toss, we send these apples back."

He spotted the quarter under the window, glinting in a streak of sunlight. She followed his gaze and ran to it. Tails.

"Oh, no . . ." she said. "Caleb? . . ."

"Don't even start," he said, taking her by the arms to turn her to look at him. "One second chance is all you get. I need to talk to you. Where's your bag? Let's go."

His eyes were like deep water in turmoil. She felt his restlessness the same way she'd felt his weariness before.

Is this what love was? Hurting when he hurt? Hurting *because* he hurt?

"Talk about what?"

Perhaps not. Maybe she was just becoming a better person and thinking of the feelings of others.

Her heart lurched. Something was wrong with her. She wasn't even fighting for different apples.

Did it mean she didn't care as much about HGK as about what happened with Caleb?

She picked up her bag off the desk and he escorted her ahead of him, hovering as if she might try to escape.

Something was wrong with her. The stab of resentment she always felt at losing hardly existed. Did she even care that the pastries might not turn out to be good enough to please the people at Morning Moments?

She could barely think. She was still tasting the kiss.

She walked fast down the hall and through the kitchen, aware of Caleb at her side every second, slowing only to say, "Jewel, we've decided to use these apples we have and add some lemon juice and zest. Would you please call Gran and work out the proportions with her?"

Jewel shot them a narrow, assessing look. Her cheeks were still pink from embarrassment. "Will do," she said. "Anything else?"

Meri shook her head no. She didn't even know when she'd be back to work. Couldn't think of anything else HGK needed or would ever need.

She truly didn't know herself anymore.

But you do know Caleb and he hasn't changed. You can't make a practice of being as irresponsible about HGK as he is.

Caleb handed her up into his truck, got behind the wheel, and turned the key in the starter.

"Thanks for coming," he said gruffly, as he backed it, crunching, onto the gravel from the grass under the big tree that grew behind the HGK building. "I know it's not easy for you to leave them to it."

He was so tense the air around him was charged. She could smell the thin sheen of sweat that shone on his skin.

"It's all right," she said, "I think this must be more important."

He threw her a quick glance as if to check her sincerity.

"Something's wrong with me," he said. "I can't talk to anybody else. Not even Gid. I realized that when I was coming out of Pete's a little while ago."

The raw pain in his voice went so deep it stunned her.

And so did the words.

I can't talk to anybody else.

No one had ever said that to her before. Except when it concerned her legal skills or her business sense.

He needed her for *herself.*

She'd never known how to give comfort. She'd hardly ever tried. She'd always been too busy trying to survive. Too busy trying to comfort herself.

She took a deep breath. "Tell me," she said, searching her memory for some of the things Lilah had said to her that day she'd found Meri crying over Caleb in the barn. "You'll feel better if you get it out of your system."

"It's nothin' but the same-old, same-old," he said, to the windshield. "I thought it couldn't touch me anymore and then I thought I could keep it to myself. I can't."

But then he stopped talking. He drove faster.

"Your dad?"

"What did you hear? Even in Rock Springs, that's pretty damn fast for word to get around."

"Nobody told me. I'm guessing."

Caleb sighed. "God knows I need your help. I want to kill him."

His knuckles were white on the wheel, his biceps tight under the sleeves of the Indian River logoed tee he wore. She'd never seen him like this. Usually she was the tense one and he tried to tease her out of it.

He was driving too fast when he turned out onto FM 2317. She was going to have to step up and comfort him whether she knew how or not.

"Well, I don't know," she drawled, trying to lighten things up. "If we should get caught in a conspiracy to murder, I'll never be able to take the Texas Bar Exam. If HGK doesn't make it I'll need to practice law again someday."

It worked. Marginally. He did relax a little and he threw her a sketch of a grin.

She was surprised at how gratifying that was. Maybe she wasn't so awkward, after all.

"Well, then," he drawled, "you'd best forget about law and bear down hard on your farmin' and bakin'."

They headed east, toward Indian River. He was hurting, so he was going home.

She could do that, too, for the first time in her life. Honey Grove was a comfort. Or maybe it was that Lilah was there to comfort her.

"Second thought, let's not," Cale said suddenly. "He's not worth the prison time."

"Exactly."

He slanted a sideways glance at her.

"No, wait. Maybe we spoke too soon. Come to think of it, the prosecution could never find a jury in Rock County that'd convict me. No matter who they put on it, there'd be at least one person that'd hang the jury for the guilty side."

"How can you know that?"

"Jake's got an enemy under every rock. He's skinned everybody, one way or another. There's no love lost between him and *any* twelve of his peers. No matter who you talk to, he's not their favorite businessman around town."

"Don't bet your life on it," she said, and he actually chuckled.

The sound warmed her.

But then his face darkened and set into such hard lines he looked like a stranger.

"I tell you, Mer, sometimes I have such a rage in me I could wreck the world. I feel just as helpless as I did when I was six years old. I hated the way Jake was to us boys, me in particular, but even more how he treated my mom. And now he's bad-mouthing her for not cooking his meals."

"I'm trying to imagine your childhood," she said. "Mine was that I always dreamed about having a father who lived with us and a mother who cooked."

He kept his foot down on the accelerator and they almost flew along the road. Thank goodness there was little traffic right now.

"Well, I had that and I can tell you those two things don't make your life *Leave It To Beaver*. I wanted to kill him then, too. To protect my mother. Her life would've been so different without him."

Meri asked quietly, "Does he abuse her?"

"Emotionally. Sometimes verbally. I've warned him. I would've stepped in long ago if it'd ever been physical. So would Gid."

"What about your older brothers?"

"Them, too. I guess. Oh, I don't know. Aaron and Tate were his favorites. He always treated them differently from us twins, but Gid not so much. I was his whipping boy."

The pain in his voice made her suck in a long breath.

It made her hurt for him and herself as a child, too.

"I should have done *something,* anyway."

"No," she said softly. "No, Cale. Don't think like that. She has to protect herself. She could leave him."

"She won't. The ranch is her home. She loves that place, the river, the trees, that land. She loved us kids, too, and she didn't want to take us away from it when we were growing up."

His pain was stirring her own, even hidden as it was behind the wall she'd built to hold it in.

"At least that's a better reason than Edie Jo's," Meri said. "She stayed every time, with every new man, for only a dream—that he'd be the one with money who'd take care of her and give her a lavish lifestyle or that he'd be the one who could make her a star 'on stage or screen.'"

"Did they hit her?"

"Mostly not. Mostly it was just that she ceded control of her own life—and *mine*—to one man after another for a dream that wasn't even real and would never be. I told her that when I got older. I was sick with fury when I realized it."

"You were young to be so smart," he said. "Fourteen when she left you, right?"

"Yes. For years, after I realized she'd abandoned me, I always thought it was because I'd told her that truth—said it out loud and burst her balloon. But now I know it wasn't. My opinion didn't mean that much. She always called me a stupid kid. Ironic, when I was the real adult in our little faux-family."

She stopped. Took a long breath. Incredibly, it still hurt—too much—to talk about her mother.

"I couldn't have changed her life. Only she could. Caleb, you need to stop beating yourself up over not doing something that was impossible."

He shrugged and drove faster. "I know you're right. And I could never kill Jake. But I *could* smash his smug face."

He turned and looked at her for so long she was torn between holding his gaze and looking for traffic ahead. She took a quick look at the road. Empty. They were almost to his turnoff.

"Sometimes I want to kill him. Sometimes I wish he . . ."

Meri waited. Then she said, ". . . loves you."

One look. Hurt, longing, knowledge, acceptance, regret, rage—all tangled in him.

He stared out the windshield again. "Usually I'd hit the road. Now I can't."

Her stomach cratered and her nagging voices woke in her head.

Why can't you? Do you care for me that much? That you'd stay?

You shouldn't've even thought that. Of course not. Nobody ever stays for you, Meri.

"I don't like to let him get to me but I can't seem to help it. I thought I was past all that but this morning, in Pete Suggs' place, I came so close to hitting him that it made me sick to my stomach. Sick not to do it and sick that I wanted to so much."

He stared into the long distance down the road.

"If I punched him out in public it'd only hurt my mother that much more."

"Lilah tells me I'll feel better if I talk about whatever's bothering me. And I do feel better. Crying helps, too, and it's all right for a man to cry. Do that. Get it out of you and then you can be cool when you see him."

He gave a rough laugh. "I couldn't cry if you held a gun to my head. What I do is move on."

Meri blurted, "But you *can't* . . ." She bit her lip and stopped herself.

What? He'd stay just because he said she was the only one he could talk to?

He threw her one of his piercing glances as they drove across the low-water bridge.

"Can't what, Mer?"

She tried to look away. She couldn't.

"*You* said you can't leave. I assumed it was because of Indian River."

"And HGK."

While he was talking, would he say how much

he'd missed her during this break? Her breath caught. Would he say again that he loved her, as he'd been so quick to do when their romance first began?

He drove slowly now, looking out for his cows that might be in the road.

"Yeah, I've gotten into too much this time," he said, in a tone that sounded as if he were talking to himself. "HGK, yes, but you and Lilah are running it anyway."

So it's you, Meri, I can't leave. You're the only one I can talk to and the only one I can't leave.

But that was not what he said.

"It's Indian River that's got me tied down. Sometimes I look around and I don't even know how I got here."

Somehow, she had a knot in her stomach now. She didn't even know if she could speak. She seemed to have no breath.

Which was ridiculous. She had never had such unrealistic fantasies in her life. One kiss, no matter how powerful, didn't necessarily change things. Maybe she was the only person he could talk to about his father and the only one he could kiss on a moment's notice.

(Well, she had to admit that Ronnie Rae probably wouldn't mind a sudden kiss from Caleb. Maybe he'd have kissed her instead if she'd happened to be in town between Pete Suggs' Diner and HGK.)

Meri. You should've stayed at work and taken care of business. You're losing your mind.

She said, "The way I hear it, you got here by way of a secret move for revenge."

He nodded. "Lilah said I shouldn't have stooped so low."

Then he shrugged and flashed his irresistible grin. "Unintentioned consequences. Gotta be careful what you wish for."

"But it's the real way to kill Jake. Prove him wrong when he says you'll never make a rancher and he'll have to stop saying it."

Caleb's whole face changed and his look went sharp.

"How do you know he said that?"

"I heard it around town," she said, as a million wild, warring feelings rose in her heart. She added softly, "*You* didn't tell me, remember?"

Now he stared at her with his old way of seeing right through her. Once again, he was reading her feelings and getting it right.

"Something like that's hard on a man's pride. He doesn't want the woman he loves to hear that."

What does that mean? He loved me then?

He still didn't tell me. I'm the one who brought it up. So he loves me now?

He looked back at the ranch road, then, driving even more slowly. He kept his eyes on the road.

Heat flowed into her cheeks. She felt unsteady, as if the truck rocked beneath her. It didn't.

All her agony had taught her to stay away from even the subject of love.

She had a long list of incidents that proved he didn't love her. She'd decided that the break would be permanent, so their love, if it was ever that, wasn't strong enough to keep them together. All their troubles proved their relationship wasn't perfect and wasn't meant to be.

He'd never said *love* since that very first time and she had never said it to him. Since the fiasco with Tim she didn't even know what *love* meant in relation to her feelings. She shouldn't even be thinking about it at this time in her life. She had far too much to do and too many responsibilities to take on a relationship she didn't even understand.

She looked away from him and looked out the window. She didn't understand men at all. She'd never known how to have a successful relationship with one.

Had she been wrong to react so strongly when he forgot to mail the IRS form?

He jerked the wheel with one hand and drove off the road and out into the pasture.

"What are you doing? Where are we going?"

"Down by the river. There's a spot I've never showed you. I found it one evening riding along the bank."

"You didn't see it before you bought the place?"

He shook his head. "I'd been on it a couple of

times and I knew it'd be a crying shame if developers got it, that's all. Then when I heard the major bidder was Jake . . . well, I couldn't resist the ugly urge to set him down a little."

"Don't beat yourself up too much. Or take Lilah's reproof too much to heart. We all give in to an ugly urge now and then, even Lilah."

He chuckled. Meri loved that sound.

"Yeah, I've seen her lose her temper once in a while."

"With your dad—the problem's not really something wrong with you at all. Not any of it, not when you were a kid and not now. It's a problem he's got that he takes out on you. It's all him. I finally learned that about me and Edie Jo, but I can't always remember it."

"You nailed it. I don't know what started it, but now Jake can't get over the fact I bought this place out from under him. And blindsided him to do it. That chapped his hide so bad, what with him being king of the mountain and all."

She nodded.

"And you and me," he said. "Part of our problems that we blame on each other come from ourselves."

Her heart made a hard, sudden thud.

They bumped over the rough ground in silence.

Finally, he braked and drifted into a slow stop.

He gestured and her gaze followed the sweep of his arm.

The sight made her draw in an involuntary breath. A grove of live oaks grew right at the moving water, bending leafy branches over to see themselves in it, holding on to the grass and mud with gnarled roots that must reach down into the depths of the river.

"These trees've been here since the War for Texas Independence," he said, "probably before. Lilah told me there was a battle here."

"And now it's the most peaceful spot I think I've ever seen," Meri said.

Caleb turned off the motor and reached for an old jacket on the backseat of his truck.

"You can sit on this," he said. "Come on. Let's watch the water and let it wash away the worries. Talk a little bit. Don't talk. Whatever."

She got out before he could come around and open her door. He hated when she did that, but it was as if that place was calling her to come.

He spread out the jacket and they sat. It was wonderful, with the breeze moving softly through the trees and the air not too hot. Meri leaned back against the trunk of one of the huge trees. Somehow, Caleb was right. The water did take her mind away if she let it.

Caleb leaned over and gently took her chin to turn her to face him.

"I said leaving's always been my go-to position. But I'm not doing it. Don't you trust me, Mer? You think I'd bail on you and Lilah like that?"

"Nooo, not really. But . . ."

"I can't blame you for jumping to that conclusion, but I'm here to stay. Jake or no Jake."

He let go and leaned back against the tree, their shoulders touching. Even that small contact warmed her like fire.

"I started running away as a kid because of Jake. Then he wanted me to go to veterinary school and somehow, I did it—"

Meri interrupted. "Oh, yeah. We always want them to love us, no matter what. I used to slave cooking and cleaning whatever pathetic place we lived in, hoping for attention from my mom."

He nodded. "I know. Anyhow, he was betting I'd be a dropout, so I had to graduate. I liked the work all right, but as soon as I graduated I started just drifting because he ordered me to come back here and be his resident veterinarian."

"Oh, no!" she said. "Never."

"Exactly. I loved new scenery, new people, new stories, new jobs . . . always had, the couple of times I hit the road while I was in high school. And I loved learning the hard jobs. The most dangerous jobs in the oil fields were my favorites because they paid more and I was determined to pay Jake back for my education."

"Even though it was his idea?"

"Right. So now, sometimes, I don't like to be tied down but I could never look in a mirror again if I left you and Lilah with all of HGK on your shoulders."

She looked into his blue, blue eyes and believed him.

And her heart hurt because it was true. He would never stay because of her. Nobody would.

He shrugged. "New adventures can't go on forever."

"And you can't leave because you'd be letting Jake win. I don't even know him but I couldn't bear to think about that, whether you were here or not."

That made him grin.

This would be a good time to set out the parameters for their relationship.

She said, "I know I complain that you don't come to HGK enough and do your share, but I have to admit I'm deeply invested in success for this ranch."

"Well, thank you, ma'am," he drawled.

"And I do trust you to be my hero if I ever get in bad trouble," she said. "I think you'd come back, even if you were in Alaska, if I needed you. I've believed that, going against the grain of my natural cynicism, ever since you told me that the first time. Remember? When we went to Taylor's Inn with Lilah and Shorty and you told me that if I ever got in trouble you'd have to rescue me because Lilah is a part of your family."

He smiled and reached to brush back her hair.

She smiled back. "Remember how angry you

were with me? Because you thought I wasn't being good to Lilah?"

He tucked her hair behind her ear, then cupped her neck with his warm hand to caress her jawline with his thumb. He leaned forward and dropped a light kiss on her forehead. He stayed there.

"I remember a lot of things," he said, his lips brushing against her skin.

Okay. That was all right. A kiss on the forehead was just sort of brotherly. Or business-partner-like. Friendly. They would be friends as well as partners in business.

He still didn't move away. He stayed there. So close. So good-smelling. So sexy.

"Believe it," he said, his voice low and strong. "You have any trouble, I'd be there in a New York minute."

A shadow moved across the blue sky of his eyes. "I'm glad you trust me for *something*. I'm sorry I forgot to mail that letter, Meri."

She didn't mean to do it, hadn't even known she was going to move, but she reached up and touched his cheek, trailing her fingertips through the intriguing stubble along his jawline.

In an affectionately friendly gesture.

But then, her hand gathered the front of his tee-shirt and pulled him to her, whispering against his lips, but keeping the subject in the territory of just-friends, "I meant what I said about Indian River. Prove you can do it."

"Don't worry," he whispered back, "it's a done deal. It's gonna take everything I've got, but I'll make Jake eat his words."

Looking deep into her eyes, he ran the tip of one callused finger along the tiny strap of her sundress.

"Everything?" she said, thrilling at the touch of his hands on her skin.

She must've lost all control because she fell helplessly into his deep blue gaze. "I'm sorry to hear that."

He quirked one brow at her. "Well," he drawled. "Maybe not *everything*."

The slight roughness of his fingertip stopped in the hollow of her shoulder and trailed up the side of her neck on a path she'd never known could be so incredibly sensitive. His fingers slipped into her hair, his hand cradled her head. His touch was as gentle as his gaze that would not let hers go.

As if he didn't want to scare her. As if she were someone precious.

His voice was soft, too, but rough with feeling as he half-whispered her name. "Mer," he was saying, "I've missed you. Bad."

The words and his sweet closeness drew the breath out of her in a heartbeat; they turned her blood into a warm, langorous river.

"I missed you, too," she whispered against his lips.

He took her mouth with his, his kiss hard and

sweet. She managed to lift her arms enough to put them around him, then she forgot everything but the hot, wild world of his mouth. Her mind was gone. She smelled his skin.

Caleb. How had she ever thought they could keep everything all business between them? Foolishness, as Gran would say. Pure foolishness.

Their mouths knew each other still, no matter how far apart their minds had been. He took his time, kissing her thoroughly as if to remind her of what she'd been missing.

When they ran out of breath and broke apart, he lifted his head and looked at her, searching her eyes in that way he had. There was no escaping it, ever, when he used it to search her soul.

When he seemed to think that he'd done so, he turned away.

For an instant, she thought, with a wild, crazy racing of her heart, that he was getting up to leave.

Instead, he stretched out full-length on the grass, put his head in her lap and looked out across the grass at the river. Meri waited for him to speak.

"Just what I needed," he said, and her heart did that crazed thing again. Was he talking about the kiss?

No. That was her insecurity demons picking at her. She still tasted its sweet sincerity on her tongue.

"That's not a very romantic remark," she teased. "You certainly didn't seem so clinical at the time."

His slow grin began. "I'm not talking about the kiss, Miss Paranoid."

She actually felt her heart—or maybe it was the world—move as it righted itself on its axis.

Oh! The relief! She'd forgotten what the warm familiarity between them did for her. She hadn't realized such a cold emptiness had been in its place.

Now she felt safe. Almost as safe as when she was in his arms.

"I've been wanting to kiss you for days and days," he said. "I almost always do want to except for the times you're givin' me a good tongue-lashin' lecture."

Heat rose in her cheeks. "I'm sorry if I'm uncivil sometimes," she said. "Gran says I get too shrill. It's just that I'm scared we'll lose everything, Caleb."

"That's how I've been feeling," he said, as his smile faded and his eyes grew serious. "The whole time you've been on this business-only kick."

He put on his most pitiful look. "I feel like I've lost everything when you don't want me to kiss you."

Her heart jumped. Was he going to say it now? For the second time over all these months? *Say you love me.*

"Don't give me that."

His gaze sharpened. The teasing grin came, too, but it didn't touch the penetrating blue eyes.

"So you agree with me? That whole idea of us as business partners only is a bunch of horse hockey? We're back together now?"

He sat up fast and turned to take her by the shoulders, his big hands as hot and intense on her skin as his eyes were on her mind.

"Meri. You can trust me to do my part from now on. I am truly sorry for being careless before."

Her lips parted but she couldn't speak. All she could do was feel his hands on her. She couldn't think in words.

Except to know that he still hadn't said, "I love you."

Twenty-five

"How in the world do other women do this?"

Meri was driven to muttering to herself, which was never a good sign, but she was so nervous about this dinner with Caleb that she couldn't think straight. It wasn't every day she declared to a man that she loved him. In fact, she'd only ever said that once before, to Tim, and then it'd been "I love you, *too*."

She sighed and pushed her hair back from her forehead with her wrist so she wouldn't get chocolate in it—she overdid the amount of milk the first time and splattered frosting everywhere—and kept the mixer whirring.

It still didn't have the right balance of powdered

sugar and milk. The recipe was wrong or the air was too dry, or something.

"I don't think they do," she told her reflection in the window that showed dusk falling faster and faster, so Caleb was due back any minute. "It's a vicious lie, all of it, the magazines, the cooking shows, the movies and their romantic dinners for two."

She *hated* not to be perfect at this. She was going to *make* it be perfect.

She glanced at her checklist. With her free hand, she measured exactly three tablespoons more of the powdered sugar and added it, seeing the minute it landed in the swirling dark frosting that she'd used too much. She reached for the little pitcher of milk.

And added too much.

She gritted her teeth. The heart-shaped cake was cool enough. She had to frost it now so it'd be ready while she made the salad dressing and put the finishing touches on the card table covered with the white cloth she'd bought. And washed. And ironed. It looked fabulous.

Her imagination wanted to run through what furniture they needed to buy first if they got married, but she stopped it. What if this idea was a bad one?

What if Caleb *wasn't* waiting for her to say she loved him before he said that to her again? What if he *didn't* want to get married?

But sometimes they talked about the future and he made remarks that made her think he was planning for them to be together forever. And everything had been so good between them these last few weeks.

He still hadn't actually said the word *marriage,* though. Just as he hadn't repeated that early declaration that he loved her.

When she realized that she couldn't go on and on in limbo as she'd done with Tim for so long, she'd realized with the next heartbeat that never, ever, had she told Caleb she loved him. She'd loved him for a long time, probably since the very beginning, but it was so very hard for her to trust anyone—to trust *life*—enough to say the words out loud.

She'd told herself over and over that it would be better to make a mistake tonight than to live like this. She wanted a home of her own and a family and her biological clock was ticking. She wanted *Caleb.*

They were opposites, yes. But they'd been getting along fantastically well since they'd begun trying to understand each other's personalities and to explain their feelings. They were doing *great.*

She frowned down at the luscious-smelling mixture in the bowl and ran one finger around the edge. Tasted it. Wonderful.

And now it seemed reasonably thick. Lilah had said it would harden a little as it dried on the cake.

So she moved the bowl to one side and pulled the cake plate with one layer closer to the cooling racks holding the other two layers. With all of it in the center of the worktable that she'd dragged out of the living room renovation project, she began to scoop icing onto the first layer of the cake.

It ran more than she'd expected. She scraped up the part that went onto the plate and put it back on top. It ran down faster than she could catch it.

She'd used too much. It was filling the rim of the plate. She worked faster so it wouldn't run off and be wasted. Moving around the table, she tripped over Caleb's long, orange extension cord, bumped into the bowl and sent it spinning almost to the edge on the other side.

Meri caught it, but barely.

Oh! The music. She had to put her phone in the speaker she'd brought, so she could use the iPod.

Bluesy music from Delbert McClinton would be perfect with the candlelight and roses on the table.

The frosting wasn't thickening fast enough.

Outside, a truck door slammed. Too late now.

The lasagna aroma filling the kitchen grew suddenly more powerful. Was that a slightly burned edge it had now?

Meri left the frosting, hopefully to thicken for a minute, and ran to the oven. She pulled open its creaky door and turned it off, then ran to the counter to get the music going.

The front door opened. His boot heels struck the floor. Two steps. Three. Pause to hang his hat on the rack.

"Hey, how come my drill's on the floor?"

More steps. "Meri? Are these . . . *rose petals?*"

She blushed. He sounded incredulous. She was, too, now.

Now she couldn't believe, either, that she'd done something so out-there. Not to mention something that was such a cliché.

She turned as he appeared in the doorway.

He looked at her, questioning, then scanned the room as if he couldn't quite take in what he was seeing. Especially the long, orange extension cord that had been plugged into his drill which now powered the mixer.

A couple of drops of chocolate frosting had fallen onto it. Probably she'd have to scrub down the whole room by the time this eternal, infernal cake was done.

It wasn't like her to make such a mess.

It wasn't like her to plan such an elaborate surprise. She hated surprises for herself. Her stomach clutched.

Most of all, it wasn't like her to take a chance like this.

Could she do it? She had to do it.

Caleb's tense, tired face broke into a grin.

"Well, bar the door," he drawled. "Meri's cooking. What brought this on?"

The cake caught his eye.

"Hey, looks like that icing's about to get away from you."

His teasing grin widened as one rivulet proved him right. It spiraled down and formed a chocolate icicle from the plate's rim to the cloth she'd used to cover the makeshift workspace.

He checked out all three chocolate layers, two of them decidedly lopsided. She hated that. She'd tried so hard to make them perfect.

"Heart-shaped? Roses on the table? I thought Valentine's Day usually comes in February."

His face serious, he looked at her then. "What's the occasion?"

"I love you."

The words came out of their own volition.

They hung there in the rose-heavy air. For maybe just a millisecond too long.

"Right back at'cha."

Then his grin returned and he crossed the room to take her in his arms. He brushed her hair back from her face in the way that she loved. He kissed her and thanked her for cooking for him, even if she didn't know how.

That made her smile as he hugged her hard and then held her with his arms tight around her in the way she liked best.

But it wasn't the same.

. . .

Caleb stared across the top of her head, watching the candlelight flicker against the wall. What the hell could he do?

He knew Meri. Those words had not been easy for her to say. And she meant them.

Or she thought she did. But trust was a big part of love and Meri had trouble trusting that she was lovable. She'd said more than once that everyone always left her.

And leaving was his game. He'd been fighting it hard lately.

He'd got himself into a box here at Indian River.

But that didn't mean he was ready to be roped, thrown and hog-tied.

He loved Meri.

But what would he do without his freedom?

Once he'd made this place a solid ranch and made Jake eat his words, then what?

He still had never been to Australia. And he'd always promised himself he would go.

"I can't get married right now," he said.

She stayed where she was but the soft pulse of her breathing stopped.

Then she stepped back so fast he almost got whiplash, pushing his arms away with both hands like she couldn't stand for him to touch her.

Her narrowed eyes held the glint of tears.

Oh, God. He prayed she wouldn't cry.

He needn't have worried.

"Did I say I want to marry you?"

He'd never heard that voice from her before. She whirled away from him and then back to blaze those violet eyes at him again.

He'd never seen her so mad.

"What did you mean," she said, teeth clenched, "that day you told me you loved me? Remember? That day you were feeling like such a big man because I sent Tim away and let you drive me home?"

"I meant what I said. I did love you. I still do."

She acted like he'd never said a word. "You even went so far as to say you thought we were soul mates. What did *that* mean?"

"What I'm talkin' about here is not that. I'm just not the marryin' kind, that's all. The idea scares me."

"Now you say."

"Well, you know that. I've never tried to hide my past. I've never made a long-term promise to any woman."

"Look," she said, and her voice broke. She pulled it back together. "I do want a lifetime commitment."

"Ha. You do not. Not with a man. To HGK, maybe."

"Oh. So you're still mad that I didn't give you a free pass on your lack of responsibility. Your behavior was beyond adolescent, Caleb."

"No, I—"

"You lied to me is what you did. You said you loved me and you didn't and you don't. I'm leaving. Enjoy the cake."

She started ripping at the knot she'd tied in her apron strings, which were so long they wrapped around her slim body twice.

He reached to help her and had all he could do to keep from putting his hands on that slim body.

"My only mistake was coming back to you after that break. The break that you did not protest, not with one single word. Remember? I should never have said temporary. This is never going to work."

His heart went through the floor. She was tearing at the knot so hard and fast she was trembling. Her body was so taut his hands begged to soothe her.

He wanted to grab her by the shoulders and turn her around and kiss her until she went limp and melted against him.

Partly because there was something irresistible about her when she was so full of emotion. Even if it wasn't desire.

"Look," he said. "You pride yourself on staying calm and analyzing every situation from every angle. And on your fairness and talking things through . . ."

The knot came loose at last and she unwound the strings in a fury of motion.

That done, she hit him with a look that would've felled his new bull.

"I'm thinking you're just pretty damned calm yourself," she said. "So calm it proves you never had anything invested in this relationship to begin with."

That hurt him in the heart. "Not true. We need to talk—"

"Oh, no. You've proven words don't mean a thing. What we need is to look at reality."

She pulled the apron off over her head and threw it at him before she headed out the door.

He went after her but she grabbed his cowboy hat off the rack when she picked up her bag and threw that at him, too. One glance from those ice-crystalled eyes froze his breath in his lungs.

Because he still had a shred of good sense left under the despair. He loved her. He truly did love Meredith Briscoe.

Probably, he'd just made the biggest mistake of his life.

Twenty-six

It took a lot to scare Lilah, after all she'd been through in her life, but the sight of that child's face, buttermilk pale, as she ran up the back steps was enough to send a chill through any grandma's blood. Meri burst into the kitchen and then stopped stock-still, breathing hard through her nostrils like a winded horse. She stared at Lilah as if she'd never seen her before.

Lilah fumbled to get her dripping hands on a towel. Meri held on to that big old leather bag of hers with both hands like it was trying to get away.

Thank goodness Lilah had the presence of mind to keep her voice calm. "Meri, honey, what happened?"

Meri looked around at the room, as if she didn't recognize it either.

"We broke up."

Real fast, she added, "I can't talk about it."

That hurt Lilah's feelings a little—a silly part of her had thought Meri had run to her for comfort—but her lungs began working again.

"Well, thank the Lord! The way you look, I thought somebody'd died."

That shot some color into Meri's face.

"My dream died. I'll never have a family of my own."

She walked on, like a person in a trance, and after a moment, Lilah heard her door close. Softly. Lilah would've felt better if she'd slammed it.

No sense going to her now. Let her have some time alone.

Lilah turned back to the sink to finish washing the beans for soaking overnight. Her hands trembled a little from the scare. She drew in a big breath of relief.

Poor baby. Meri didn't know it probably wasn't over, at all. Every love had its ups and downs and Lilah knew love when she saw it.

But it would be wasted breath to try to tell Meri that now. Maybe before bedtime, so she'd have a scrap of hope to sleep on.

Bless her, Lord. And show me how to help her. She takes everything so hard.

She opened her mind to listen for an answer as she took the beans through the third wash, letting the water run through her fingers. The days and nights she'd had with Ed had gone just that fast. She hoped Meri and Caleb wouldn't waste too much of their time.

Lilah covered the beans in the pot with fresh, cold water and set it on the stove. Meri needed something in her stomach. Sometimes tea was sickening and sometimes it was just the ticket for an upset. It'd be worth a try. Meri was a coffee lover but that just didn't feel right for her now. Too strong.

And she needed food. Something very light.

Honestly, the girl was rail-thin and that was not an exaggeration.

Lilah fixed fresh, hot tea with sliced lemon on the side and lightly buttered toast with fresh honey in the little pot that looked like a beehive. She wet a washcloth in cold water, laid it to the side and took the tray down the hall to her granddaughter's door.

"I've brought tea," she said, balancing the tray on one knee to knock and turn the knob. She was taking this food in whether Meri wanted her to or not. "I won't stay unless you want me."

Meri lay flat on her back on her bed, staring up at the ceiling. Her face bleak and pale enough to scare Lilah all over again.

Lilah set the tray on the cedar chest, then picked up the cold rag and spread it over Meri's forehead.

She used her most soothing voice. "There's times in a woman's life when nothing will help except to lay down with a cold rag on your head."

Lilah reached for the pillows. With a little urging, Meri finally sat up and let her stuff them between her back and the knobby spindles of the iron bedstead.

"You're limp as a rag doll," Lilah said. "That's not like you. Go on and cry it out."

Meri had not breathed one word to her. Not one. Much less told her to leave her alone.

Oh, Lord. Be with us here. Bring the right words to my tongue.

Lilah took a chance and gave the child a light hug as she finished with the pillows.

Meri stared into the distance.

Lilah unfolded the legs of the tray and set it across Meri's lap, poured a cup half full of tea, then went to sit in her mother's rocker by the window. Meri didn't move, didn't lift a hand.

"It's all my fault," Meri said softly.

"No," Lilah said, careful to use that same low tone, "whatever happened, it's *not* all your fault. Last time I looked, there were two people involved."

Meri did turn her head against the pillow to look at her. To say she didn't believe that.

"Anytime it's a couple, there's two sides to it," Lilah said.

"I started it," Meri said. "I called the first break. He must've liked being free more than he liked being back with me."

Oh. So. This time it was Caleb who needed space.

Her haunted eyes found Lilah's.

"Caleb's a free-born man, all right," Lilah said. "But he's one with deep feelings. And I can see the need in his eyes when he looks at you."

Meri picked up the cup with both hands. "A long time ago, he told me he loved me."

She took a tiny sip of tea. And waited.

Lilah's heart constricted, not only from pity but from guilt. Of course, Meri, being Meri-the-abandoned-child, hadn't been able to believe him. She wanted to know what Lilah thought.

Wise Lilah. Oh, *yeah*. The grandmother who hadn't looked for her hard enough to find her and save her childhood.

Silently, she prayed for the wisdom she hadn't had back then.

"I see love in his eyes, too," Lilah said. "Every time he looks at you or speaks your name."

Meri's words came out in a jerky rush. "He never said it again. Ever. I said it to him. Tonight. Big mistake."

She took the cloth off her head, dropped it on the bed and poured herself more tea in that way she moved when she *had* to have something to do.

Lilah prayed to say the right thing.

"Lots of people—really, most everybody—gets scared when they start thinking about making the commitment to marry . . ."

"I didn't *say* . . ."

"But that's the crossroads, right?" Lilah kept her tone soft and reasonable. Meri was one to respond to logic.

"When both people have declared their love? And no matter how sure they think they are, it's scary. Everybody, when they're right up on the wedding day, is liable to get cold feet."

Another small sip. "Did you and Grandpa Ed?"

"I did. The day before the wedding. After we'd been sweethearts all our lives. He never would own up to it, but I think he did, too. It's nothin' but natural."

"What were you thinking when you thought about not going through with it?"

"That I'd like to travel some. See the world. See what other people were like. Other men, too. Maybe."

"Did you tell him that?"

Lilah chuckled. "Not the other men part."

"If you loved him so much, why did you feel that way?"

"It was cutting off all my possibilities. I well

310

knew how farming ties you down. It's a way of life. It's just that simple."

"What did he say when you told him you had cold feet?"

"He promised to warm them for me, winter or summer. Then he said we couldn't put off the wedding until later. We had a crop to put in."

"Very romantic."

Lilah laughed. "You know, turned out it was. Your grandpa was a very *romantic* farmer-man."

"Now I know Cale doesn't want marriage . . ."

Lilah held Meri's eyes with hers. "Don't jump ahead of yourself. You can't know the future. And . . ."

Meri looked at the tray, grabbed it and thrust it in Lilah's direction as she tried to get out from under it. Lilah jumped up to take it as Meri rushed out of the room. She ran across the hall, into the bathroom, and slammed the door. Lilah heard the sounds of retching.

She picked up the washcloth, carried the tray back to the kitchen and wet the cloth again. She hurried to the bathroom to hold Meri's head.

The child had very little in her stomach, so it was soon emptied. She went back to her bed and threw herself on the bed again, but facedown this time.

But then she was up and running for the bathroom again. Lilah held her head and washed her face and led her back to bed. Meri lay there like a stone.

For a few minutes. Until she started gagging again.

There were times in between when Meri lay unmoving with her eyes closed and Lilah hoped she was falling asleep, but then she'd leap up, retching again, and finally it all became a circular routine from bed to bathroom and back again that wouldn't stop. Lilah tried blackberry juice and everything else she could think of, but nothing completely stopped it.

Meri was pale as paper and shaking, down to nothing in her stomach but bile and hardly that.

Lilah looked at the clock. It was nearly midnight.

This whole thing was way past home remedies.

Meri hadn't opened her eyes for a while and her arms lay limp at her sides.

"Come on," Lilah said. "Get up, Meri. I'm taking you to town. You're getting dehydrated."

"No."

"Yes."

Lilah picked up the afghan that lay across the foot of the bed and ran her arm under Meri's shoulders to make her sit up. She wrapped the soft throw around her pitiful little granddaughter.

"Okay. Stand up."

"Gran, I just can't . . ."

"I'll drive you to Doc's house or I'll call Sissy and Buck," Lilah said, pulling her to her feet. "How much publicity do you want?"

Twenty-seven

The stall aisle of the barn was black as the inside of a cow. Caleb stopped in the doorway and just stood there for a minute, not even reaching for the light switch. Something was really wrong with him.

(Besides the stupid point of honor that he and Gideon shared: the leader of the outfit should set an example by being at the barn every morning when the help arrived. That was pure insanity.) His new help, Delmer, wasn't too smart but he was smart enough to be asleep right now.

And here Caleb stood with the grit of no-sleep in his eyes.

He had a terrible rock in his gut, too. Dread. Regret. Fear.

Who knew? It could be anything but it'd appeared the minute Meri walked out of his house last week.

Where was that old lifting feeling of happiness when a relationship fell apart? The old looking forward to the fact anything could happen, anybody could come into his life, anywhere could be his next home.

He flipped on the lights and made his feet move toward the stack of hay bales. All that was still true, no matter how he felt. He could hire a manager for Indian River and let himself be free. He could sell it and let Jake win.

It was a futile effort, anyhow, to try to win Jake's respect. He would never change his opinion of Caleb, anyhow. Or if he did, he'd never admit it.

He'd still be heaping the same old insults on him and saying the same old hurtful words.

So Caleb might as well have his freedom.

He had to feel free. Always before, in his whole life, that had been his best comfort.

Caleb reached for the wire clippers hanging on the barn wall and forced his hands to work, cutting the nylon strings that had taken the place of baling wire.

Where was that sense of freedom he always felt when he broke up with a woman? The *relief?*

He couldn't find it, couldn't feel it, and God knew, he'd tried. Even if the ranch held him here, he should be able to laugh and sleep more than four hours at a stretch and take joy from physical labor and eat heartily and maybe go out dancing. At least go listen to a good band.

But none of that had happened in the whole week since Meri had tried to cook him a good dinner and he'd acted like a jerk.

His gut clenched around the rock of regret. But, *damn!* What could he do?

She'd never, ever said she loved him before and

he knew her well enough to know that it took every bit of nerve she could scrape up to do it. Meri didn't risk her heart easily. If at all.

It was too hard for her to trust anyone.

Probably, she was mistaken about loving him. She just thought she did. Maybe she was in love with the idea of love or whatever that saying was.

Because she didn't trust him. She'd told him that in so many words.

He tore off some flakes from the hay bale and started throwing them into stalls on both sides as he walked down the aisle. Today he'd quit thinking about her. If he didn't get her off his mind pretty quick, he might as well stay up around the clock. Wear a headlamp and just keep on trucking, 24/7.

He needed to get so tied up in some project that he couldn't turn loose today or he'd be on the phone or in the truck hunting her down. He *did* need her, terribly. More than he'd known was possible.

He missed her like he would miss one of his arms or legs.

But even if it proved out that he *could* stay in one place for the rest of his life, how could he possibly commit to something as sacred and permanent as marriage? He couldn't stand to feel like he had no options.

Always, through his whole life, a day came

when he just had to go find something new. If Indian River was all that was holding him here, he could hire a manager and go anyway. He could say the hell with Jake's opinion of him.

But he did have responsibilities at HGK. He really did contribute to it, whether Meri thought he did or not.

This whole ranching project had started out as in-your-face-Jake and, except for the fact that he loved it, it still was.

But it was a project with an end to it, good or bad.

Marriage wasn't. And he was far better equipped to be a successful rancher than a good husband. How could he be? The only example he'd ever had was a father who was the furthest thing from it.

He forced himself to finish the hay and go get the scoops of sweet feed.

Today he'd use Socks, the horse Joe Dan Payne gave him a couple of days ago. The old sorrel was watching him over his shoulder, ears pinned, butt to the stall door.

"Aw, come on," Cale said. "You've gotta earn your keep like everybody else around here."

Poor old guy gave a halfhearted kick at the stall door. He was a one-man horse and he missed his true owner.

Caleb's gut twisted for Joe Dan. He loved this ornery horse but he had a wife, three children and another one on the way. Welding jobs were scarce these days and the money didn't stretch far enough for him to keep both humans and horses fed and shod.

So Cale gave Socks a home. Riding him out through the dark this morning might be stupid—and it was—but Cale needed something to get his adrenaline going and focus his mind on something different besides Meri.

He was free. *Free.* So why didn't he feel like it?

His phone sounded off. His pulse flashed to racing speed. What if Meri couldn't sleep either? What if . . .

He fingered it out of his front pocket and read the time, 4:47, and the caller's name, Gideon Burkett.

This couldn't be good. Not this time of day. His heart dropped into a rhythmic thump of dread.

He forced his thumb to move, then stuck the phone to his ear. *"What?"*

"Mom. They think she's having a heart attack or something."

All his blood chilled. "God, no! What happened?"

Cold rolled through him in a tumbling wave. His *mother*.

"Sissy and Buck just picked her up. Meet us at the hospital."

No. This cannot be. Oh, God please help her.

"How bad is it?"

His feet were moving on their own. He was running for the truck, slapping the lights off as he passed the switch. Thank God he hadn't already been out in the pasture with no cell service.

"Don't know yet. I'm headin' out."

Caleb smashed the phone against his ear as he ran.

"So 'm I. Where's Jake?"

This was his fault, no matter what anybody said.

"In the ambulance with her."

"At least he was home."

"You said it."

Gid was in the waiting room when Caleb got to the hospital.

"Doc's with her. They've got her on an IV and Sissy and Buck say she's pretty much stable. Still unconscious, though."

The twins started pacing the floor in sync, from the windows that showed it was still dark outside to the rows of plastic chairs by the door. And then back again.

"You call Aaron and Tate?"

Gid shook his head. "Jake said they're both in Canada, working on that fracking deal, be back in a couple of days. We'll wait and see if we should bring them home now."

"Gid, what happened?"

"Who knows? She's always been under a lot of stress, dealing with him."

"My first thought," Cale said.

He turned on his heel and stared at Gid. "He shouldn't be the only one with her. I'm going in there."

"The doc said . . ."

Cale waved that off. He left the waiting room and strode down the freshly waxed hallway to the double doors of the ER, pushed them open and stepped inside. Three cubicles were empty. The one on the far end had the curtains pulled and he could hear somebody talking.

A nurse pushed her way out, rattling the curtains' rings on the rod, and headed in the opposite direction from him, so intent on her errand that she didn't even see him. He walked faster, hoping that her hurrying didn't mean that his mother was worse.

Two long strides more and he heard words.

"*Don't* die. *Please.*"

Caleb stopped short. It was Jake's voice, but weird. Thin.

"Dulcie, do you hear me? Hold on. Don't let go."

Could he be *crying?* No way. Not possible. This was Jake Burkett.

Yes, he was weeping. That was so hard to get his mind around that Caleb didn't even realize he should walk away. He stood frozen, not even breathing.

"We'll go to an art show—is that what they call them? I'll hire you an agent." He sniffed. "Hell, I'll build you a gallery or whatever it is where they market that stuff. I'll do anything."

The rhythmic wheezing of a machine was his only answer.

"Dulcie, I'm sorry," he said, his words lower now. Slower.

"None of the rest of them meant a damn to me. Ever. You're the only woman I ever loved."

He sniffed and cleared his throat. "I've been a rotten husband and a worse father. I'm a selfish bastard. I've been a self-centered SOB. Oh, God! Don't die."

Silence. Then Jake moved and the curtain slid, rattling, on its crescent rod. Its edges separated and Jake moved into partial view as he threw himself to his knees beside the bed.

Jake Burkett *kneeling?* First, weeping, now kneeling?

He tossed his hat brim-down on the floor and it skidded almost to the edge of the curtain.

"Regrets are hell," he said, his voice rough and unsteady at the same time. "I'll make it all up to you, Dulcinea."

Caleb had never heard him call her that before. There was a new tenderness in his tone that made Cale feel he should walk away, yet he couldn't move. Was that really his mother's name? Or a pet name?

Jake cleared his throat.

"Remember when we first got married? Remember the time we chased each other hell-bent through the river? Nearly drowned us and the horses, too?"

He gave a rusty, teary chuckle. "Nearly drowned us both dead but we couldn't stop laughing."

Caleb's jaw dropped. *What?* He tried to picture that in his mind.

When had Jake ever laughed?

Jake kept his eyes on Dulcie. "Listen to me. I'm telling you the God's own truth. I'll change. Live. Stay with me and I'll change. I've proved it, time and again. I can do anything I want to and I'm gonna change."

Cale stepped sideways so he could see his mother's face. Her eyes were closed. Her face didn't show any pain.

"I choose what I do," Jake said. "By God, I've always gone after what I wanted and got it. I'm a changed man from this minute on. You can take that to the bank, Dulcie."

Caleb could hear someone coming, but he couldn't move.

"None of it—not the money, not the power, not the property, not the respect—not one bit of it makes a dime's worth of difference if you're gone, Dulcie girl, and I didn't know that 'til now. Don't die."

Jake got to his feet and stood looking down at his wife.

"I just now figured it out," he said. "When the chips're down, family's all that's important. Nothin' else means a cotton-pickin' thing. You tried to tell me that for years."

Caleb stepped back and away, staying silent on the balls of his feet, and pivoted to go meet whoever was coming. It was the same nurse.

Behind him, Jake rasped, "We'll hire a cook. You don't ever have to cook again if you don't want to, Dulce. We'll take a trip. We'll *both* go down and sit by the river—maybe ride the horses through it. You *can't* leave me here alone."

Caleb and the nurse met a few yards from the cubicle. She was very young, evidently new to town. He couldn't recall ever seeing her before.

"How is my mother?"

At first he thought she wasn't going to answer but then he tried a smile.

It couldn't have been much, but it worked.

"I can tell you that she's comfortable now and in no immediate danger," she said. "The doctor will come out and talk to you soon . . . Mr. Burkett?"

"Yes," he said. "I'm Caleb Burkett."

"I'm Holly Johnson," she said. "Please don't worry. I'll take very good care of your mother."

She was a beautiful brown-eyed redhead and she was giving him a warmly inviting smile but Caleb noticed those details only with the analytical corner of his brain. That was another thing that was wrong with him since he lost Meri. He didn't want to socialize with anybody, not even pretty young women.

Twenty-eight

Something was really wrong with her, Meri decided. Deeply wrong.

If Lilah walked into the barn and saw her now, sitting in the battered rocking chair cradling the very-pregnant stray cat against her shoulder, she'd rush her granddaughter to Doc again. This time, for a referral to a mental health professional.

Anybody who'd known the real Meredith Briscoe before this strangely sentimental alien took over her body would do the same.

But she didn't care what anybody thought, including her old self. The cat's purring in her ear and its incredibly soft fur under her hand gave her some rare comfort. Which explained why only the name Serena came to her, no doubt.

Meri's heart clutched. She had a feeling today was the day for the kittens to arrive. Serena had appeared over a week ago and today was the first time she'd followed Meri through all the barn chores, begging to be picked up. The thin cat was hugely pregnant.

Meri rocked and stroked the cat in rhythm while

she evaluated the wooden fruit box full of old towels and soft rags she and Lilah had placed next to the cat's food and water. Lilah had insisted that Serena would take care of everything else.

Still, Meri felt responsible. After all, she'd talked Lilah into letting Serena stay instead of taking her to the shelter as they usually did for the dogs and cats people dumped out on the highway.

Serena wiggled free and jumped down. Meri just sat there and watched her prowl her restless way along the aisle of the barn.

Get up. Working from home does not mean sitting in the barn all day. You should already have those expense projections done.

She'd lost her will to work. She truly was sick. She couldn't even find the drivers inside that had kept her moving forward since she was fourteen. All her life, really. She still couldn't believe she had let her despair take her over until she actually threw up. And she knew Doc's diagnosis of emotional distress had been right.

Maybe it ran in the family. Lilah had said the same thing happened to her when Grandpa Ed died so suddenly. She said Meri's body had been trying to get rid of the truth.

Meri stopped the rocker and stood up. She still didn't want to see anybody, so she'd given herself until next Monday to go in to work at HGK. But there was lots she could still do online and she had to get to it. Work—and Lilah—were all she had left in her life.

But first, the birthing box could use a little more bedding, so she'd get more from the house. As big as Serena's belly was, there must be five or six kittens at least.

Meri made herself run from the barn to the house. That was another thing she'd let slide—her daily run. It always made her feel better but somehow she'd let herself sit around and wallow in misery instead.

When she reached the edge of the yard, the sound of wheels on the gravel drive made her look up the long driveway. A big white pickup was turning in off the road. Looked like Caleb's.

No. He hadn't called, hadn't come to see her and it was too late now.

Whatever he wanted, it was too late. She'd see him when necessary on business at HGK.

But she slowed enough to see that the truck had a winch on the front like his. She could only see the driver's silhouette—the shape of his hat, not his face. But it was he. She could tell by the way he held his head.

She ran faster, crossed the yard and pounded up the back steps like a madwoman. No way. No way was she strong enough yet to deal with him.

She stopped on the porch. What was she doing? *Running* from him.

She wouldn't. But she wouldn't stand here and

wait for him, either. She opened the screen, went in at a dignified pace and latched it behind her so he couldn't just knock and come on in, which was what most people did at Honey Grove.

Meri stood still just inside the kitchen and tried to remember what her errand was. She wouldn't even think about Caleb again, after she told him to go away.

Her blood was pounding in her ears. She took three deep breaths to calm herself and clear her mind, then she went into the mudroom just off the kitchen and rummaged in the antique meal box for more rags.

His boot heels rang on the porch. He knocked on the door, then tried the screen.

"Meri?"

The low, silky sound of Caleb's voice saying her name made her catch her breath.

"Lilah's campaigning door-to-door," she said, glad to hear the frost in her tone, "since there's only a week to go until the election. You can catch her at HGK . . ."

"I didn't come to see Lilah."

That squeezed the blood out of her heart that he held in his hand.

You are stronger than this, Meri. You used to love him but you don't anymore. You. Do. Not. Love. Him.

"Then go away."

She grabbed some towels without looking at them, straightened up and took a deep, ragged breath while she stared at the wall. This room needed painting. She'd do that tonight.

"Come here and say that to my face."

"You heard me."

"First you run when you see me and now you hide. What's the matter, Mer? You scared?"

Yes.

But she'd die before she would admit it. Holding on to the soft worn towels like a child with a teddy bear, she forced her feet to move and her legs to carry her to the door. His big frame filled the screen.

She stopped one step before she reached it but his eyes blazed so blue distance was no protection.

She reached for her long-ago courtroom-attorney persona.

"Why are you here, Caleb?"

"I have something to say to you."

"I have a phone."

"It's personal."

She waited.

"Open this door."

Just catching the scent of his cologne made her feel shaky. He was all starched and pressed and solemn as could be. She had to get rid of him.

"Step aside," she said. "I have to get back to the barn."

He eyed the towels. "To wash the water

buckets? Polish the saddles? Clean the feeders? I'll help. I can do any of it."

She flipped the latch up. "Thanks but no, thanks. Go away."

He pulled the screen open and stepped back. She went out past him and down the steps.

He followed.

She ignored him until they reached the driveway, where she stopped and turned to look at him.

"Get in your truck and leave Honey Grove, Caleb. My cat's about to have kittens."

His eyes widened. "Henry? That'd be something I could write a paper about for the veterinary journals."

"Go," she said. "And don't try to be funny. It's a stray named Serena. I've gotten attached to her."

His jaw set in that stubborn way of his. "I'm here until you've heard me out."

"Shall I call for help?"

He grinned. "Nice try. For somebody who hates to be the subject of gossip."

She tried to stare him down.

"Hey," he said. "You're a lawyer. You know both sides get their day in court. Where's your sense of justice?"

"Go," she said.

"I'm trained as a veterinarian, remember? I can be useful to have around in case of cats giving birth. Miss Lilah tells me this one's malnourished and footsore."

Meri's chest tightened. "I resent the two of you talking about me. What else did she tell you?"

"We were talking about stray animals. She won't talk about you, no matter how hard I quiz her about your state of mind."

He held her gaze and wouldn't let it go.

"Say what you came for," she said. "Then get off the farm."

She couldn't breathe. The way he was looking at her was making her dizzy.

Something was *wrong* with her. He'd broken her heart. She hadn't even begun to recover the pieces of it, much less put it together to heal, yet she was craving his touch. And his kiss.

As if she had no memory in her mind. Or in her emotions. Only her body could remember. And it had forgotten nothing.

"I love you, Meri," he said. "I'm miserable without you. I can't *live* without you. I want to marry you. I want you to be the only woman in my life and the mother of my children."

Her rage roared to life. The words *marry* and *children* pierced her through the gut as well as the heart.

"And no doubt you want me to take good care of them for you when you head off to Alaska or Australia," she said, turning her temper loose on him. "Plus feed your dogs and keep your horses ridden every day and take good care of your cattle.

Right? Should I go ahead and finish the house renovations, too?"

Blood pounded in her ears from the fierce feelings that filled her.

"This," she said, "from Mr. Footloose. Mr. Don't-Tie-Me-Down. It's ludicrous. You're making a fool of yourself, Caleb."

"I don't care." His tone was so flat it left no doubt that he meant what he said. "Sad thing is, I love you. I could get on a plane and go to the other side of the world and it wouldn't help. This misery has got to stop."

Exactly the way you feel about him.

Hey, whose side are you on?

"But what if one day you get up with the wanderlust uppermost in your feelings? You always do what you feel like doing."

"And what if one day you get up and look at me and the life we have and you see it isn't perfect? You always want everything to be perfect."

They exchanged a long look. She tried to keep her guard up.

"Caleb, you're forgetting who you are. Now, if you'll excuse me, I have to fix this bedding for my cat."

"Who I am is the man I choose to be," he said, falling in beside her as she walked on to the barn. Somehow, that simple gesture soothed her a little. It made no sense, but it did. "I'm willing to change my way of living for you, Meri."

She threw him a straight look. "Why?"

"Mainly because my life's a living hell without you and I'm selfish and I like to be happy. Deep down, I haven't been deep-down happy for one minute when we're apart. Ever since the day I met you."

"You don't know how hard it is to change. You have to have your freedom, remember?"

"Freedom's not in it. Hard's being separated from you. If you'll marry me, I'll be the best husband on earth."

Meri walked on ahead of him and went to work adding the extra towels to Serena's bed.

"I never did think I could be a decent husband. Jake was such a rotten one I guess I thought I'd be the same. My older brothers haven't done so well at it, either."

"So what changed your mind?"

She finished arranging the towels and stood up. Serena was still roaming the barn.

"Come on. If your cat's ready, she's needing some privacy. I want to tell you what happened to Jake and what I've learned from him."

"But . . ."

"We'll check on her in a few minutes. She doesn't want us here."

So they walked up the orchard path, the same trail they'd run down, hand in hand in the pouring rain that day so long ago when they barely knew each other. That day of their first kiss, soaked to the skin and trembling, arms wrapped around each other as if they could never let go, right there at the top of the steps on Lilah's back porch.

Now, with the yellow and gold leaves blowing off the trees, swirling to catch the sunlight and scatter it over the hill, Cale told her what he'd overheard at the hospital.

"My father's one of the wealthiest men in Texas. A powerful man. But he's learned that he has nothing if he doesn't have the love of his family."

Meri nodded. "My mother never did know that."

"When I heard him say it, the whole truth hit me hard," Caleb said. "Not that I'll ever be the businessman he is, but if I lose you, all I'll have at his age—*if* I keep working 24/7 and have good luck—is Indian River."

They climbed to the top of the hill and sat down under one of the trees.

"Why does it have to be me? You'd have no trouble finding someone else."

He leaned back against the trunk and smoothed Meri's hair, tangling in the wind.

"Not an option," he said. "Not anymore."

He took her face in both his big hands.

"I'll trade my freedom," he said. "Gladly. I can't live if I lose you, Meri."

She searched his eyes, clear and blue as the autumn sky. She shook her head.

"You just want me to raise your children and

take care of your cows," she said. "I might wake up some morning and find a note that you've gone to Antarctica."

"No way. I already have too much invested here to buy two tickets to a place that far." He grinned. "If I go, you go. And all six kids, too."

"Six?"

She loved to make him laugh. But laughter didn't take away the truth in his eyes. She, who didn't trust anyone, couldn't stop believing him.

He took her hand with his and reached into the pocket of his shirt with the other.

"Meri," he said, "all I can tell you is that we have choices. We decide to be together, we get married and then every day, we'll choose to stay that way. I'll choose it, even if I'm feeling just a tad restless and you'll choose it even if you're lookin' at me thinkin' he's not perfect."

Tears filled her eyes.

"Every rolling stone has to stop sometime. What I want is to be at Indian River with you. I don't want to wind up like Jake . . ."

He grinned. ". . . except for the money and power."

She smiled. "Hey, now," she teased, "you're a partner in HGK, don't forget. You're gonna be a wealthy man."

"If you say yes, I already am," he said. He fingered a ring from his pocket. "Meri, will you marry me?"

The guards around her heart gave up and laid down their spears. "Yes."

He slipped the ring onto her finger.

"It's a purple diamond to match your eyes," he said. "I bought it the day after we ran down this hill in the rain."

She gasped. "You *did?* That long ago?"

Sunlight flashed from the stone and went spinning in all directions.

"I knew the minute I met you," he said. "It just took me awhile to bring you around to my way of thinking."

"Oh, yeah . . ."

But then he kissed her and she gave up trying to think of a comeback.

Twenty-nine

Even though the room was filling up fast and Lilah was trying to keep an eye on Dulcie and Jake—not to be nosy, of course, but to judge the sincerity of his new change of heart for herself—she saw Shorty when he came through the door at Taylor's Inn. He stood and gawked like he'd never been in there before.

Barbara Jane watched him, too, while she uncovered the pans of baked beans. "What's Shorty looking for? You're right here in plain sight."

Lilah snorted. "And I'd like to walk right over

there and slap his silly, jealous face. He's looking for reasons to complain we've overdone this watch party for Elbert. I tell you what, B.J., if those two don't quit it with this stupidity, either they're gonna stroke out or I'm gonna kill 'em both."

"I thought they made friends over a bottle at y'all's drunken picnic."

Lilah stared at her. "B.J.! It's not *my* picnic. *I* didn't get drunk. I got out of there just as soon as I could."

Her friend flashed her most aggravating smile, which Lilah ignored.

"But yes. They're even fishing buddies now. Yet that doesn't stop 'em from acting like teenaged boys trying to get my attention."

She didn't say it to B.J., but, here lately, Lilah was starting to go around with a knot in her stomach all the time, feeling like her whole life was out of control. Try as she would, she couldn't stop these men from making nuisances of themselves, owning a business was turning out to be a 24/7 job with lots of worries and decisions to share, which was always hard for her, and so she had so little time left over for the work on Honey Grove Farm that it was pathetic.

Not to mention the gigantic threat of the infernal zoning change hanging over the neighborhood.

Well, this evening would tell the tale. It

wouldn't be long now until the polls closed and the ballots were counted.

The only good thing—and it was huge—was Meri's and Caleb's engagement.

Lilah clung to that bright spot. It vindicated her. Hadn't she said all the time that they were meant for each other, opposites or not?

Now, if only they could be tolerant of each other and hold their tempers and trust their love and make it all the way to marriage, she could relax at last. Then Meri would be here in Texas for good and Lilah could start dreaming about great-grandchildren.

B.J. started talking to Suzy Clinton's cousin, JaneAnn, and Lilah finished with the bread baskets, so she went to the dessert table to make a tray (she'd brought two of her silver ones) of HGK goodies. No sense serving food out of a box if you didn't have to. A little touch of graciousness was always a good thing.

While she worked, she watched Dulcie and Jake sitting at a table over by the window and actually talking to each other. They'd gone everywhere separately for so many years that this was hard to believe. He'd *better* be a changed man, or Lilah would have to shoot him, too.

"Looks like you done throwed your feet out. This here's quite a party for the Judge."

Lilah jumped. She'd tried so hard to put

Gladys rang her handbell and everyone quieted down.

She looked at the paper Dottie handed to her and called out in her scratchy voice, "Ballot box: Trammell's Corner! The Judge: Fifteen votes! Missy Lambert: Three votes!"

She waited for the cheering to stop, which didn't take long, and then, smiling, she made her commentary. "That makes half our precincts reporting," she said, "and so far, the Judge is ahead by a comfortable lead. One hundred and fifty votes ahead!"

More cheering.

Shorty took a cowboy cookie and stood beside Lilah while he ate it.

He was scanning the tables, now. Dallas and Addison were decorating them one by one with the centerpieces they'd made from flowers and autumn leaves and Texas and American flags.

It'd been their own idea to do that for community volunteer credit in their 4-H state record books and Lilah had encouraged it whole-heartedly. Not only would it help them develop an interest in the political process, it was refreshing to find young girls who even thought of such niceties as decorating tables.

Shorty said, "How about if I go save that one over there for us?"

"I told you, I'll have to help B.J. serve, so I can't sit there all night . . ."

The door blew open and the wind started whipping the tablecloths around.

Talk died down as people turned to look. Meri and Caleb stood, arm in arm, in the doorway, tall and slim and very close to each other. Lilah thought of the couple on top of a wedding cake.

The picture imprinted on Lilah's mind. A little moment in time. Her two beautiful young people who still didn't know enough about life to appreciate it fully. If only they had enough sense to grab onto their love and hang on.

Then talk started up again and the kids came on in. They separated when they spotted Dulcie and Jake. Caleb went to his parents and Meri came toward Lilah.

Oh, Lord. What now?

Lilah searched her granddaughter's face as she reached the table. Behind her, she glimpsed the Burketts getting up from the table.

"Gran? Shorty? Do y'all have a minute to step outside with us?"

Lilah's mind was racing but it had no idea where to go.

Shorty must be worried, too. He put his hand on her back as they made their way across the room and kept them going, nodding and speaking to people but not letting anyone stop them to chat.

The Burketts were there when they got to the

side door and Jake held it for them. One quick glance told Lilah he didn't know, either. Outside on the patio with its wrought iron tables, she went to Dulcie.

"What's going on?"

"I have no idea."

Caleb got a chair for his mom but she waved it away.

"Enough mystery," Jake boomed. "What's going on?"

Caleb put his arm around Meri. "We just got married this afternoon in San Antonio. We wanted to tell y'all right now before you hear it from somebody else."

Lilah looked at Meri's dress. It and her shoes, too—even with their high heels—were all business. So, yes, it must've been an impulse decision.

"Where?" she said.

Something in her wasn't even surprised. And she had proof that her intuition had known it all along. She'd predicted to Doreen the day of the ice cream social that Meri and Caleb would elope and, at the time, she hadn't even known why she said it. Sometimes a grandmother just knows things.

"Who else knows?" Jake said. "You said 'before we heard it from somebody else.' "

"Doreen's cousin, Trace. He saw us on the street right after. Meri was carrying flowers and we were brushing off the confetti Judge Nolan's staff threw on us."

"Trace congratulated us," Meri said, with a teasing grin and a significant look all around. "He even hugged us."

That brought all the old folks out of shock and back to themselves. The group erupted into squeals and laughter and hugs and congratulations all around. Even Jake got in on it.

Then he went inside to the bar to get glasses and something to drink for a toast, which made Lilah and Dulcie exchange amazed glances. Maybe he really was trying to make up for lost time.

They sat around one of the outdoor tables, then, toasting and talking, looking at Meri's plain platinum band that looked fabulous with the purple diamond and wishing the kids well.

"Y'all come out to Honey Grove when all this is over tonight," Lilah said. "I want to give my mother's scrapbook to Meri on her wedding day."

She looked at Meri. "In spite of the fact I didn't get invited to the wedding . . . and we all didn't get to help plan it, either."

"That's one reason we did it this way," Caleb said.

Lilah clapped her hand to her chest. *What?!!*

"No offense," he drawled, grinning at her with all the mischief in the world in his eyes. He looked so happy. She didn't know when she'd seen him like this.

Don't ruin it, Lilah. How selfish can you be? What's done is done and not yours to judge. Never was.

Meri took Lilah's hand. "Really, Gran, it wasn't because of you. Think about doing that on top of running HGK and the farm. It would've made me even more crazed than I already am. You know how I obsess over every detail and how I work to make everything perfect."

"Yeah," Caleb said. "I say she should save her strength to finish renovating our house. I've got outside work to do."

Meri pretended to slap his arm but she smiled at him, literally dewy-eyed, and said, "I love the way that sounds. '*Our* house.'"

Dulcie groaned. "Oh, Lilah! What'll we do with them? They've got it bad."

"But the main reason we married today was my fear she'd change her mind," Caleb said, and leaned over to kiss his bride.

"That's what I thought from the start," Jake growled. "It was one of your wild-hair impulses."

He looked at Meri as if he were her kindly uncle. "Meri, are you sure he didn't push you any? Did he give you time to think it over?"

Everyone there turned and stared at him.

"Who are you," Dulcie said wryly, "and what have you done with Jake Burkett?"

He threw her an annoyed look as B.J. opened the door into the inn and stuck her head out.

"Lilah, the Judge is calling for you. Missy Lambert conceded! He won!"

Relief surged up in Lilah through the mix of happiness and disappointment and surprise she'd been trying to sort out ever since Meri and Caleb appeared in the doorway.

"Come on," Caleb said, to Meri. "Let's go in and have a big glass of sweet tea and tell everybody our news."

They all laughed then, and the next thing Lilah knew, they were filing back into the inn. She felt almost dizzy. Her wishes seemed to be coming true, one after another, on the same day. Her hard work was paying off. Now her life didn't feel so out of control, after all.

The Judge was standing by the chalkboard where Gladys had printed a wobbly WINNER beside his name. Everybody was looking at him.

"Miss Lilah! Come over here to me, please, ma'am. I want to tell these fine supporters of mine what all you've done during this campaign and thank you for your hard work."

As she made her way through the crowd toward the Judge, Lilah realized that Shorty was not going with the other four to sit at the Burketts' table. He was sticking to her like a burr to a saddle blanket. She stopped beside the Judge and Shorty flanked her on the other side.

"I swear," she muttered in his ear. "Didn't you hear a word I said earlier? And I don't need a bodyguard."

"You don't know that," he muttered without moving his mouth.

"All of you know this fine lady," Elbert boomed. "Folks, I give you the Queen of Rock County, Miss Lilah Briscoe of Honey Grove Farm and Honey Grove Kitchens. Let's give it up for one of Rock County's finest citizens!"

She wanted to roll her eyes. Now he was using slang the young people used. "Give it up." Pitiful. That, on top of all this trying to date her, was enough to make a person wonder whether he was having a late—very late—midlife crisis or a touch of early—very early, since he wasn't much older than she—senility.

And same with Shorty. Lord! Dogging her tracks like he couldn't think where else to go!

But she put a smile on her face and waved her thanks at the people "giving it up" for her. Many of them truly loved her. From time to time she'd offended some but most of them had come to see she'd been right.

There was a lot of love in Rock Springs and she was so happy Meri would be living here. It was exactly what she'd needed all her life.

Lilah pushed away the little stab of guilt that came with that thought. Now wasn't the time for it. Plus the Lord had forgiven her and she needed to forgive herself.

She smiled. And, he had given her a *yes* answer to her prayers about Caleb and Meri. And, she assumed, this election result meant she was vindicated on the zoning change question, too.

Two out of three wasn't bad. Now all she had to do was straighten these men out and get things back to normal in that area and she'd have a handle on her life again.

"All of y'all know Miss Lilah," the Judge was saying, "*and* her position against the proposed zoning change for Jones Orchards which is right across the road from her Honey Grove Farm."

He cast a quizzical look at Shorty. Shorty smiled at him.

"And you know Shorty Grumbles, who . . . also lives in that neighborhood."

Shorty, grinning, nodded to the crowd and lifted a hand.

The Judge kept glancing at him but he kept talking, too. "Miss Lilah has been a big factor in my reelection," he said. "I want to thank you, Lilah. And I want to announce that I am taking the same position as you on the proposed change for Jones Orchards' zoning. My vote will be a resounding NO!"

The crowd started cheering and the Re-treads burst into a rousing rendition of, for some unknown reason, "The Orange Blossom Special" instead of "The Eyes of Texas." That put an end to the speechifying because no way could anybody be heard over all that racket.

Lilah did the only thing she could do, which was leave Shorty to the Judge and go help B.J. and Verna Carl replenish the food on the buffet. A crowd was gathered around Meri and Caleb with everybody hugging her and slapping him on the back. Real joy began rising in Lilah, now that she was getting used to the idea they'd eloped instead of letting her throw a big wedding.

It was almost as if she, too, was starting a whole new life, what with this hope of great-grandchildren running in and out of her house. And this comfort of knowing she'd have Meri and Caleb right here nearby from now on.

Lilah finished putting the last of the brisket in the pan on the bar and took the empty one back to the kitchen so she could have a little more chance to think about it all.

She slumped against the worktable, weak with relief. Her campaigning had paid off. Her house would still be the old one on Honey Grove and her land would still be a farm when Meri and Caleb's children came to see her. The way the morning light came in and fell across the kitchen, the sound of the screen door slamming, the persimmon tree rustling in the wind—all of that would be passed down one more generation.

She'd teach those babies to ride and get them a

puppy no matter what Henry thought about that and she'd enroll them in 4-H and haul their horses to shows. They'd play in the springhouse and camp out in the yard. They'd come over for the weekend and make tents out of blankets and giggle and fuss and fight and keep their great-grandma up all night.

Thank You, Lord.

She had so much to be thankful for.

Her efforts had paid off and her prayers had been answered *yes* and she was about to figure out what to do with Shorty and Elbert. Just throw them together every time and bring up the subject of fishing.

Yes. Her life was manageable again.

She puttered around the kitchen, throwing out the trash, washing the empty casserole dish with Suzy Turner's name sticker on the bottom, enjoying the sudden solitude and thinking about it all, letting the problem of her "boyfriends" perk in a peaceful mind and daydreaming about the future.

Miraculously, nobody came in to disturb her for a good while. But then, just outside the door, somebody started yelling, "Lilah! Lilah!"

Doreen's screech was unmistakable.

She rushed in and grabbed Lilah by the arm to pull her out into the big room again. Frantically, Lilah reached for a dish towel as they passed, yelling back, "Just let me dry my hands!"

Doreen didn't even hear that. "Come on. You have got to see this. It's terrible. I don't know what I'm going to do!"

As soon as they got to the end of the bar, Lilah stopped in her tracks. "What in the world?!"

Now it was Missy Lambert standing by the chalkboard with, of course, Simone in her arms.

Somebody called out, "So did you say, a minute ago, that you're moving to Rock Springs?"

Missy had on her big, star-powered smile and Simone looked happy, too. Maybe Missy didn't care if her daddy and brothers and uncles and cousins got to build houses all over the country or not. She turned her head to twinkle at somebody. Lilah looked. Oh, Lord. Lawrence. And he was smiling back.

"Look at him," Doreen hissed. "He looks happier than she does. I tell you what, I nearly . . ."

But she had to hush so they could hear Missy.

"Yes, I am." She threw a coy look at the Judge. "That's why I wanted to come over here and concede the race again. In person. Because I want everyone to know there's no hard feelings on my part."

"Are you going back to your television job?"

"Nooo," Missy said. "I've been wanting to do something else, maybe like start a business of my own—something fashion-related—and then when my wonderful realtor, Lawrence Semples,

349

showed me a wonderful house I fell in love with, I decided it would have to be a *Rock Springs* business!"

She let go of Simone with one hand to pump her fist in the air. Everybody—well, all the men—cheered for Rock Springs. And for Missy's low-cut, u-shaped neckline that could not, in a million years, hold her bosoms in. Much less cover them up.

"Has she lost her mind?" Lilah whispered.

Doreen just stood there, her eyes frozen, staring at Missy.

Finally, she spoke in a low, fierce tone Lilah had never heard before.

"No, she's crazy like a fox. I came to get you when she said she was fixing to move here. I was worried about Lawrence. But now I see she's after my marriage *and* my business."

Doreen could shed tears at the drop of a hat, but she was dry-eyed now. This went too deep for tears.

Lilah had never seen Doreen this doubtful of herself. She hadn't been this undone since Ed married Lilah. Only then did Doreen accept the fact that he would never love her instead.

It scared Lilah, somehow.

"We—our generation—we can't start going soft now," she said, and that came out just as fierce. She took Doreen's upper arm in both her damp hands and shook her a little.

"Buck up. Hold your head. You're about to throw a runaway. Get a grip, here, Doreen."

She took her by the chin and turned her friend's eyes from Missy's face to her own.

"Listen to me. We're Doreen and Lilah. We can deal with one little hussy before breakfast."

A little of the freeze went out of Doreen's eyes.

"Think about it," Lilah said. "We're the ones who always had to take care of everything in and around Rock Springs and we've done good. One heavily mascaraed, has-been-celebrity floozy's no more than another blip on our radar screen, girl."

That made Doreen smile and come around a little more.

She took her by both shoulders and got in her face because there was so much noise in the room behind her. The Re-treads had started playing softly while Missy fielded more questions.

Lilah said, "She who scares you conquers you."

Doreen rolled her eyes. "Lilah. You know your Bible better than that. It's 'He who angers you conquers you.'"

"Am I gonna have to slap you? What I said's just as true. Women are a lot like horses. They know fear when they smell it."

"But—"

Lilah spoke through gritted teeth and shook her

a little more. "Where is your *backbone?* You are *Doreen Semples,* for heaven's sakes. Act like it!"

Doreen stared at her in shock. "Well, that's a first," she said. "All my life you've criticized me for the way I act."

They looked at each other for a long minute and then burst out laughing. When they finally got it under control, they had to wipe their eyes.

They hugged. Lilah held on after they pulled apart.

"I think this is a really good thing," she said. "I mean that you're starting to fall apart over this."

Doreen's eyes widened. "You *do?*"

Lilah nodded and spoke more softly so no one else could hear. "I think it means that you love Lawrence every bit as much as he loves you."

Doreen's eyes teared up again.

"Think about it, honey. Everybody could see that it was a little bit one-sided when y'all got married so soon after we did. And you've outright said it, once or twice over the years, that he loved you more at the start."

Doreen was choked up now, so she just nodded.

"Remember he's been crazy about you since we were all little bitty kids and how much he's *always* loved you and still does—or he wouldn't put up with all your antics.

"Remember it's not easy for a man to realize he's getting older.

"Remember how people are drawn to glamorous celebrities.

"And . . . remember that your Lawrence is Central Texas Realtor of the Year and he's thrilled beyond words to sell that house that's been on the market for two years. *That's* his interest in her."

That brought on another good laugh, one that brought Shorty to them, asking what in the world was so funny.

"Why don't y'all go on out to the house?" Lilah said. "It's about time. Ask Dulcie and Meri to look in my big freezer and pull out those brownie cupcakes I made. They're one thing that warms up good in the microwave."

"Where're you goin'?"

"I don't want to leave my car here. And I've got a couple of loose ends to tie up. It won't take long."

She smiled at him. "And I need a minute to myself."

"Got it," he said, smiling back. "See ya in a little while."

Doreen hugged her again. "Oh, Lilah," she said. "I'm so glad we're not enemies anymore. Thank you."

"Even if we had been, I'd've told you the same thing," Lilah said. "No woman worth her salt's gonna let another woman suffer like that."

They exchanged a long look.

Then Doreen nodded, squeezed Lilah's hand, and went to find Lawrence.

Lilah went back into the kitchen to help wind things up. She was so happy she wanted to whistle like she did when she was a little girl. Every time her grandmother heard her, she'd say, "Whistling girls and crowing hens always come to some bad end."

Probably, that was the only one of her grandmother's sayings that didn't prove true. At least, not for Lilah, who was feeling truly blessed.

She wondered if Missy Lambert ever whistled. Bless her heart, she was liable to come to some bad end, what with Doreen up and running again.

The whole time Lilah was stacking the personal dishes to be picked up and putting the Taylor's Inn trivets back in the bin, she was thinking how good it felt to have her life back in order again. With the added blessing of Meri and Caleb settling down.

She finished her part of the cleanup, picked up her purse and headed out. Her grandmother was probably spinning in her grave, but Lilah let herself whistle "Roly Poly" as she went out the front door and across the porch of Taylor's Inn.

As she crunched across the parking lot, somebody stepped away from a car and came to meet her.

Oh, great. Tol Weddle. He probably wanted to quiz her for details of the elopement to put in his gossip machine. Well, she didn't have time to mess with him now.

She walked faster. He turned and fell into step beside her.

"Hey, there, Lilah," he said. "I know that here lately you've started dating. I was just wondering if you'd give me a chance."

July 19, 1950

Meredith Kathleen Rawlins
Honey Grove Farm, Rock County, Texas

Canning tomatoes today—for the third day in a row—and I've got the jars scalded and the canner on the stove with the rack in it, waiting. But I can't shake off the dream I had last night where my Lilah is a woman grown, with daughters and granddaughters of her own.

I'm still picturing our long line of Texas Steel Magnolias, marching on down the years, screaming with laughter in the good times and holding each other up in the hard times.

This scrapbook is for all of y'all.

Courage for the great sorrows of life, and patience for the small ones; and then when you have accomplished your daily task, go to sleep in peace—

God is awake.

—VICTOR HUGO

While the earth remaineth, seedtime and harvest, and cold and heat and summer and winter, and day and night shall not cease.

—GENESIS 8:22

The wheel of fortune is greased with labor.

—MARCELENE COX

How to Make Gram's Fried Corn

Take fresh sweet corn and cut the kernels off the cob, then scrape the cob to get all the milk out of it. Heat butter in a heavy iron skillet, add water and salt and pepper, bring to boiling. Add corn and corn milk, reduce heat and cook twenty minutes or so, being careful to keep it stirred. Then thicken it with a small amount of flour in water, add that to the corn along with some cream skimmed from cow's milk.

Flossie's Cake Sauce

*(Guaranteed to be good,
never mind what kind of cake)*

1⅓ cups of granulated sugar
1 stick of butter
1 small can of evaporated milk

Cook until thick.

Especially scrumptious on a wedge of chocolate pound cake.

Sparkling Watermelon Lemonade

Makes 6 1-cup servings
(which probably won't be enough,
so be warned)

4 cups seeded, chopped watermelon
Make ¾ cup of lemonade concentrate out of lemon juice and sugar (whatever proportions you usually make your lemonade, depending on however tart you like it)
1 (25 ounces) bottle of lemon sparkling water, chilled
6 lemon wedges

Combine chopped watermelon and lemonade concentrate in a blender. After it's processed smooth, pour into a pitcher. Add lemon sparkling water and stir gently. Serve immediately over crushed ice. Squeeze a lemon wedge into each serving.

All right, there's a good treat for summer. Now, here's a good one for winter—if it ever cools off enough for us to see cold weather again.

Geneva's Syrup for Popcorn Balls

1 cup white or dark corn syrup
1 cup sugar
¼ cup water
1 teaspoon vinegar
2 tablespoons butter
2 quarts popcorn

Boil ingredients without stirring until the mixture spins a thread from a spoon, then pour over popped corn. Butter your hands to make the balls and be careful not to burn your palms. (Or your mouth, if you're greedy.)

I've often thought that marriage definitely is from God because it's a miracle that any man and woman can live together for any length of time.

Keep two things in mind, Girls.

One is that you and your husband must always stay friends, no matter what, and the way to do that is to follow Proverbs 17:17, which is

"A friend loveth at all times."

The other is that you both must stay busy. If you marry a farmer or a rancher that just naturally takes care of itself, since you'll both be working from cain't see to cain't see. And that's not all bad. It makes for partners, in every sense of the word.

The earth is full of the goodness of the Lord.
—Psalms 33:5

Yes, work is good, but also make sure you two always have some fun to leaven the work and plenty of loving to keep the flame burning.

Remember Proverbs 13:12 says, "Hope deferred maketh the heart sick: but when the desire cometh, it is a tree of life."

And Proverbs 17:22, "A merry heart doeth good like a medicine."

St. Teresa says,

"Mirth is from God, and dullness is from the devil. You can never be too sprightly. You can never be too good-tempered."

My mother always told me this. "Sharp words have cut many a marriage tie."

One more thing and then I'll quit preaching. At least for today.

It gives me a lot of joy to pass on to y'all whatever little bits of wisdom I may have learned in my life and I hope there'll be more and deeper wisdom to come. I hope it'll help smooth y'all's paths so y'all will be free to make different mistakes from mine.

(My thought is that the reason the human race never makes progress in any meaningful way, like improving our human nature, is that every generation makes the same mistakes as the one before it and never learns from anybody's experience but their own.)

Anyhow, this last quote holds the key, Girls, to your own satisfaction in marriage. No, in your whole life.

And it's the key for men, too. Written by a man.

"To know what you prefer instead of humbly saying Amen to what the world tells you you ought to prefer, is to have kept your soul alive."

—R. L. Stevenson

My Darlings. Figure out what it is you really, really want in life and get after it. Time runs like a river.

While you're thinking about that, make this for a treat for summer supper.

Gone With the Wind

2 tablespoons sugar
1 stick butter, melted
2 cups graham cracker crumbs
½ cup pecan pieces

Mix these four ingredients and press into the bottom of a 9x13 pan.

Combine 2 sticks butter and 2 cups powdered sugar and 1 teaspoon vanilla by beating with mixer for 15 minutes on medium speed. Pour this over the crumb crust.

Then add layers in this order:

2 ripe bananas, sliced thin
1 (20 ounces) can crushed pineapple
1 cup shredded coconut
1 ½ cups sliced strawberries
1 cup broken pecan pieces

Then whip 2 cups heavy cream with a little sugar and spread on top. Garnish with extra strawberries.

Refrigerate for several hours and serve cut in 3-inch squares.

About the Author

Genell Dellin grew up in a household of seven, which included Grandpa Grady, who raised vegetables in a big truck patch and hauled fruit from the Rio Grande Valley to sell door-to-door, and Gram (Ara), well-known for her down-home Southern cooking. Several of her recipes are now Lilah's. Genell has written both historical and contemporary romance novels. She loves to hear from her readers. Please visit her website at www.genelldellin.com.

Center Point Large Print
600 Brooks Road / PO Box 1
Thorndike ME 04986-0001 USA

(207) 568-3717

US & Canada:
1 800 929-9108
www.centerpointlargeprint.com